YOU'VE

REACHED

SAM

YOU'VE

REACHED

SAM

DUSTIN THAO

WEDNESDAY BOOKS
NEW YORK

First published in the United States by Wednesday Books, an imprint of St. Martin's Publishing Group

YOU'VE REACHED SAM. Copyright © 2021 by Dustin Thao. All rights reserved. Printed in the United States of America. For information, address St. Martin's Publishing Group, 120 Broadway, New York, NY 10271.

www.wednesdaybooks.com

Designed by Devan Norman

Case stamp art © Shutterstock.com

Library of Congress Cataloging-in-Publication Data

Names: Thao, Dustin, author.
Title: You've reached Sam / Dustin Thao.
Other titles: You have reached Sam
Description: First edition. | New York : Wednesday Books, 2021. | Audience: Ages 12–18.
Identifiers: LCCN 2021017546 | ISBN 9781250762030 (hardcover) | ISBN 9781250836748 | ISBN 9781250836748 (international, sold outside the U.S., subject to rights availability) | ISBN 9781250762047 (ebook)
Subjects: LCSH: Bereavement—Juvenile fiction. | Future life—Juvenile fiction. | Interpersonal relations—Juvenile fiction. | Cell phones—Juvenile fiction. | Romance fiction. | CYAC: Love—Fiction. | Grief—Fiction. | Future life—Fiction. | Cell phones—Fiction. | LCGFT: Romance fiction.
Classification: LCC PZ7.1.T44725 Yo 2021 | DDC 813.6 [Fic]—dc23
LC record available at https://lccn.loc.gov/2021017546

Our books may be purchased in bulk for promotional, educational, or business use. Please contact your local bookseller or the Macmillan Corporate and Premium Sales Department at 1-800-221-7945, extension 5442, or by email at MacmillanSpecialMarkets@macmillan.com.

First Edition: 2021

10 9 8 7 6 5 4 3

TO MY PARENTS, GRANDMA, AND DIAMOND

YOU'VE

REACHED

SAM

PROLOGUE

The second I close my eyes, the memories play, and I find myself back at the beginning.

A few leaves roll in as he enters the bookstore. He wears a
denim jacket, with the sleeves pushed up, a white sweater un-
derneath. It's the third time he's come in since I started working
here two weeks ago. His name is Sam Obayashi, the boy from
my English class. I've been staring out the window throughout
my shift, wondering if he'd come in again. For some reason,
we haven't spoken to each other yet. He just browses the store
as I ring up customers and restock the shelves. I can't tell if he's
looking for something. Or if he likes that feeling of being inside
a bookstore. Or if he came to see me.

As I move a book from the shelf, wondering if he knows my
name, I catch the glint of brown eyes through the gap, looking
back at me from the other side. We're silent for a moment too

long. Then he smiles, and I think he's about to say something— but I shove the book between us before he has the chance. I grab the crate beside me and hurry to the back room. *What's wrong with me? Why didn't I smile back?* After scolding myself for ruining the moment, I gather some courage to go back out and introduce myself. But when I return from the back room, he's already gone.

On the front counter, I find something that wasn't there before. A cherry blossom, made of paper. I turn it over in my hands, admiring the folds.

Did Sam leave this here?

If I hurry outside, I might still catch him. But as soon as I rush out the door, the street vanishes, and I find myself entering a noisy café on the corner of Third Street, nearly two weeks later.

Round tables pop up from a wooden floor as teenagers crowd around them, snapping pictures and drinking from ceramic cups. I'm wearing a gray sweater, slightly oversized, and my brown hair is pinned back and brushed smooth. I catch Sam's voice before I see him, behind the counter taking someone's order. The swoop of dark hair. Maybe it's the apron, but he appears taller from behind the register. I head for a table on the other end of the café, and set my things down. I take my time as I spread out my notebooks, summoning up courage to approach him, even if it's only to order my drink. But when I look up from the table, he's there beside me, holding a steaming cup.

"*Oh*—" I'm startled by his sudden presence. "This isn't mine."

"Yeah I know, you ordered this last time," Sam says, setting it down anyway. "A honey lavender latte, right?"

I stare at the cup, at the busy counter, and back at him. "Should I pay up there?"

He laughs. "No. I mean, it's on the house. Don't worry about it."

"Oh."

A silence between us. *Say something, Julie!*

"I can make you something else instead," he offers.

"No, this is fine—I mean . . . *thank you.*"

"No problem," Sam says through a smile. He slides his hands into his apron pockets. "Your name is Julie, right?" He points to his name tag. "I'm Sam."

"Yeah, we're in the same English class."

"Right. Have you done the reading yet?"

"Not yet."

"Oh good," he sighs. "Me neither."

Some silence as he stands there. He smells faintly of cinnamon. Neither of us knows what to say. I look around. "Are you on a break?"

Sam stares back at the counter, rubbing his chin. "Well, my manager isn't in today, so I guess you could say that." He adds a smirk.

"I'm sure you deserve it."

"It would be my fifth one today, but who's counting?"

We both laugh. My shoulders relax a little.

"Is it okay if I sit here?"

"Sure . . ." I slide my things out of the way, letting him take the chair beside me.

"Where did you move here from again?" Sam asks.

"Seattle."

"I hear it rains a lot there."

"It does, yeah."

I smile as we sit together, talking for the first time, about school and the classes we're taking and little things about ourselves—he has a younger brother, likes music documentaries, and plays the guitar. From time to time, his eyes dart around the room, as if he's nervous, too. But after a few hours, we're both laughing like old friends. Outside the sun lowers itself, turning his skin almost golden in the window light. It's hard not to notice. It isn't until a group of Sam's friends come through the door, calling his name, that we both look up and realize how much time has passed.

A girl with long blond hair puts an arm around Sam's shoulders, embracing him from behind. She glances at me. "Who's this?"

"This is Julie. She just moved here."

"Oh—where from?"

"Seattle," I answer.

She stares at me.

"This is my friend Taylor," Sam says, patting her arm that's still around him. "We're all about to see a movie. I get off work in an hour. You should come."

"It's a psychological thriller," Taylor adds. "You're probably not into that."

We look at each other. I can't tell if she's being rude.

My phone vibrates on the table and I glance at the time. It feels like I've woken from a daydream. "That's okay. I should probably head home."

As I get up from the table, Taylor slides into my seat, making me wonder if they're together. I wave good-bye, but before I go, I head to the front counter. When I think Sam isn't looking, I pull a paper flower from my bag and place it beside the register. I spent a week watching tutorials on how to fold a cherry blossom like the one I found at the bookstore. But the steps were too hard to follow for my untrained hands. A lily was easier.

I zip my bag and hurry out the café door, and suddenly I'm on the front porch of my house, staring out at the lawn. The early morning dew still hangs on the grass. Sam's car pulls up with the window down. He texted me the night before.

Hey. This is Sam. I just got my license!
Do you want a ride to school tomorrow?
I can pick you up on the way if you want

I climb onto the passenger seat and shut the car door. A pleasant scent of citrus and leather hits me. *Is that cologne?* Sam moves his denim jacket as I buckle myself in. A USB cable connects the stereo to his phone placed inside the cup holder. There's a song playing in the background, but I don't recognize it.

"You can change the music if you want," Sam says. "Here— plug your phone in."

A shock of panic hits me and I squeeze my phone tight. I don't want him knowing what I listen to yet. *What if he doesn't like it?* "No this is fine."

"Oh, you like Radiohead too?"

"Who doesn't?" I say. It's a quiet drive through neighborhood streets. We exchange glances from time to time, as I think of things to say. I look at the backseat. A suit jacket hangs from the grip handle. "Is this your car?"

"No, it's my dad's," Sam says, lowering the volume. "He doesn't work Thursdays, so this is the only morning I get to drive it. I'm saving up to buy my own, though. That's why I'm working at the café."

"I'm trying to save up, too."

"For what?"

I think about it. "College, I guess. Maybe an apartment, after I move or something."

"Where are you moving? You just got here."

I'm not sure what to say.

Sam nods. "So it's a *secret* . . ."

I smile at this. "Maybe I'll tell you another time."

"That's fair," Sam says. He looks at me. "How about next Thursday?"

I hold back a laugh as we turn into the school parking lot. Even though the drive doesn't last long, Thursdays are becoming my new favorite day of the week.

The memory changes again. Lights dance across a gymnasium floor and music blares as I step through an archway made of silver and gold balloons. It is the night of the school dance and I don't know anyone here. I'm wearing the new dress my mom helped pick out, dark blue satin that flows out at the waist. With my long hair pinned up, I hardly recognized myself when I looked in the mirror. I wanted to stay home, but my parents forced me to go out and make friends. I didn't want to disappoint them. I spent the last hour standing against the cold cement wall, watching the floor fill with people dancing and laughing. I check my phone from time to time, pretending I'm waiting for someone, but it's just an empty lock screen. Maybe this was a mistake.

Something keeps me from leaving. Sam mentioned he might be here tonight. I texted him a few hours ago but he hasn't responded—maybe he hasn't checked his phone yet? When the music slows down and the crowd disperses, I leave my spot at the wall and make my way through the dance floor, searching for him. It takes me a while, but the moment I see him, my heart drops. There he is, with his arms wrapped around Taylor, slow-dancing. There's a sinking feeling in my stomach. *Why did I come here?* I should have stayed home. I shouldn't have texted him. I turn away before anyone sees me, and rush toward the gym doors.

The night unfolds around me as the loud music muffles, letting me breathe easier. The parking lot, lit up by a few streetlamps, seems so still compared to the dance floor. It's misty out tonight. I should head home before it turns into rain. I think about texting my mom to pick me up, but it's too early. I don't want her asking me what's wrong. Maybe I'll walk home and sneak into my room. My heels are starting to hurt, but I ignore the pain. As I make my way down the parking lot, the gym door swings open behind me, followed by a voice I recognize immediately.

"*Julie—*"

I turn around and it's Sam, looking more serious than usual in a black suit.

"Where are you going?" he asks.

"Home."

"In the rain?"

I don't know what to say. I feel like an idiot. So I force a smile. "It's just a little mist. I'm from Seattle, remember?"

"I can give you a ride if you want."

"That's okay. I don't mind walking." My cheeks are warm.

"Are you sure?"

"Yeah, don't worry." I want to get out of here. But Sam doesn't move.

I try again. "Your date is probably waiting for you in there."

"What?" He stutters a little. "Taylor isn't my date. We're just friends."

There's so much I want to say, but the knots in my stomach

keep me from speaking. I shouldn't feel this way. Sam and I aren't even together.

"Why are you leaving so early?"

I remember him under the colored lights, his arms around Taylor, but there's no way I can tell him the truth. "School dances aren't really my thing. That's all."

Sam nods and slides his hands into his pockets. "Yeah, I know what you mean. They can be pretty lame."

"Does anyone have a good time at these things?"

"Well, maybe you haven't gone with the right person."

My breath catches as I take this in. Even from outside the gym, we can hear the music through the walls, melting into another slow song.

Sam stands at the door, rocking back and forth on the heels of his dress shoes. "Do you not like . . . to dance?"

"I don't know . . . I'm just not very good at it. And I don't like people watching me."

Sam looks around us. After a moment, he smiles a little, and holds out a hand. "Well, no one's watching us now . . ."

"*Sam—*" I start.

His familiar smirk appears. "Just *one* dance."

I hold my breath as Sam steps forward and takes my hand, pulling me close to him. I never imagined my first dance would be like this, the two of us swaying outside in the school parking lot. His face is slightly dewy from the mist, and I inhale his familiar sweet scent, resting my cheek against his chest. As I move my hands onto his shoulders, he notices something.

"What's this?"

The paper cherry blossom. It's tied around my wrist with a ribbon.

My cheeks feel warm again. "I didn't get a corsage. So I made one myself."

"I gave this to you."

"I know you did."

Sam smiles at this. "You know, I wanted to ask you to the dance tonight, but I was worried you'd say no."

"What made you think that?"

"Because you never texted me. That day we met at the bookstore."

I squint at him, thinking back. "But you never gave me your number."

Sam drops his head, chuckling to himself. "What's so funny?" I ask, slightly annoyed, as he takes my hand. He plucks the cherry blossom from my wrist, and begins unfolding it. I start to protest, but fall silent when it's just a sheet of paper in his hands. Inside is a note with Sam's name and number.

"I never thought to open it . . ." I say.

"I guess that's my fault."

We both laugh at this. Then my smile fades.

"What's wrong?" Sam asks.

"It's ruined now."

The paper is torn and wet from the mist.

"Don't worry," Sam says. "I can make you another one. I can make you a thousand more."

I put my arms around him as we continue our slow dance in the parking lot, listening to the music through the gym wall, as the mist swells around us like clouds before it shifts and fades into a clear night sky, and the memory changes again.

Clothes fly out the second-floor window as I run onto the lawn that's covered with my father's things. My parents have been shouting for the past hour, and I can't stand to be in the house anymore. I always knew things would end eventually, but I never expected it to happen so soon. *Where else can I go?* I asked Sam to come pick me up, but he isn't here yet. I feel the neighbors watching me from their windows. I can't wait around any longer. I turn down the block and start running until everything disappears behind me.

I don't even know where I'm going. I keep running until nothing looks familiar. It isn't until I reach the edge of town, where the farm grass stretches toward the mountains, that I realize I forgot my phone. A pair of headlights shine down the empty road. As I move out of the way, the car slows to a stop in front of me and I realize it's Sam.

"Are you okay?" he asks as I climb into the passenger seat. "I showed up at your house but you weren't there."

If I remembered my phone, I would have sent him my location. "How did you even know where to find me?"

"I didn't . . . I just kept looking."

We sit in his car with the engine humming for a long time.

"Do you want me to take you home?" Sam asks eventually.

"No."

"So where do you want to go?"

"Anywhere else."

Sam starts driving. We circle through town until we lose track of time. Shop lights turn off one by one as the roads begin to darken. With nowhere else to go, Sam turns into a parking space of a twenty-four-hour minimart, and shuts off the car. He doesn't ask me anything about what happened. He just lets me rest my head against the window glass and close my eyes for a moment. Before I drift off, the last thing I remember is the fluorescent light of the minimart sign, and Sam laying his denim jacket over me as I fall asleep.

I wake up on the grass at golden hour. Sunlight warms my cheeks as I push myself up and look around. The trees are full of hand-folded blossoms, hundreds of them, tied up with long strings, swaying in the breeze like willow. Once I'm on my feet, I notice a trail of petals leading toward the sound of a guitar playing in the distance. I follow the sound, passing through a curtain of paper blossoms, and remember where I am. Our secret spot at the lake. The place we've met a hundred times before. The moment I break through the trees, and catch the sunlight shimmer across the water, I find him there waiting for me.

"Julie—" Sam calls my name as he sets his guitar down. "I wasn't sure if you were coming . . ."

"I wasn't sure if you'd still be here," I say.

He takes my hands. "I'll always be here for you, Jules."

I don't question this. At least, not right now.

We sit near the lake and stare out at the water. Clouds move slowly across a pink sky. Sometimes, I wish the sun would never set, so we could stay here, enjoying each other's company, talking like we always do, laughing at inside jokes, pretending like nothing could ever go wrong. I look at Sam, and take in his face, his beautiful smile, his black hair that sweeps across his forehead, his tan skin, and wish I could freeze this moment and hold on to it forever. But I can't. Even in a dream, I can't seem to stop time. The clouds are thickening above us, and there's a strange tremble beneath the earth. Sam must have noticed this, too, because he rises to his feet.

I grab his hand. *"Don't go yet."*

Sam looks at me. "Julie . . . if I could stay with you, I'd never leave."

"But you *did* leave."

"I know . . . I'm sorry."

"You never said good-bye . . ."

"That's because I never thought I had to . . ."

Out of nowhere, a wind sweeps in from behind us, as if it's come to take him away from me. Behind the trees, the sun starts to fall, casting shadows across the water. It isn't supposed to end like this. This was just the beginning. Our story has barely started. My heart pounds inside my chest. I squeeze Sam's hand harder to keep him from leaving.

"This isn't fair, Sam—" I start, but my throat catches, as I feel tears forming behind my eyes.

Sam kisses me one last time. "I know this wasn't part of our plan, Julie. But at least we had this time together, right? I want you to know . . . if I could do it all over again, I would. Every second of it."

If the ending is this painful, I don't know if this was worth it all.

My grip loosens as I think about this. "I'm sorry, Sam . . ." I say, stepping back. "But I don't think I can say the same . . ."

Sam stares at me as if he's waiting for me to take back my words. But there's no time left. Sam starts to disappear before me, dissolving into cherry blossom petals. I stand watching as the wind picks up and pulls them through the air. Before he's completely gone, I reach out to grab a single petal and hold it tight against my chest. But somehow it slips through my fingers and vanishes into the sky. Just like the rest of him.

CHAPTER

ONE

NOW

MARCH 7 11:09 P.M. Don't bother picking me up anymore. I can walk home.

I did walk home. All five miles from the bus station, dragging an overstuffed carry-on with a broken wheel in the middle of the night. Sam kept trying to reach me. Twelve unread messages, seven missed calls, and one voice mail. But I ignored them all and kept walking. Reading these back again, I wish I hadn't been so angry at him. I wish I had picked up the phone. Maybe then everything would be different.

Morning light comes through the curtains as I lay curled in bed, listening to Sam's voice mail again.

"Julie—you there?" Some laughter in the background, and crackling from the bonfire. *"I'm so sorry! I completely spaced. But I'm*

leaving now! Okay? Just wait there! Should only take me an hour. I know, I feel terrible. Please don't be mad. Call me back, okay?"

If only he'd listened to me and stayed with his friends. If only he didn't forget about me in the first place. If only he just this once let me be upset instead of always trying to fix things, no one would be blaming me for what happened. *I wouldn't be blaming me.*

I play the voice mail a few more times before I delete everything. Then I climb out of bed and start upending drawers, looking for anything that was Sam's or reminds me of him. I find photos of us, birthday cards, movie ticket stubs, paper blossoms, stupid gifts like the stuffed lizard he won at the town fair last fall, as well as every mix CD he made me over the years (who even burns CDs anymore?), and cram them all into a box.

Every day these little reminders of him get harder to look at. They say moving on becomes easier with time, but I can barely hold a photo without my hands trembling. My thoughts go to him, they always do. *I can't keep you around, Sam. It makes me think you're still here. That you're coming back. That I might see you again.*

Once I have everything collected, I take a long look at my room. I never realized how much of him I had lying around. It feels so empty now. Like there's a void in the air. Like something's missing. I take a few deep breaths before I grab the box and leave my room. It's the first time this week I managed to get out of bed before noon. I only make two steps out the door before I realize I forgot something. I set the box down and turn back to get it. Inside my closet is Sam's denim jacket. The one with the wool collar and embroidered patches (band logos and flags of places he's traveled) along the sleeves that he ironed on himself. I've had it for so long, and wear it so often, I forgot it was his.

I pull the jacket from the hanger. The denim feels cold to the touch, almost damp. Like it's still holding in rain from the last time I wore it out. *Sam and I race down puddle-filled streets as bursts of lightning lit up the sky. It is pouring on our way home from the Screaming Trees concert. I pull the jacket over my head as Sam holds his signed guitar tight to his chest, desperate to keep it dry. We waited three hours outside for the band's lead singer, Mark Lanegan, to come out and hail his taxi.*

"I'm so glad we waited!" Sam shouts.

"But we're soaked!"

"Don't let a little rain ruin our night!"

"You call this a little?"

Out of everything I'm throwing out, this reminds me of him the most. He wore it every day. Maybe it's all in my head, but it still smells like him. I never got the chance to give it back like I promised. I press the jacket against me. For a moment, I consider keeping it. I mean, why does everything have to go? I could shove it in the back of the closet, hide it beneath my coats or something. It seems like a waste to throw out a perfectly nice jacket, regardless of whom it once belonged to. But then I catch a glimpse in the mirror and come back to myself.

My hair unbrushed, skin more pale than usual, wearing yesterday's shirt, cradling Sam's jacket like it's still a part of him. A chill of embarrassment goes through me, and I look away. Keeping it would be a mistake. Everything has to go, or else I'll never be able to move on with my life. I shut the closet door and hurry back out before I change my mind.

Downstairs in the kitchen, I find my mother leaning over the sink, staring out of the window. It's Sunday morning, so she's working from home. The bottom step creaks under my foot.

"Julie—is that you?" my mother asks without turning around.

"Yeah, don't worry." I was hoping to sneak the box right by her. I'm not in the mood to have a talk about what's inside. "What are you looking at?"

"It's Dave again," she whispers, peering through the blinds. "I've been watching him set up new security cameras outside his house."

"Oh?"

"It's exactly like I expected."

Dave is our neighbor who moved in six months ago. For some reason, my mother thinks he was sent to watch us. She's been paranoid ever since she received a letter from the government a few years back, the contents of which she refuses to share with me. "It's better if you don't know," she said when I asked. I think it has something to do with a lecture she gave at her old job that incited protests. Her students went around campus smashing clocks on every wall. What were they protesting? The concept of time. To be fair on her part, she said her students "didn't get it." But the university decided her teaching style was too radical and let her go. She is convinced they reported her to the government. "The same thing happened to Hemingway," she explained to me. "But no one listened to him. Fascinating story. You should google it."

"I heard someone broke into his garage the other week," I say to relax her. "That's probably the reason for the cameras."

"How convenient," my mother says. "We've lived here for almost, what, three years now? No one has taken as much as a lawn gnome."

I readjust the box that's starting to feel heavy. "Mom—we've never owned a lawn gnome," I say. *Thankfully.* "And we also don't collect vintage sports cars."

"Whose side are you on again?"

"Ours," I assure her. "Just tell me our plan to take him out."

My mother releases the blinds and sighs. "I get it . . . I'm being paranoid." She takes a deep breath, releases it like her yoga instructor taught her, and looks at me. "Anyway, I'm glad you're up," she says. Her eyes flash to the clock above the fridge. "I was about to head out, but I can make you something if you're hungry. Eggs?" She slides toward the stove.

The electric kettle begins to boil. A bag of coffee sits near the sink beside a teaspoon.

"No—I'm fine."

"Are you sure?" my mother insists, her hand hovering over the handle of a clean pan. "I can make you something else. Let me think . . ." She seems more rushed than usual. I glance down the counter and see a stack of ungraded papers. They recently finished midterms at the university in town where my mother works. She is an assistant professor in their philosophy department. It was one of the few places that interviewed her after the incident. Thankfully, one of her old colleagues is tenured there and put his name on the line. One mistake and they both could lose their jobs.

"Actually, I'm on my way out." I keep glancing at the clock, trying to appear to be in a hurry. The longer I linger around, the more questions she can throw at me.

"Out of the house?" my mother asks. She shuts off the electric kettle and wipes her hands with a dish towel.

"Just for a walk."

"Oh . . . Okay. I mean, that's good." For the past week my mother's been bringing meals up to my room and checking in several times a day. So I'm not surprised to hear the note of concern in her voice.

"And I'm meeting a friend."

"Fantastic." My mother nods. "You could use the fresh air, get some decent coffee. And it's good to see your friends. That reminds me, have you talked to Mr. Lee at the bookstore?"

"Not yet . . ." I haven't really spoken to anyone.

"You should check in with him if you can. At least let him know you're okay. He's left a few messages."

"I know—"

"Some of your teachers, too."

I grab my bag from a hook on the wall. "Don't worry, Mom, I'll talk to them tomorrow."

"You mean, you're going back to school?"

"I have to," I say. "If I miss another week they won't let me graduate." Not to mention I'm behind on all my schoolwork, which keeps piling up. I really need to focus again, and pull myself together, because what else am I supposed to do? The world keeps moving, no matter what happens to you.

"Julie, don't you worry about any of that," my mother says. "They'll understand if you need more time. In fact"—she holds up a finger—"let me make a call." She turns in a circle, looking around. "Where is that thing . . ."

Her phone is sitting on the kitchen table. As my mother walks over to grab it, I jump in her way.

"Mom, listen, I'm *fine.*"

"But Julie—"

"*Please.*"

"Are you sure?"

"I promise I am, okay? You don't have to call anyone." I don't want her to worry about me. I can deal with this on my own.

"Alright then," my mother sighs. "If you say so." She cups my face with her hands, running her thumbs along my cheeks, and tries to smile. The silver in her hair shines beautifully in the light. Sometimes I forget she was once blond. As we take each other in, my mother glances down. "So what's in the box?"

I was hoping she wouldn't notice. "It's nothing. I was cleaning out my room."

Without asking me, she lifts the jacket off like a lid and glances inside. It doesn't take long for her to connect the pieces. "*Oh,* Julie—are you sure about this?"

"It's really not a big deal . . ."

"You don't have to get rid of everything," she says, riffling through it. "I mean, you can always store some of it away if you want—"

"No," I say firmly. "I don't need any of it."

My mother lets go of the jacket and steps back. "Alright. I won't stop you on this."

"I have to go. I'll see you later."

I leave the house through the garage door. Down by the curb, I drop the box of Sam's things beside the mailbox and recycling bin. It hits the ground with a clatter like change and bones. The sleeve of his jacket hangs limply over the side of the box like the arm of a ghost. I straighten my shirt and begin my morning walk toward town, letting the sun warm me up for the first time in days.

Halfway down the block, a breeze rolls leaves across my path as I pause on the sidewalk, struck with a strange thought. If I were to turn around, would he be standing there holding his jacket, staring down at the rest of his things? I imagine the look on his face, and even wonder what he might say, as I cross the street and continue down the block without once looking back.

There is a slight chill as I make my way into town. Ellensburg lies east of the Cascades, so occasional gusts of mountain air blow right through us. It's a small town made up of historic redbrick buildings and wide open space. It's a town where nothing happens. My parents and I moved here from Seattle three years ago when my mother received a new job at Central Washington University, but only she and I stayed after she was offered a full-time position. Dad returned to his old job in Seattle and didn't look back. I never blamed him for leaving this place. He didn't belong here. Sometimes I feel like I don't belong here, either. My mother describes Ellensburg as an old town that's still figuring itself out in an age where everyone wants to be in the city. As much as I can't wait to leave the place, I admit it has its charm.

I cross my arms as I enter downtown, noticing the changes brought by spring these last few weeks. Flower baskets bloom beneath streetlamps. A line of white canopies runs down the main block for the weekly farmers market. I cross the street to avoid the crowd, hoping not to run into anyone. Downtown Ellensburg is usually beautiful, especially during the warmer months. But walking these streets again, I am reminded of him. *Sam waits for me to get off work and we grab falafels at the food stand. We watch a movie on "five-dollar Sundays" at the theater and then wander through town together.* When I sense him standing around the corner, waiting for me, my heart races, and I think about turning back. But no one is there except a woman lost in her phone. I pass by without her even noticing.

My friend Mika Obayashi and I arranged to meet for coffee at the diner on the other side of town. There are plenty of coffee shops around, but I texted Mika last night saying I'm in no mood to run into anyone. She replied, *Same.* Inside the diner, I am seated at a booth by the window near an old couple sharing a menu. When the waitress comes, I order a cup of coffee, no cream, no sugar. Usually I add some milk, but I'm training myself to drink my coffee black. I read somewhere online that it is an acquired taste like wine.

I've only had a few sips when the bell jingles from the ceiling, and Mika comes through the door, looking for me. She's wearing a black cardigan over a dark dress I've never seen her wear before. She looks better than I expected, given the circumstances. Maybe she just came from one of the services. My mom told me she spoke at the funeral. Mika is Sam's cousin. That's how she and I met. Sam introduced us when I first moved here.

Once Mika sees me, she comes over and slides into the red booth. I watch her set her phone down and throw her bag beneath the table. The same waitress reappears, sets down a cup, and pours a long stream of coffee.

"Extra sugar and milk would be great," Mika requests. "Please."

"Sure," the waitress says.

Mika holds up her hand. "Actually, is there soy milk?"

"Soy? No."

"Oh." Mika frowns. "Just milk then." As soon as the waitress turns, Mika looks at me. "You didn't reply to my messages. I wasn't sure if we were still meeting."

"Sorry. I haven't been the most responsive lately." I don't really have another excuse. I have a habit of leaving my phone on silent. But this week, I've been especially disconnected.

"I get it," she says, frowning a little. "For a second, I thought you might have canceled without telling me. You know I don't like being stood up."

"Which is why I came early."

We both smile. I have a sip of coffee.

Mika touches my hand. "I missed you," she whispers, giving me a squeeze.

"I missed you, too." As much as I tell myself I like being alone, I feel a rush of relief to see a familiar face. To see Mika again.

The waitress arrives, sets down a small pitcher of milk, tosses some sugar packets from her apron, and disappears again. Mika rips open three sugars and pours them into her cup. She picks up the pitcher and holds it out. "Milk?" she offers.

I shake my head.

"Because it isn't soy?"

"No . . . I'm trying to drink my coffee black."

"Hmm. Impressive," she says, nodding. "Very Seattle of you."

At the word *Seattle*, Mika's phone lights up as notifications pop up on her screen. The phone vibrates on the table. Mika glances at her screen, then back at me. "Let me put this away." She hides the phone in her bag, and picks up a menu. "Did you want to order something?"

"I'm actually not hungry."

"Oh, alright."

Mika sets down the menu. She laces her fingers together on the table as I have another sip of coffee. The jukebox blinks orange and blue from across the room but no music plays. An air of silence nearly settles between us until Mika finally asks the question.

"So, did you want to talk about it?"

"Not really."

"Are you sure? I thought that's why you wanted to meet."

"I wanted to get out of the house."

She nods. "That's good. But how are you handling all of this?"

"Fine, I guess."

Mika says nothing. She looks at me, as if expecting more.

"Well, what about you," I ask her instead. "How have you been?"

Mika's gaze falls onto the table as she thinks about this. "I don't know. The services have been hard. There isn't really a temple around here, so we're doing what we can. There's a lot of traditions and customs I didn't even know about, you know?"

"I can't imagine . . ." I say. Mika and Sam have always been connected to their culture in a way that I haven't. My parents are both from somewhere in northern Europe, but it's not something I really think about.

Things quiet again. Mika stirs her coffee for a long time without saying anything. Then she goes still, as if remembering something. "We held a vigil for him," she says without looking at me. "The day after. I stayed the night with him. I got to see him again . . ."

My stomach clenches at the thought of this. At *seeing* Sam one more time after he . . . I stop myself from imagining it. I have another sip of coffee, and try to blink the image away, but it doesn't fade. I wish she wouldn't tell me about this.

"I know. Not a lot of people wanted to see him like that," Mika says, still not looking at me. "I almost couldn't do it, either. But I knew it was the last time I would get the chance. So I went."

I don't say anything. I drink my coffee.

"There were a lot of people at the funeral, though," she continues. "We didn't have enough seats. There were people from school I didn't even recognize. There were so many flowers."

"That's really nice."

"Some people asked where you were," Mika says. "I told them you weren't feeling well. That you prefer visiting him on your own."

"You didn't have to explain anything," I say.

"I know. But some of them kept asking."

"Who?"

"It doesn't matter who," Mika says, brushing it off.

I have the last sip of my coffee, which by now has lost all of its warmth, intensifying the bitterness.

Mika looks at me. "So have you visited him?"

I take my time to respond. "No . . . not yet."

"Do you want to?" she asks, taking my hand again. "We can go now. Together."

I pull my hand back. "I—I can't right now . . ."

"Why not?"

"I have things to do," I say vaguely.

"Like what?"

I don't know what to say. *Why do I need to explain myself?*

Mika leans into the table, her voice low. "Julie, I know this whole thing's been terrible for you. It's been terrible for me, too. But you can't avoid this forever. You should come, pay your respects. Especially now." Then, in almost a whisper, says, "Please, it's *Sam*—"

Her voice cracks at his name. I can hear a cry rising up her throat as she manages to hold it down. Seeing her this way sends an ache of pain to my chest, making it impossible to speak. I can't believe she would use this against me. I can't think straight. I have to hold myself together.

I clench my empty cup. "I told you, I don't want to talk about this," I say again.

"For god's sake, Julie," Mika scolds me. "Sam would have wanted you to come. You haven't been there for him this entire week. You weren't even there when they had him buried."

"I know, and I'm sure everyone has a lot to say about that, too," I say back.

"Who cares what everyone else says," Mika cries, her body half rising from the seat. "It only matters what *Sam* would say."

"Sam is *dead*."

This quiets the both of us.

Mika stares at me for a long time. Her eyes search mine for signs of guilt or regret, as if she's waiting for me to somehow amend my words, but all I have to say is, "He's dead, Mika, and me visiting him isn't going to change anything."

We hold our gaze for what seems like a long time before Mika looks away. From her silence, I know she is both stunned and disappointed. It is at this moment I realize the tables around us have hushed as well. Our waitress passes by without a word.

After a moment, once the tune of the diner resumes, I gather my words.

"This isn't my fault, you know? I told him not to come but he wouldn't listen to me. I told him to *stay there*. So everyone needs to stop expecting some apology from me, and blaming me for any of—"

"I'm not trying to blame you for this," Mika says.

"I know you aren't. But everyone else probably does."

"No. Not everyone thinks that, Julie. And I'm sorry, but this isn't about you—it's about Sam. It's about missing his funeral. It's about how the one person who was closest to him, who knew him best, wasn't even there to speak about him. Sam deserved more, and you know it. That's what everyone expected. But you weren't there, through *any* of it."

"You're right. Maybe I do know him better," I say. "And maybe I think he doesn't believe in any of this stuff. The ceremonies, the vigil, the people from school—*please*. Sam doesn't care about any of them. He would have hated all of this. He's probably glad I didn't show up!"

"I know you don't believe that," Mika says.

"Don't tell me what I believe," I say. That came out sharper than I wanted it to. I almost take it back, but I don't.

Luckily, our waitress reappears to take our order before this goes further. Mika looks at me, at the waitress, then back at me.

"Actually, I should go," she says abruptly, and gathers up her things. Our waitress steps aside as Mika rises from the booth. She lays some money on the table, and turns to leave. "I almost forgot," she says. "I picked up your assignments from school the other day. Wasn't sure when you'd be back." She unzips her bag. "Yearbooks also came. Ours were the last to get picked up, so I got yours, too. Here—" She drops everything on the table.

"Oh—thanks."

"I'll see you later."

I don't say good-bye. I just watch Mika disappear through the entrance door, ringing the bell behind her, leaving me alone again. The waitress offers to refill my coffee, but I shake my head. I suddenly can't stand to be in here anymore, inside this noisy, cramped, syrup-stained diner that's making me anxious. I need to get out of this place.

There goes my afternoon. I don't know what else to do but wander outside again. I try not to think about Mika and what I should have said differently, because it's too late. I walk through town, letting the caffeine kick in. At least the morning chill is gone. Shop windows glisten in the afternoon sun. I pass by without going inside. There's the antique store. Sam and I used to go in and furnish our imaginary apartment together. I pause at the window. Through the dusty glass are long shelves crowded with paintings and figurines, floors swathed with Persian rugs and old furniture, among other things. Then despite myself, another memory comes . . .

Sam hands me a gift. "I bought you something."

"For what?"

"Your graduation present."

"But we haven't even—"

"Julie, just open it!"

I tear off the wrapping. Inside is a silver bookend in the shape of a single wing, outstretched.

"Shouldn't this be a set?" I ask. "Where's the other piece? It's missing."

"I could only afford one at the time," Sam explains. "But I just got paid. We can go back for it now."

When we return to the antique store, the other half was already sold.

"Who on earth buys half a bookend?" Sam asks the woman behind the register.

I turn to him. "You."

It became an inside joke for us. But it doesn't matter anymore. I threw it out in the box with the rest of his things.

This town is full of memories of us. There's the record store where I'd always find him when I got off work. The red door is propped open with a chair. A few people are looking through the aisles of old records. Someone is changing the strings of an electric guitar. But no Sam sitting on the counter by the speaker, adjusting the music. He didn't even work here. He just knew everyone. I hurry off before someone sees me and tries to start a conversation I don't feel like having.

I don't know how much longer I can stand to be in Ellensburg. I'm tired of reliving these memories in my head. Graduation isn't far away, I remind myself. Only a couple more months, and I'll be out of here. I don't know where exactly I'm heading yet, but it doesn't matter as long as I never have to come back to this place.

I don't remember how I ended up at the lake. It's nowhere near town. In fact, there are no trails leading up to it, and no signs pointing toward it, meaning you have to go and find it yourself. From the long list of places I planned on avoiding today, this was the last spot I expected to end up.

A few leaves fall from a tree as I throw my things on the bench and sit, facing the lake. Sam and I used to meet here in the warmer months. It was our little escape from the world. Our secret getaway when we couldn't afford to leave town. Sometimes, I would sit with a notebook, trying to write something, while Sam was out swimming. If I close my eyes, I can hear him paddling in the water, see the blades of his glinting shoulders cut across the lake. But then I open them and see the glassy, flat surface of the water, and find myself alone again.

Stop thinking about Sam. Think about something else.

Writing often helps me keep my mind off things. I brought a notebook with me. But how do you write when it's hard to focus? Maybe if I sit here long enough, something will come to me. I touch my pen to a blank page and wait for the words to pour out. We don't have spaces for creative writing at school, so I try to do it on my own time. You never get the chance to write what you want in class anyway. I understand you have to know the rules before you break them, but writing should bring you joy, right? I think teachers forget that. Sometimes, I forget that. I hope college will be a different experience.

I should be hearing back from colleges soon. Reed College is my top choice. It's where my mother went. You would think that might help me in this situation. "I don't have the greatest reputation there, so I wouldn't mention me," my mother warned.

"When you're old enough, I'll tell you the story. Other than that, Portland is a wonderful city. You'll love it there." It doesn't hurt that it's only four hours away, so we won't be too far from each other. I went through their course catalog the other day, and it's full of creative writing classes, all taught by established writers from all over the world. I think I can be myself there, find out what I'm good at. Maybe I'll end up writing a book for my creative thesis. But I'm thinking ahead of myself. I found out they need a writing sample from me. So even if I do get accepted to Reed, I might not make it into the program. I have some pieces of writing I could look through, but I'm worried none of them are good enough. I should work on something new. A strong sample that will impress them. But this last week has made it so hard to be creative. I can't get Sam out of my head, no matter how hard I try. He won't be there when I open my acceptance letter. He'll never know if I get in.

An hour passes and the page remains blank. Maybe I should try reading instead, at least for inspiration. The yearbook sits beside me. I tried to leave it at the diner earlier, but the waitress followed me out and nearly threw it at my head. The cover is a tacky gray-and-blue design. I skim through some pages. Club and sport photos take up a good portion, but I skip through them entirely. Next are senior favorites, class clown and best friends, that I didn't care to see who won. There were several people from our class who went around campaigning. A little embarrassing, if you ask me. The next section is senior portraits, but I don't feel like looking through them. I skim all the way to the end until there's nothing left but blank white pages for people to write in. And then I realize someone did, there on the second-to-last page. I guess Mika must have found time to sign it before she gave it to me. But then I look closer at the handwriting and notice it isn't hers. No, it's someone else's. It takes me a second to recognize it. But that can't be right.

Sam. It's his handwriting, I know it. But how did he get ahold of this? When was he able to write to me? I can't seem to wrap my mind around it. I shouldn't read this, at least not right now when I'm trying so hard to forget. But I can't help myself, my hands start to shake.

His voice fills my head.

Hey.

Just to make sure I beat everyone to it, I wanted to write in this first. I hope that's some more proof of how much I'm in love with you. I still can't believe it. How did three years go by so fast? It feels like yesterday I was sitting on the bus behind you trying to build the courage to say something. It's crazy to think there was a time before we knew each other. A time before "Sam and Julie." Or "Julie and Sam"? I'll let you decide that one.

I know you can't wait to leave this place, but I'm gonna miss it. I get it, though. Your ideas were always too big for a small town, and everyone here knows it. But I'm happy your path somehow made you stop in Ellensburg along the way. So you and I could meet each other. Maybe it was supposed to happen, you know? I feel like my life didn't start until I met you, Julie. You're the best thing to happen to this small town. To me. I realize it doesn't matter where we're going next, as long as we're together.

I'll be honest. I used to be scared of leaving home. Now I can't wait to move on and make new memories with you. Just don't forget the ones we made here.

Especially when you make it big. And whatever happens, promise you won't forget me, okay?

Anyway, I love you, Julie, and always will.

Yours forever,

Sam

Forever . . .

I shut the yearbook and stare out at the water as this sinks in.

A family of ducks has appeared on the other side of the lake. I watch them make tiny rings in the water, and listen to a breeze stir leaves from the branches behind me, as the full weight of Sam's words echoes through me.

It's been one week since Sam died. And in my attempt to move on, I've been trying to erase him from my life like a terrible memory. After everything we've been through together. I threw out all of his things. I skipped his funeral. And I never even said good-bye. In his death, Sam asked for only one thing, and that was for us to remember each other. Yet here I am trying so hard to forget.

A shiver goes through me as the first clouds begin to appear. The chill from this morning returns as I sit unmoving on the bench, watching long shadows appear on the surface of the lake, as this sudden feeling of guilt sinks into my bones. I don't even know how much time has passed since I sat down. But the next thing I know, I'm on my feet again, dashing back toward town.

The farmers market is packing up as I cut through it—it's a flash of falling produce, toppling bread loaves, and turning heads. I don't care who I bump into as I make my way down the neighborhood streets toward home. By the angle of the sun and the still traffic, it must be late afternoon. The garbage truck that makes its rounds probably came by hours ago. But schedules often change, and things run late, and somewhere by the curb the box of Sam's things might still be there.

As soon as I turn the corner and my house is in view, I look for the curb and realize it's gone. Everything. All of Sam's things. I nearly stumble as this heavy, sinking feeling falls over me, like water filling my chest, and I forget how to breathe.

I run inside the house and check the kitchen. The counters are empty. I search the living room in the chance that my mother had saved me from making a horrible decision, and brought some of Sam's things back inside. But nothing's here.

I pull out my phone. My mother's at her office, but still manages to answer on the fourth ring.

"Mom—where are you?"

"Why? Julie, is something wrong?"

I realize how out of breath I sound. But I can't seem to collect myself.

"The box of Sam's things from this morning. The one I left outside. Did you bring it back in?"

"Julie, what are you talking about? Of course I didn't."

"So you don't know where it is?" I ask desperately.

"I'm sorry, I don't," she says. "Are you alright? Why do you sound like that?"

"I'm fine. It's just I . . . I have to go—"

I hang up the phone before she can say anything else. My stomach sinks. It's too late. Everything I had left of Sam is gone.

I suddenly remember how I skipped every service and ceremony that was held in his memory—memories I abandoned. I didn't even bother to visit his grave. I can't seem to stand still. I keep pacing back and forth through the empty house as these sudden emotions, the ones I've been holding back, cycle through me like ice water in my veins, making my hands shake. Mika was right. What would Sam think of me if he knew how I treated him?

As I replay the last few days in my mind, I begin to understand something I didn't before. All my pent-up anger was nothing more than a wall to hide my guilt.

It wasn't Sam who left me that night. It was *me* who abandoned him. The second I realize this, I'm back outside and running.

An overcast sky has appeared while I was inside, painting shadows over the neighborhood as I cross the streets. Ellensburg is not the smallest town in central Washington. But there's one main road that runs through the whole town, and if you follow it straight through, you've seen everything. A few blocks before you reach the university, there's an unmarked trail that cuts straight across the entire north side. I follow the trail toward the hill as more clouds roll in, and I feel the first sprinkling of rain.

It's about an hour's walk to memorial hill from the neighborhoods, but the trail cuts the time by nearly a third. And because I haven't stopped running since I left the house, I reach it in no time.

It's drizzling out, but the rain has resolved into mist. I can hardly see in front of me. My clothes are half soaked from the run, but it's not enough to bother me as I stride toward the memorial park's entrance.

Sam is buried somewhere up there. I have to see him at least once, pay my respects, and tell him I'm sorry for not coming sooner and what a terrible person I've been. I have to let Sam know that I haven't forgotten him.

An image plays in my head like a film reel. I see him sitting on top of his headstone, in his denim jacket, waiting for me for the past week. A dozen conversations play through my mind as I think of what to say to him, how to explain why I've kept away for so long. But two feet before I reach the main gate, I stop short.

The lamppost hanging above the gate creaks, unlit in the rain.

What am I doing here? The hill is more than four hundred acres of folded land. I look up and see a thousand grave markers lined up for miles. I don't know how long it would take to find him or where to begin. My feet stay frozen on the wet concrete. I can't go in there. I can't make myself do this. *Sam isn't here.* There's nothing to see but a newly laid plot where he's supposed to be. But I don't want that to be the last image I have of him. I don't want this memory. I don't want to think of him having to spend the rest of eternity buried somewhere up on that hill.

I take a few steps away from the gate, wondering why I came here. This was a terrible mistake. Sam isn't there. I don't want him to be.

Before I even realize it, I've turned away from the gate and nearly slip as I break into another run.

The evening mist has turned into a shower as the brick walls that run along the cemetery fade behind me. I don't even know where I'm going this time. I want to get as far away as I possibly can. The sky is pouring as I enter the woods. I keep on running until the view of houses and roads is long gone.

Rainfall has softened the ground and filled it with puddles. As I'm running, I start imagining myself emerging into an alternate world where everything's still okay, and wishing I could leap through time so I can go back and change everything. But no matter how hard I try, I can't seem to *will* time and space and undo the fabric that is twisting and pulling me apart.

Suddenly my foot catches on something and I slam to the

ground. My body stings in a million places before it goes numb, and I feel nothing at all. I try to get up but I can't seem to move a muscle. So, I don't bother. I just stay there on the floor of stones and leaves as the sky continues to pour.

I miss Sam. I miss the sound of his voice. I miss knowing he would always answer me if I called. I don't even know where I am or who I can talk to. This isn't one of my finest moments. And tomorrow, I will regret ever letting it get to this point. But right now, I'm so desperate and alone, I pull out my phone and turn it on. The light blinds me for a few seconds. I forgot I deleted everything this morning—all of my photos, messages, and applications, so nothing's there. I go through my contact list, trying to think of someone else to call, but there aren't many options. When I notice Sam's name isn't even there, I remember I deleted it, too. I'm not sure if I even remember the number anymore. I don't even know what I'm doing when I dial it anyway, hoping to hear him again through his voice mail one more time. Maybe I can leave him a message, let him know I'm sorry.

The ringing startles me. It's a strange sound to hear in the emptiness of the woods. I shut my eyes and shiver from the cold. The phone rings for a long time, slowly drowning out my thoughts, and I feel as though it will go on and on forever, until suddenly the ringing stops.

Someone picks up the phone.

There is a long silence before a voice comes through the line.

"Julie . . ."

Raindrops patter against my ear. I become aware of the sound of my own heart beating against the earth. I turn my face up slightly toward the sky and keep listening.

". . . Are you there?"

That voice. Faint and raspy like the murmur of the ocean in a seashell. I know it. I've listened to it a thousand times before to where it's become as familiar as my own. That voice. But it couldn't be.

Sam . . .

CHAPTER
TWO

"Can you hear me . . ." he says. *"Julie?"*

The ocean fades and his voice comes through more clearly. *"Are you there?"*

I blink off raindrops. I must have played one of his voice mails by mistake. But I thought I deleted them this morning.

"If you can hear me—say something. Let me know if this is you . . ."

I don't remember that line from before. So this must be something else. Maybe I hit my head and am suddenly imagining things. My vision blurs, so I close my eyes again to stop the trees from spinning. I'm not sure if his voice is coming through the phone or my own head, but I answer it anyway.

"Sam?"

Silence fills the woods. For a second, I think he's gone. That he was never there. But then I hear a breath that isn't mine.

"*Hey . . .*" he says with an air of relief. "*I thought I lost you there . . .*"

My eyes crack open to reveal a sliver of the world. I'm too numb from the cold to know which way is up or down or where the sky is. I reach into the back of my mind for some sense and come up empty.

"*Sam?*" I say again.

"Can you hear me, okay? I wasn't sure if this would work."

"What's going on?"

"I wondered if you'd ever call me back," he says, as if nothing is out of the ordinary. As if we are continuing a conversation we left off yesterday. "I missed you. I missed you infinity."

I can't think straight. I don't know what's happening.

"Did you miss me, too?"

I take in his familiar voice, the rain against my skin, the feeling of my body sinking into the ground, the sudden dizziness in my head, and try to make sense of what's happening. As strange as this all seems, I can't help asking, "Is this . . . really you, Sam?"

"It's me," he says, and laughs a little. "I thought I'd never hear from you again. I thought you might have forgotten about me."

"How am I talking to you?"

"You called me." His voice is as calm as water. "And I picked up. Like I always do."

Always.

"I don't understand . . . How is this possible?"

The line goes quiet. Raindrops roll off my skin like sweat. Sam takes a moment to respond.

"To be honest with you, Julie, I don't understand this, either," he admits. "I don't know how this is happening right now. Just know that it's really me. Okay?"

"Okay . . ." I manage to say.

I decide to go along with this, let his voice cover me like an umbrella, even though this can't be real. I feel my mind slipping, and myself sinking deeper into the earth as I hang on to Sam's voice like rope. Even though I don't know where it's coming from. I want this to be him, but it can't be. It's impossible. And then it hits me. *I'm dreaming . . .*

"This isn't a dream," Sam says, his voice filling the woods. "I promise."

"Then how else are we talking?"

"The same way we always have. Through the phone, just like this."

"But Sam . . . I still don't—" I start.

"I know," he goes on. "It's a little different this time, but I promise to give you a better answer soon. But for right now, can't we just enjoy this? This phone call, I mean. Getting to hear each other again. Let's talk about something else. Anything you want. Like before."

Before. I close my eyes again, and try to go back there. Before I lost him. Before any of this happened. Before everything was ruined. But when I open them again, I'm still here in the woods. And Sam is still a voice on the line.

"You still there?" he asks. His voice is so clear, I turn my head, expecting to see him.

It's only me out here. A question comes to me. "Where are you?"

"Somewhere," he answers vaguely.

"*Where?*" I ask again. I adjust the angle of the phone, listening for background noises on his end, but the rain drowns everything out.

"It's hard to explain. I mean, I'm not entirely sure if I know

myself. Sorry I don't have all the answers. But none of that matters, okay? I'm here now. And you and me are connected again.
You don't know how much I missed you . . ."

I missed you, too. I missed you so much, Sam. But the words
won't come out. A part of me still thinks I'm dreaming. Maybe
I've fallen through some rabbit hole and entered an alternate reality. Or maybe I hit my head harder than I thought. Whatever
it is, I'm afraid that if our conversation ends, I will lose him
again and never get my answer.

The rain continues. But the sky has reduced it to a soft
drizzle.

"What's that sound?" Sam asks, listening. "Is that rain? Julie,
where are you?"

I glance around. For a moment, I forgot how I ended up
here. "Somewhere outside."

"What are you doing out there?"

"I don't remember . . ."

"Are you near your home?"

"No . . . I—I'm not sure where I am." I'm not really sure of
anything at the moment.

"Are you lost?"

I think about this question. There are so many ways I could
answer it. Instead, I close my eyes to shut out the rest of the world,
focusing on Sam's voice, trying to hold on to it for as long as I can.

"You should get out of the rain, Julie . . . Find someplace
safe and dry, okay?" Sam says. "And as soon as you do, give me
a call back."

My heart jolts and I open my eyes.

"*Wait!*" My voice cracks. "Please don't hang up!"

I'm not ready to lose him again.

"Don't worry, I'm not going anywhere," he says. "Get somewhere safe and call me back. As soon as you do, I'll pick up. I promise."

He's made promises before that he didn't keep. I want to refuse but I can't seem to speak. I wish I could keep him on the line forever. But Sam repeats these words over and over until I start to believe them.

"As soon as you call me back . . . I'll pick up."

I can't stay out here forever. I'm drenched and am beginning to lose the feeling in my hands. I need to get out of these woods, and out of the cold, before the sun goes down and I can't find my way back.

I don't remember how the call ended or what happened after. That part remains a blur in my mind like a missing page from a book. All I know is that I kept walking until I made it out of the woods and found the main road again.

It's late evening by the time I reach town. I hurry along wet sidewalks, passing beneath store canopies to avoid the rain. The lights from the diner where I met Mika this morning are off, but the café down the street is still lit up. It is the only light on for blocks. I cross the street and make my way inside. Even at this hour, the place is half filled with students from the university, coupled together beneath Moroccan lamps. Raincoats hang over the backs of bar stools. Laptop screens illuminate blank faces. I make my way toward a table in the back without ordering anything. Once I settle down, I turn my chair away from the others and face the window. There are no mirrors in this café, so my pale reflection in the glass catches me by surprise.

I blow out the tea candle and the image of me vanishes. I run a hand through my wet hair. My clothes are dripping onto the hardwood floor. Maybe I should have wrung them out a little before I came in. Thankfully this corner of the café is dark enough to keep me unnoticed.

I take a few deep breaths to calm myself, and glance around the room. The woman at the table near me is reading a book. I don't want her to overhear the phone call, so I wait a little. She is sitting alone, dressed all in black, and I wonder if she works here. Maybe she's reading on her break. She sips her tea slowly, making me anxious. It isn't until she gets up to leave that I breathe easier. I pull out my phone. It's almost nine. How did it get this late? This is the first I've been aware of the time since I left the house. There are no new messages or missed calls. I guess no one noticed I was gone.

I set my phone down on the table and pick it up again. I do this several more times until I lose count. The smell of caffeine and chai singes my nose. Now that I've made it out of the woods, and am thinking more clearly, the thought of calling Sam again seems ridiculous. Whatever happened out there was probably all in my head. At least, I think so. Have I completely lost it?

I must have, because I pick up the phone again and dial his number.

The call goes through. I hear the first ring and hold my breath. But he picks up almost instantly.

"*Hey* . . . I was waiting for you."

The sound of his voice floods me with relief. I bring my fingers up to my mouth to contain a sound. I don't know whether to feel confused or relieved or a mixture of both.

"*Sam—*" I say his name without thinking.

"I wasn't sure if you'd call back," he says. "Thought you might have forgotten."

"I didn't forget. I wasn't sure where to go."

"Where did you end up?"

I turn my head and look up at the stained-glass transom above the door without thinking. From inside the café, the mosaic letters reflect backward in gold and blue lantern light.

"Sun and Moon."

"The café where I used to work?" he asks. I almost forgot. It's been a while since I've been back here. Sam goes quiet for a moment, and I feel him listening to the background noises through the phone. Suddenly I become aware of them, too—the sound of stools scratching against wood floor, the clink of a spoon on a ceramic plate, the low murmurs of a conversation from across the room. "That's where I first talked to you. You were sitting in the back of the café. Do you remember?"

My mind flashes back to that day. A black apron, the steam from a warm latte, a paper lily on the front counter. Sam brought over my drink before I could order and we talked for hours. That was almost three years ago. This is the same table, isn't it? The one in the back, by the window. I almost didn't notice.

"You used to order a honey lavender latte. I still remember. You never order that anymore, though. You drink coffee now. At least, you try to," he says with a laugh.

It feels like yesterday we were sitting here together. But I can't think about this right now. "Sam . . ." I say to bring him back.

"Remember that time you wanted an espresso to finish your paper, but I said it was way too late for that?" he goes on, almost reminiscently. "You kept insisting, so I made it anyway, and you couldn't sleep the entire night. You got so mad at me . . ."

"I wasn't mad at you. I was just cranky."

"Remember the concert, that night I got my guitar signed? We ended up at the café, too, isn't that right? We shared one of those half-moon cookies . . . you know with the white icing? The ones you said don't look like moons at all? Remember that?"

Of course I remember. The memory is fresh in my head, sending a flutter to my stomach. I was wearing his denim jacket, the one I threw out this morning. We were soaking wet from the rain. Exactly like I am right now. My heart is pounding. Why is he bringing these things up again? These memories. I don't think I can't hear any more of them. "Why are you doing this?" I ask.

"What do you mean?"

"Reminding me of all this . . ."

"Is that a bad thing?"

"*Sam—*" I start.

Something interrupts me. A shoulder with black sleeves emerges as someone pulls a chair around, taking the table behind me. At the same moment the door swings open as another couple comes in, folding down an umbrella. It's getting too crowded in here. I turn back to face the window, and lower my voice. "I wish you could tell me what's going on," I say. "How do I know if this is real?"

"Because this is real. *I'm real*, Julie. You just have to believe me."

"How do you expect me to do that? I feel like I'm going crazy."

"You're not crazy, okay?"

"Then how am I talking to you?"

"You called me, Julie. And I picked up. Like always."

It's the same thing he said before. But it isn't enough.

"I didn't expect you to answer. I didn't expect to hear from you again."

"Are you disappointed?" he asks.

His question surprises me. I'm not sure how to answer it. "That's not what I meant. I only meant . . . I—" I don't know what to say. My mind is too far away and scattered to concentrate. Someone drops a spoon and it echoes across the room, and I hear laughter at the other tables. It's getting too loud in here. More people pour in through the door, and I feel the café shrinking and myself about to get crushed.

"Julie . . ." Sam's voice pulls me back. It's the only thing holding me together. "I know nothing makes sense right now. The two of us talking again. I'm sorry I don't have all the answers for you. I wish I did. I wish there was a way to prove this is real. You just have to believe me, okay?"

"I don't know what to believe anymore."

More voices fill the room. Then comes the sound of footsteps, followed by a blur of jeans and blond hair. The couple who came in appear with hot drinks, taking the table across from me. I try to steal a glance from the corner of my eye without them noticing. The second I recognize a voice, my stomach drops.

Taylor settles into her chair as Liam sets their drinks down. Sam's old friends. They've been dating for almost a year now. They were there at the bonfire the night he died. I turn myself toward the window and lower my head a little, letting my wet hair fall across the side of my face. Of all the people from school I could have run into, it had to be them. I'm sure they noticed I wasn't at the funeral. I bet they have a lot to say about it.

Sam practically grew up with them. They formed a close-knit group that used to hang out before I moved here. The group fizzled out a little once Sam and I started seeing each other. I suspect Taylor had her own reasons for this. When I asked Sam why they didn't like me, he said people around here have a thing against those who grew up in the city. Probably because of our families' "political" differences. Taylor's dad drives a gas-guzzling truck while mine drove an environmentally friendly car. Kids rolled their eyes when he used to drop me off in front of school. My dad hated it here. He couldn't wait to leave this place.

Maybe they haven't noticed me. I'm too scared to check. I'm deciding whether to wait until they leave or move to the bathroom when a bright light blinds the side of my face, and I look up. Taylor lowers her phone that's pointed right at me. Her eyes widen as she realizes she forgot to turn the camera flash off. Liam sips his drink, pretending nothing happened. They don't apologize or say a word to me. My body trembles.

I can't deal with this right now. I just can't.

"Julie, what's wrong?"

Sam's voice comes back and I remember he's still on the phone.

A car appears outside and throws headlights into the café window, illuminating me like a spotlight. *I have to get out of here.* I rise abruptly from my seat, nearly knocking over my chair. Taylor and Liam are silent but I feel their stares as I move between tables, bumping coats and shoulders as I make my way toward the door and throw it open.

It finally stopped raining. People are moving toward me from all sides. I duck beneath someone's umbrella and hurry down the sidewalk with the phone pressed to my chest. As soon as I reach the corner, I break into another run. I run until the café noise and lights are behind me, and not a single passing car is in sight.

A single streetlamp barely lights this side of the block as I lean against it. The bulb flickers above me as I catch my breath. I remember Sam is still on the line. I put the phone back to my ear.

"Julie—what's wrong? Where did you run off to?"

My head is pounding. I don't know what to say, so all that

comes out is a breathless, "I don't understand what's happening to me—" I am never like this, even when Sam died, I held myself together.

"Julie . . . are you crying?"

It isn't until Sam asks this that I realize I am. And I can't stop. What's wrong with me? What am I doing out here? Nothing makes sense anymore.

Sam's voice softens. "I'm sorry. I really thought that if I picked up, everything would be better. This is all my fault. I wish I could fix this."

I take in a deep breath and say, "Please tell me what's going on, Sam. Tell me why you picked up."

There's a long silence before he finally answers this. He says, "I wanted to give us a chance to say good-bye."

I nearly crumble to the floor. There's a lump in my throat that makes it almost impossible to speak as I fight back more tears. "But I never wanted to say good-bye," I manage to get out.

"Then don't. You don't have to, okay? You don't have to say it right now."

I wipe my eyes and keep breathing.

"Listen," Sam says after a moment. "How about this. Let me show you something. I think it'll make you feel better, okay?" Before I ask what it is, he says, "Just trust me."

Trust him. I don't think Sam realizes how much trust I'm already giving him by staying on the phone. I don't know what else to say so I say nothing at all. I stand there in silence beneath the light of the lamppost, as I hold on to Sam's voice and tell myself everything is okay when I'm no longer sure what's real and what isn't anymore.

I take back what I said earlier about the lake. *This* is the last place I expected to end up tonight.

Sam's driveway is empty of cars. Not a single light shines from the windows of the house. His family must be staying with relatives outside of town. I'm not sure what I'm doing here. Sam asked me to come get something he's been meaning to give me. *"Trust me,"* he kept saying. There is a spare key taped beneath the mailbox, just like he told me. I find it and open the front door, hoping no one's inside.

It's too dark to see anything. The scent of flowers and incense overwhelms me. I step over his little brother's shoes as I feel around for a switch. A single lamp flickers on and I look around. The living room is filled with flowers that are beginning to wilt. A beautiful wreath of chrysanthemums hangs near the mantel. This must all be for Sam.

Sam's voice comes on the line. "Is anyone home?" he asks me.

"I don't think so. It's too quiet in here."

"That's weird. Where is everyone?"

"There are a bunch of flowers for you, though," I tell him. "The house is full of them."

"Flowers?" Sam repeats, a note of surprise in his voice. "Interesting . . . Are yours there, too?"

"Mine?"

I look around the room anyway. Knowing full well nothing here is from me. Not even a card. A knot of guilt forms in my chest, and I feel terrible again. "I don't see them here," is all I say.

"I'm sure my mom kept them somewhere else," Sam says.

"Maybe . . ."

I don't want to be in here anymore. So I take my shoes off and head upstairs. It's so strange to be alone in the house. I tiptoe past his little brother James's room, even though he isn't there. Maybe it's out of habit. Sam's room is at the end of the hall. His door is covered with band logos and NASA stickers. The doorknob is cold to the touch. I take a deep breath before I twist it open.

I don't need to turn on the light to know something is different. The curtain is drawn, giving me enough moonlight to see the boxes in the room. Some of the shelves have been cleaned. It looks like Sam's parents have started to pack things, leaving only the bedsheets and the smell of him. I take another breath. *I never thought I would be back here again.*

"You still there?" Sam's voice brings me back to him. "Sorry if my room's a mess." He always said this right before I came in.

"What am I looking for?"

"It should be somewhere on my desk," Sam says. "I wrapped it up for you."

I go through his desk. Behind the computer, under folders, in the drawers. But nothing's there.

"Are you sure? Try the middle drawer again."

"Nothing's there, Sam," I tell him. I glance around the room. "It might be in one of the boxes."

"What boxes?"

I almost don't want to tell him. "There are boxes in your room. I think your parents are packing things up."

"Why would they do that?"

I give him a moment to think this through.

"Oh . . . Right. I guess I forgot for a second there."

"I can look through them, if you want me to," I say.

Sam doesn't hear me. "Why would they pack my things up so soon . . ." he says more to himself than to me. "I haven't been gone that long, have I?"

"You know, I can't speak for your parents . . . but sometimes, it's just hard to look at these things," I try to explain.

"I guess so . . ."

I turn on the desk lamp to see the room better. The boxes are half filled with Sam's clothes, books, CDs and record collection, and rolled-up posters—so many things I thought I'd never see again. I suddenly remember the things I threw out this morning. Here they are right in front of me. Sam's Radiohead T-shirt. His Mariners hat he bought when we were in Seattle, even though he knows nothing about baseball. It all still smells like him. For a second, I forget what I'm even looking for.

"Did you find it yet?" Sam asks again.

I open another box. This one's full of recording equipment. Sam must have spent the last six months saving up for this microphone. He always talked about recording his own music. I told him I'd help him with lyrics. Sam wanted to be a musician. He wanted his song to play on the radio someday. He wanted to make it in the world. Now he'll never get the chance.

I find the gift eventually. It's wrapped with magazine pages and filled with tissue. It's heavier than I expected.

"What is it?"

"Just open it, Jules."

I tear it open, letting the wrapping paper fall to the rug. It takes me a second to realize what this is.

"Wait a second . . ." I turn it over in my hand, trying to make sense of what I'm holding. The winged bookend. The same one I threw out this morning. But it can't be. "Sam . . . where did you get this?"

"At the antique shop. It's the other half you were missing."

I examine it closely. He's right—this isn't the same one I

kept in my room. It's the long-lost half we couldn't find. "But, I thought someone bought it by the time we came back."

"That was me."

"What do you mean?"

"That's the surprise," Sam says with a laugh. "I went back and got the other piece for you. I let you think it was gone. That way, it would be more special when you finally get to put them together. When the wings are complete. It's pretty romantic, right?"

Except I don't have the other wing anymore. Because I threw it out, and now the two pieces will never be reunited. I can't believe I ruined his gift. I ruined everything.

"I was expecting a big reaction," Sam says, noticing my silence. "Did I do something wrong?"

"No, you didn't, it's only, I—" I swallow hard. "I don't have the other piece anymore, Sam."

"Did you lose it?"

I clench his bookend. "No . . . I threw it out."

"What do you mean?"

"I threw everything out," I tell him. "All of your stuff. I couldn't look at it anymore. I was trying to forget you. I'm so sorry, Sam."

Silence fills his room. I know he's hurt by this, so I tell him, "I tried to get them back. But it was too late. Everything was already gone. I know, I'm terrible. I'm sorry—"

"You're not terrible," Sam says. "Don't say that. I'm not mad at you, okay?"

My eyes water again. "But I ruined your gift . . ."

"You didn't ruin anything. You can still keep it. It'll be like before."

Before. What does he mean by that? There's no going back there anymore. "But the rest of your things are still gone. I'll never get those back again . . ."

Sam thinks about this. "Well, how about you take something else of mine? Anything you want from my room."

I had already thought of this. But I was afraid to ask. "Are you sure?"

"Of course. Anything at all," he says. "I want you to have it."

I keep him on the phone as I go through the boxes again. This is so strange, a complete reversal of what I was doing this morning. I take the Radiohead T-shirt and a few other little things—a guitar pick, band bracelets, the hat he bought on his trip to Tokyo. Then I head to the closet, and slide it open. There are still some clothes hanging, but I find it immediately. There it is, his oversized plaid button-down shirt. Sam wore it almost every day, regardless of the season. I guess even his parents couldn't throw it away.

I take the shirt from the hanger and put it on. For a brief second, I feel his hands on me, but it's only in my head. I wipe my eyes with his sleeve. After a moment, I walk over to the bed and lie down. The phone feels warm against my cheek.

It's been a long day, and an even longer week, and I don't realize how exhausted I am until my body rests on the mattress that feels as safe as my own. Sam tells me I can stay in his room as long as I need. I don't even have to say much. I just stay on the phone, listening, and *feel* him there on the line with me. After a moment, almost out of the blue, Sam says, "I'm sorry."

"For what?" I ask him.

"For all of this."

At first, I still don't know what he is apologizing for. But then I realize what he meant. At least, I think so.

"Me, too," I whisper.

Sam stays with me on the phone for the rest of the night and we talk until I fall asleep. Just like we've done a thousand times before.

CHAPTER
THREE

BEFORE

It's too dark to see anything. A hand moves across my face and pulls a string, illuminating the desk lamp on the floor between us. White sheets hang down from the ceiling light in Sam's bedroom as we lay on the carpet with pillows stacked around us like walls. We are hiding in the fort he built with his little brother, James. Sam reaches over and moves my hair out of my face to see me better. He's wearing his favorite royal-blue tank, the one that shows his shoulders and brings out his summer tan skin. He whispers, "We can do something else if you're bored."

James pokes his head in through the opening of the sheets with a flashlight. "I heard that."

Sam drops his head, groaning. "We've been in here for two hours."

"You promised to hang out tonight," James says. He just turned eight years old. "I thought you guys were having fun."

"We are," I assure him, and give Sam a nudge on the arm. "Sam, relax."

"Yeah, Sam. *Relax*," James repeats.

"Alright. Another hour."

I look up nervously at the ceiling lamp that's holding the weight of the sheets, and glance around the fort. It looks like it could fall apart at any moment. "Are you sure it's safe in here?"

"Don't worry," Sam says with a laugh. "We've done this a million times. Right, James?"

"Nobody's safe out here in the wastelands," James says in his creepy voice.

"That's right," Sam says to play along. He looks at me. "We should really be worried about what's out *there*. Better cuddle up, and keep each other safe," he whispers playfully. He leans in and kisses me on the cheek.

James winces. "Ew. Not in the *fort!*"

"It was just the cheek!"

I break out with laughter, then go quiet again. "Do you hear that?" I pause to listen. "I hear rain."

"Acid rain," James corrects me.

I look at Sam and sigh. "I'm gonna have to walk home in that."

"Or you can stay the night," he says through a smirk.

"*Sam.*"

James points the flashlight at our faces. "Mom says to tell her if Julie ever stays past midnight."

"You would do that to me?" Sam asks, looking hurt. "My own brother?"

"She said she'd give me ten dollars."

"So you're taking bribes now, eh," Sam says. "What if I gave you fifteen?"

"Mom said you'd make an offer. She says she's willing to match anything, plus tickets to the Rockets game."

Sam and I look at each other. He shrugs. "She's good."

"Let's focus," James says, looking out through the opening of the fort for signs of trespassers. "We need to figure out what the aliens have done with the others they kidnapped."

"I thought we were hiding from the zombie apocalypse," Sam says.

". . . That the aliens started. Duh," James says, rolling his eyes. He repositions his arms, holding the flashlight like a light saber. "We need to hurry and get the ingredients for the antidote. We can't lose any more men." Behind us lays the body of Mr. Bear wrapped inside a pillowcase. Together, we had to make the hard decision of putting him down before the virus spread to the rest of us.

"Oh. You mean—this antidote?" Sam holds up a glass vial that looks a lot like his bottle of cologne.

James lowers his light saber slowly. His voice darkens. "You've had that all along . . . while one of our men was infected?"

"Been in my pocket the entire time."

"You traitor."

"Worse," Sam says. "I'm the alien."

James narrows his eyes. "I knew it."

I gasp as James throws himself onto Sam, pulling down the fort with him. The sheets fall over me, covering my face, and then rise again in the air before they shift and fall into flakes of snow as the scene changes around me.

I am sitting in Sam's car with my door open. We are parked across the street from the Reed College campus. The ground is

covered with leaves and a thin layer of snow. Sam opens his door
and walks around to my side of the car. He squats down to look
at me, and offers a hand.

"Come on, Julie. Let's check it out," he says. "We drove all
the way here."

"I said we don't need to. It's already starting to snow. We
should go."

"I'd hardly call this snow," Sam says.

"Let's just go, Sam," I say again, and face the front of the car,
ready to leave.

"I thought you wanted to look around the campus? I mean,
isn't that why we drove *four* hours?"

"I only wanted to get a *sense* of the place. And I got it."

"From the seat of my car?" He rests a hand on the roof, and
looks down. "I don't get it. You were so excited when you planned
this. Now you want to leave already."

"It's nothing. I want to check out downtown before everything
closes. Let's go," I say.

"*Julie . . .*" Sam says. He gives me the look that means he
knows me too well. "Tell me what's wrong."

I cross my arms and sigh. "I don't know. What if I hate it? It
already doesn't look like anything from the pictures. I'm under-
whelmed."

"But you haven't even seen all of it yet."

"What if it's worse?" I point out at a redbrick building that
resembles a barn near an empty field. "Look, that's straight out
of Ellensburg."

"You're not giving your dream school a fair shot, Jules," Sam
says. He stands and glances around at the people walking by.
"Don't you want to at least talk to some students? Ask them questions about what it's like here, about the social life and stuff?"

"Not really," I say. "What if they're all a bunch of rich elite snobs who keep asking me what my parents do for a living?"

"That's what we're here to find out."

I take a deep breath and let it out. "I don't know, Sam . . . There's this air about the city that's—what's the word?" I pause to think. "Pretentious."

"I thought you liked pretentious," Sam says.

I give him a look.

"Kidding." He smiles. "So now you don't like Portland at all, I see."

"Overrated. As far as I can tell."

Sam sighs, and then squats down to my level again. His voice softens. "You're scared about leaving your mom, aren't you?" he says.

"I don't want her to be alone," I say. "My dad already left, so maybe I should take a year or two off and work at the bookstore. Mr. Lee said he'd promote me to an assistant manager."

"Is that what your mom would want?" Sam asks.

I don't say anything.

"Is that what *you* want?"

Nothing from me.

"She's gonna be fine, Jules," Sam says. "Okay? You can't name a more independent person. I mean, your mom teaches a class called *Distorting Time*. She literally does Pilates in other dimensions."

"I know," I say.

Sam takes my hand and our fingers lace. "Portland's gonna be great," he promises. "We'll find a cool little apartment downtown . . . fix it up . . . look for coffee shops where I can play music and you can sit and write . . . it'll be like we planned."

"Maybe."

"Let's see what this campus is all about," he says.

"We *really* don't have to," I say. "I'm fine with what I see from the car. Really."

"Fine." He sighs. "Then I'll drive the car onto the quad." He pulls out his keys and stands.

"What? *Sam—*"

It's something he would absolutely do. I grab him before he steps around the car. "Okay—I'll go."

Sam smiles as he takes both my hands and helps me out of the car as fog begins to rise around us. I follow Sam into it like walking through a wall of smoke, as strobe lights flash all around me and music begins to blare, growing louder until I realize I've gone somewhere else.

The smoke fades as Sam takes me down to a crowded basement in someone's house while their parents are out of town. It's my first high school party and I don't know anybody here. There's a Ping-Pong table littered with red and blue cups. People are not really dancing, but swaying to the music. Several guys are wearing sunglasses indoors. It looks like I came late.

"Did you want something to drink?" Sam asks through the music.

"Sure—what do they have?"

Sam looks at the bar against the wall. "Do you like beer?" he asks.

"Yeah," I lie. I'm not planning to drink anything. I just wanted something to hold. I remember a trick my mother told me she used back in her day. *"Dump it out and fill it with cranberry juice,"* I hear her voice in my head.

Sam leads me through the crowd toward a red couch in the back where a girl in a white sweatshirt is sitting with her legs crossed.

"This is my cousin Mika," Sam introduces us. "This is Julie. She just moved here."

Mika stands to shake my hand. "Nice to meet you," she says. "Where are you from again?"

"Seattle."

"Right. I can tell."

"You can?" I ask, unsure of what to make of that.

Sam looks at her then back at me. "So how do you like Ellensburg so far?" he asks. I can tell he's already had something to drink.

"I don't know yet," I say. "There isn't really a lot to do around here."

Sam nods. "Yeah, I guess. You're probably used to like, what, laser shows and holograms and 3D arcades and stuff like that."

"She said she's from Seattle, not the future, Sam," Mika says.

"No, we have some of those things," I say.

Sam looks at Mika. "See."

Someone bumps into me, almost knocking over my drink, so I step out of the way.

"This is a senior party," Sam says to impress me. "I had to ask Spence if you could come. He's the one that lives here. It's his older brother's party."

I can't think of anything else to say but, "Cool."

A minute passes without saying anything. Sam tries to make small talk.

"So, what do you like to do for fun?"

"Uh, I like to write," I say.

"Like books?"

"I guess so. I mean, I haven't written one yet. But someday."

"What's your favorite book?" he asks.

"I like *The Buried Giant*."

"That's my favorite too," Sam says.

"He's lying. He's never read that," Mika says.

Sam shoots her a look.

Mika mouths, "I'll leave you two alone," and disappears through the crowd.

"Okay—maybe I haven't read that yet," Sam admits. "But I know the author. He's Japanese, right?"

"Yeah. Ishiguro."

"I knew it." Sam nods. "My mom has all his books in our living room." The loud music slows down to something more palatable. The blues of an electric guitar with a Lennon-esque voice swaying through it. "It's Mark Lanegan. Do you know him?"

"Of course," I lie.

"He's from here, you know. Ellensburg. My dad ran into him at the gas station once."

"How cool," I lie again.

"Yeah, see, exciting things happen here, too. Ellensburg is a great place. You're really gonna like it," he says with some confidence. "I've been to Seattle, and it sucks. You're so lucky you left."

"I love Seattle," I say.

"Oh . . . yeah? I've heard good things." He tries to smile.

"This is a good song," I say.

"It's 'Strange Religion,'" Sam says, nodding to the melody. "One of my favorites."

We listen to the song, nodding along, awkwardly looking at each other from time to time, while others in the basement have coupled together, slow-dancing. When Sam nearly stumbles, I catch his arm.

"You should sit down," I say, and help him to the couch. Sam rests the back of his head against the wall, and I can't tell if he's about to fall asleep. He seemed fine a moment ago.

"You don't drink often, do you?" I ask.

"No," Sam says.

"Me either," I say.

"I'm really glad you came tonight," he says. "I wasn't sure if you would."

"Well, I did," I say. I take the cup from his hand and place it on the table.

"Maybe we can hang out sometime. Like, after school or something."

"I'd like that."

"Do you drink . . . coffee?"

"No, but I'm teaching myself to," I say.

"I'm really glad you came tonight."

"You just said that."

Sam smiles at me and shuts his eyes.

Suddenly the music cuts off. Someone flickers the lights on and off. A voice shouts down from the top of the stairs.

"*Dudes*—cops are outside! Back door—everybody!"

"Sam, wake up, we have to go—"

"Huh—" He yawns as I wrap his arm around my neck and lift him up from the couch. A stampede of bodies races toward the backyard as I limp and stumble, trying to follow them out. Eventually, I make it through the door and emerge into complete darkness as the weight of Sam vanishes from around my shoulders. The scene changes again, and I find myself somewhere else.

A breeze blows against my skin, and when I look up through the dark, I see I've made it outside. I blink and a baseball diamond emerges through the moonlight. A telescope stands in the middle, angled toward the sky. Leaning down beside it is Sam, who is trying to adjust something.

"This isn't going to work," he says.

"What's wrong?" I ask.

He looks up at me, his eyes flashing with disappointment. "It's too cloudy out. You can't see anything. I thought this would work. I wanted to surprise you," he says.

I squint at the sky. "Surprise me with what? Stars?"

"No. I wanted to show you Saturn's rings. For that story you're writing in class. You said you wished you could see it so you could describe it better." He leans down, checking the lens of the telescope again. "Dang it."

"I can't believe you went out of your way to do this."

"I emailed the astronomy department at the university and everything," he tells me. "And they're only letting me borrow the telescope for tonight."

"Sam . . ." I whisper, and touch his back. He looks up from the lens. He and I have never kissed before. I'll never forget his look of surprise when I pulled his face up slowly with my hands and pressed my lips to his, and we felt a slight shock of static from the metal of the telescope.

"Thank you for this," I whisper.

"But you didn't even get to see it."

"I'm good with my imagination."

We both smile. Sam puts his hands around me, and pulls me in for a longer second kiss beneath the cloudy night sky and bars of moonlight breaking through it.

I remember he said later, "I'll show you them another time. I promise."

He never kept that promise.

CHAPTER FOUR

NOW

The bell echoes down the empty hallway as I arrive late to school. I missed the bus this morning. Now I have to make an entrance to a class that's already started, and draw more attention to myself. I consider skipping first period to avoid this altogether. But I've been absent for an entire week of school now, and I'm already here. I might as well get this over with, since I'll have to face everyone sooner or later. At least I remembered to set my alarm yesterday. But I never planned to wake up in Sam's bed and have to rush home.

Sam.

I'm still trying to wrap my head around last night. *The phone call in the woods. Hearing his voice again.* It was all real, wasn't it? How else would I have ended up in his room? Only seven hours of this place, I remind myself. Then I can call him again. It's all I can think about. It's what's keeping me together as I brace myself for the rest of the school day without him here.

I take a deep breath before I step through the door to first period. All heads turn slowly toward me as the room silences. Mr. White pauses his chalk on the board, and opens his bearded mouth as if he's about to say something. But he looks away and continues his lecture, allowing me to go find my seat. As I slip between desks, no one makes eye contact with me. When I see the empty table by the window with two chairs, my heart stops. It's where Sam and I usually sat together. But I don't stall for too long because I sense people staring. I take another breath before I walk over and set my things down. I don't look at anyone. I just stare at the front of the room and watch the minutes *tick, tick* away on the clock.

After class, everyone ignores me. No one asks how I'm doing or looks my way. I don't know what I was expecting coming back. It's hard not to let it bother me. Maybe they all noticed I wasn't at the funeral. Maybe they think I'm some cold, heartless person who feels nothing after her boyfriend died. The rest of the day goes like this. Hallways grow silent as I walk through them, and whispers follow. But I keep my chin straight and pretend I don't hear anything. I suddenly remember the photo Taylor took of me and wonder who she sent it to. Probably their senior group, everyone at the bonfire that night. I'm sure it made them feel better, seeing me like that. Thankfully I don't have any classes with her or Liam. I've been trying hard to avoid those two all day. I even took the other stairs to avoid passing by their lockers.

At lunch I don't know where to sit. I take my time placing food on my tray as I look around for Mika. I haven't seen her all morning. Maybe she's still taking time off from school. She hasn't contacted me since we met at the diner yesterday. If only she knew what happened last night. *After I called Sam and he picked up.* But I can't possibly tell her anything yet. Would Sam want me to? I should ask him before I make any decisions. If our phone calls are real, I don't want to risk anything.

There are plenty of chairs open but nowhere to sit. I consider eating outside, but I feel everyone watching me. I don't want them thinking I'm afraid to eat alone. I won't be one of those girls who ends up hiding in a bathroom stall.

I search for an empty table in the back of the cafeteria. Something catches my eye. Behind a chair, rose jewels glitter along a white silk backpack. It belongs to my friend Yuki. Her smooth black hair flows down her back, long and beautiful. She is sitting by the window with two other exchange students—Rachel from Vietnam and Jay from Thailand. I head over and set down my tray.

"Is anyone sitting here?"

Blinking eyes look up from cafeteria food and lunch boxes. Jay, who is a head taller than the rest of the table, removes his headphones and brushes his dark waves from his forehead. He's wearing a striped blue baseball jersey he bought on his trip to Seattle.

"No—of course," Rachel says. Her hair is tied back in a ponytail today. She moves her bag to make room for me. "Please join us."

"Thank you," I say.

Awkward smiles are exchanged as I take a seat between her and Jay. Yuki and I share a nod from across the table. We eat in silence. Usually, the three of them are bright with conversation. But there's a weight at the table that keeps us quiet and somber.

Without saying anything, Jay slides a box of mango slices in front of me. A sympathy offering. I smile at him and take a slice. Then Jay pushes a bag of homemade cookies toward me, along with those mini green tea Kit Kats that he knows are my favorite. They're his favorite, too. I try to push them back but he insists. "How about we split it," he says. He's always been sweet this way.

Rachel smiles at me. "We missed you, Julie," she says. "We've been thinking about you. We're glad to have lunch with you again."

"And we miss Sam, too," Jay says mournfully. "We're really sorry . . . about what happened."

The table goes silent again. Yuki's eyes flash between me and Jay, as if she's reading my reaction to Sam's name. To make sure it's okay to bring him up. It does feel strange to have them talk about him like this. Like I wasn't on the phone with him last night.

"Sam was a great friend," Yuki adds, nodding. She tries to smile. "To all of us. We'll always remember him."

"Always," Rachel says.

It warms me to hear this, especially coming from Yuki. She knew Sam longer than the others. She lived with his family during the first year of her exchange program. Sam was the first person she met when she arrived in Ellensburg, and he showed her around. His mother hoped it would help him improve his Japanese. The day after the funeral, she stopped by my house to drop off soup and tea for me even though I ignored all her messages.

Jay and Rachel moved here a few months ago. It's their first year in Washington. We have a few other international students. The ones from Europe are treated like royalty and get invited to all the parties. Yuki, Jay, and Rachel, on the other hand, have had a more difficult time finding their place. They get the alienation treatment, despite their fluency in English. No one makes the effort to talk to them like the French and German students, so they rely a lot on each other. The terrible thing is when people see them together all the time, they accuse them of isolating themselves from the rest of school. I never noticed this until Sam mentioned it to me. Sam told me his friends would refer to them as *those* Asians. When Sam finally said, "You know, I'm Asian, too," one of his friends replied, "Yeah, but you're . . . *different.*" Because Sam was born here and didn't have an accent. Sam never said anything back. He just grabbed his things one day and moved to Yuki's table, and I went with him. Now lunch feels empty without him here. *Like something's missing.* I know the others sense it, too.

Jay passes me another Kit Kat and leans into me. "Let us know if you need anything," he whispers. "We're always here for you."

I don't know what else to say to everyone but "Thank you." I poke at my salad with my fork as we continue to eat in silence. Much later, almost out of nowhere, I say to the table, "I think Sam would be happy to know what you guys said about him." I know in my heart this is true. And I plan to tell him later.

At the end of school, I hurry to my locker to grab my things. I'm trying not to run into anyone. I just want to head home and call Sam as soon as I get to my room. It's what we have planned. As I'm standing there, I sense someone behind me. There's a tap on my shoulder.

"Julie?"

I turn around to meet dark green eyes. It's Oliver, Sam's best friend, standing a bit too close. He's wearing his blue letterman jacket. His backpack hangs over a single shoulder.

"You're really back . . ."

"Did you need something?"

"I wanted to say hi."

"Oh. Hi," I say quickly. I turn back to my locker and grab another book, hoping he'll take the hint.

Oliver doesn't move. "How have you been lately?"

"Fine."

"Oh . . ." He waits for me to say more but I don't. Maybe he was expecting a different answer. I'm not in the mood to have that conversation right now. Especially with him. But he keeps talking. "It's been a real week, hasn't it?"

"I guess you could say that."

"Are you sure you're okay?" Oliver asks again.

"I said I'm fine."

I don't mean to be so rude. But Oliver and I have never been good friends, despite his relationship with Sam. There was always some tension between us I never completely understood. It always felt like the two of us were competing for Sam's attention. There was a time when I wanted to get to know Oliver. Whenever we were together with Sam, I remember trying to start a conversation with him, but he'd always be short with me or pretended not to hear it. He would invite Sam somewhere and say there was no room in his car or spare ticket for me. So forgive me if I'm in no mood for a chat. Especially since Sam isn't around anymore. I don't have to be friendly. I don't owe him anything.

Oliver was also one of the people there at the bonfire that night. Maybe that's what he wants to talk about. I'm not looking for a confrontation right now. I shut my locker. "I have to go."

"But I was hoping you and I could talk, or something," he says somewhat tensely.

"I don't really have time right now. Sorry." I walk off without saying anything else.

"Wait—just for a second?"

I keep walking.

"*Please*," Oliver calls after me. Something sharp and wounded in his voice cuts me, making me stop. "Please . . ." he says again, almost desperately this time. "I don't really have anyone else to talk to."

I turn around slowly. The two of us stand there, looking at each other as people walk right past us. Now that I'm looking at him, I can read the pain in his face. *He lost Sam, too.* Except he isn't connected to him like I am. I step toward Oliver, closing the distance between us, and whisper, "Is it about Sam?"

Oliver nods. "Nobody else gets it," he says. Then he leans into me. "Why did it have to happen to him, you know?"

I touch his shoulder and feel how tense he is. Like he's holding something in. Neither of us say any more because we don't need to. For the first time, it's like we understand each other.

"I know . . ." I say.

"I'm really glad you're back," Oliver says. "It was weird not having you around, either." Then out of nowhere, he puts his arms around me and hugs me tight. The leather of his jacket is soft against my cheek. I usually shy away from this sort of affection, but for this occasion, I allow it. We both lost somebody we loved. After a moment, Oliver pulls away and readjusts his backpack. "Is it okay if I text you sometime? Just to talk?"

"Of course you can."

Oliver smiles. "Thanks. I'll see you tomorrow."

I watch him disappear down the hall. It almost feels like we just met for the first time. It's too early to say if Oliver and I might be friends after all of this, but at the very least, maybe things will be different.

At home, I find my mother's car in the driveway. She's in the kitchen washing dishes as I make my way inside. As soon as I close the door, I hear the faucet shut off, followed by my mother's voice.

"*Julie?*" she calls from the kitchen. Before I can answer, she storms down the hall with a look relief on her face. "Where have you been all day?"

I take off my jacket. "I was at school. I thought I told you yesterday."

"But why didn't you answer my messages?" she asks.

"What messages?"

"I texted you last night. I even called."

"You called me?" I don't remember waking up to any notifications. The only person I've spoken to since last night was Sam. I check my phone again. "Are you sure? I never got anything from you."

I hand her my phone to see for herself.

"Of course I'm sure," she says, scrolling through it. "That's so bizarre. I definitely texted you. Do you think it's your phone? I guess it could be mine."

"Maybe it's the service."

"Maybe . . ." my mother says, thinking. She hands me back my phone. "You know, no matter how smart they try to make these things, they never work." She lets out a long breath.

"I'm sorry to worry you."

"It's alright," my mother says. "I'm just glad you're fine." She takes my jacket from me, and hangs it on a hook on the wall. "Thankfully I noticed your backpack was gone this morning, so I figured you were at school. How late did you come home last night?"

"Oh—" My eyes shift to the floor. She doesn't realize I never came home at all. "Not too late . . ." I say.

"You know, I could have given you a ride this morning."

"I don't really mind the walk." I turn toward the stairs.

"Wait." My mother stops me. "How was school? Is everything okay?"

I pause on the first step. "It was . . . fine," I say without turning around.

"You don't want to talk about it?"

"Maybe not this second. I'm a little tired."

My mother nods. "Alright. You know I'm always here, Julie," she says as I head upstairs. "But we should get your phone checked out soon! Mine, too, now that I'm thinking about it. I've had a suspicion that someone's been trying to hack it. It's probably been *tapped*. Then again—what isn't these days . . . They're probably recording everything we're saying right now. Be careful!"

"I will!"

I shut the door behind me and look around the room. Everything's exactly like I left it. I returned this morning from Sam's house to change and grab my things before school. That's why I was late to class. I didn't mean to spend the night in his room, but I was so exhausted, and Sam told me it was okay. I haven't spoken with him since then. I sit at the side of my bed, and take out my phone. We made plans to talk after school once I got home. I remember making him promise me he'd pick up again. Otherwise, I couldn't fall asleep. I stare at the blank screen of my phone. While this rational part of me keeps thinking last night was all a dream, I look over and see his plaid shirt hanging on the back of my chair. On my desk is the other bookend he gave me last night. His Radiohead shirt is folded and tucked away in the middle drawer. I checked a second ago to make sure it was still there.

I check my phone. For some reason, Sam's number doesn't appear in the call history. I noticed this in the morning when I woke up. It's as if there's no record that it happened. There's no way this could be all in my head, could it? How else would I have known about the key under the mailbox? I guess there's only one way to be sure. I take a deep breath and dial Sam's number. The sound of the ringing makes me tense. But it only rings twice before he picks up.

"*Julie* . . ."

The knots in my chest undo themselves, and I breathe easily again. "*Sam.*"

"You still sound relieved to hear me," he says with a laugh. The warmth of his voice pulls me back to the beginning and it's . . . like *before*.

"Can you blame me?" I whisper, as if someone might hear us. "I don't expect you to pick up."

"But I promised I would, didn't I?"

I swallow my breath, taking his voice in like air. "I know you did . . . And that's why I called back. But you realize how crazy this is, right? You are supposed to be gone . . ."

"What do you mean?" he asks.

My stomach hardens. I can't tell if he's being serious. He has to know what happened that night one week ago, right? *The bonfire. The missed calls. The headlights on the road.* There's no possible way he and I should be talking on the phone again. I'm almost afraid to ask this. But I have to know. The words are heavy in my throat. *"You died, Sam* . . . You know that, don't you?"

There's a long silence before he answers.

Sam lets out a breath. "Yeah I know . . . I'm still processing it."

A chill goes through me. A part of me wanted to hear a different answer. Something that could bring him back to me. "So am I imagining all of this?"

"You're not imagining anything, Julie. I promise, okay?"

Another promise. Without an explanation. I grip the phone tight, trying to keep it together. "I still don't understand how this is possible. How are we talking to each other?"

Sam goes quiet again. I move the phone to the other ear, waiting for his answer. "Honestly, Jules, I don't really know," he says. "All I know is that you called me and I picked up. And now we're connected again."

"It can't be that simple, though—" I start.

"But why can't it be?" Sam asks me. "I know this doesn't really make sense right now. But, maybe we don't need to complicate it with questions we don't know the answers to. Maybe we can just enjoy this chance for what it is. For as long as we have it."

I glance at the walls, thinking this over. *Another chance. To be connected again.* Maybe he's right. Maybe this is a gift or a glitch in the universe. Something far outside the realm of our understanding. I remember something from last night. "When I was outside the café, you said something else. You said you wanted to give us a second chance at good-bye. You said that's why you picked up. Did you mean that?"

Sam takes his time to answer this. "At some point, I think we both need to say it. But you don't have to worry about that right now, okay?"

"So . . . until then, I can still call you?"

"Of course. Whenever you need me."

"And you promise to pick up?"

"Always."

Always.

I close my eyes and take this all in. It doesn't take long for my mind to drift back to *before*. Before everything changed and all the plans we made were still in place. Before Sam died and I could reach out to touch him and know he's there. Before everything was taken from us. On the other line, I sense Sam is doing the same. When I open my eyes, I find myself alone in my room. As I think of Sam, and this second chance we have, a question comes to me. I know I asked this before, but he never gave me an answer. "Where are you, Sam?"

"Somewhere," he answers vaguely.

"*Where?*"

"I can't really say. At least, not right now."

For some reason, I sense I shouldn't push him on this. "Is it anywhere I've been?"

"I don't think so . . ."

I try to listen to the sounds on his end. But I can't hear anything else.

"Can you at least tell me what you see?"

He takes a moment. "An endless sky."

I look over to the window. The curtain is partly drawn, so I walk over and pull it out of the way. The window is already unlatched when I push it open, letting a breeze roll in as I look out past the roofs of the houses, beyond the tops of the distant hills, and out toward the sky. I feel Sam *listening*. I ask him, "Are we looking at the same one?"

"Maybe. I'm not entirely sure."

"I'm guessing this is all you can tell me."

"For now, at least. I'm sorry."

"It's okay," I say to ease him. "I'm just glad you picked up the phone."

"I'm glad you called me," he says. "Thought I'd never hear from you again."

Tears form behind my eyes. "I thought I lost you forever. I missed you."

"I missed you, too. I missed you infinity."

I don't question him further on what's happening. At least, not right now. I just take this for whatever it is, and breathe in this impossibility of being reconnected to someone I thought I lost, no matter how ridiculous it seems. The rest of our phone call goes on like a daydream, as I continue to question what is real and what isn't. I'm wondering if any of it matters. We talk about ordinary things, and it feels like old times again. I tell him what Yuki and the others said at lunch. I tell him about the rest of my day at school, like my conversation with Oliver. Seems like something from my imagination, but there are things I can't explain. It would be easier to tell myself none of this is real, but then I see the physical objects in the room that shouldn't be there. *The shirt, the bracelets, the other bookend.* How could I have gotten these if he hadn't told me where the spare key was?

Questions fill my mind, but I push them aside for now and allow myself to live in this beautiful strange rabbit hole I've fallen into. I don't care how any of this is possible. I have Sam back. I don't want to let him go.

CHAPTER
FIVE

I've been working at Mr. Lee's bookstore for almost three years now. It is a relic of a place, filled with leather-bounds, rare foreign books, and collectables, and has been around for two generations despite more people shopping online these days. It is the last bookstore in town. I found it by accident the first week I moved here. The store is nameless with no storefront signs outside. The only indication are the books stacked in spiral towers in the windows. Many of our customers wander in out of curiosity.

To be honest, I wasn't sure how long the job would last when I applied. Every time I turn that corner on my way to work, I worry I'll find the lights off and the CLOSED sign unturned at the door. I'm surprised Mr. Lee still manages to keep us around when there's so little to do. I can't thank him enough for his kindness.

The crystal wind chime jangles against the glass door as I

come in. It's the next day, and I decide to stop by after school to check in on things. After a week of radio silence on my end, it's time. When I step inside, it feels like I've gone through a portal. Light bulbs hang from strings at different heights in the air, blinking occasionally. The place looks small from the outside, but the sixteen long rows of hand-painted bookshelves that nearly touch the ceiling make the store seem massive.

The store looks empty at first. More quiet than usual. Then I hear the struggling of a box being torn open, followed by the ripping of tape, then the sound of several books tumbling onto the floor, and someone's voice.

"*Oh geez.*"

I figured Tristan would be working today. I follow the voice and find him crouched down in the back of the fantasy section, mumbling to himself, picking up fallen books. I kneel down to help him out.

"Need a hand?"

"Huh? *Ouch—*"

Tristan turns too fast, bumping his head against the bookshelf ladder.

"Oh my god—are you okay?"

"Yeah, totally fine." Tristan winces, smiling through some pain. He blinks at me with recognition. "*Julie?* When did you get here?"

"Just a second ago," I say as I check his forehead. "Maybe we should put something on that."

Tristan waves it off. "No, really, I'm fine," he says again, and laughs a little unconvincingly. "It happens to me all the time around here."

"That worries me a little."

"Don't worry! It's only a bump."

After we stack the books together, I help Tristan to his feet. He straightens up and runs his hand a few times through his brown curls, even though they bounce right back. It's a nervous tic of his.

"I'm sorry I scared you," I say.

"You didn't scare me," he says, dusting his sleeves off. "I was little surprised, that's all. Didn't know you were coming in today."

"I felt like checking in. I know it's been a while." I glance around the store for changes. But it's exactly as I left it. I turn to Tristan. "Sorry for leaving you guys out of the blue. I heard you volunteered to take over my shifts. I never thanked you."

"Oh, no need to thank me. I mean, I'm glad I could help."

Besides Mr. Lee, it's only me and Tristan working here. If one of us is sick, the other one is responsible for their hours and closing the store. We rely a lot on each other, especially around finals when we have to coordinate our exam schedules. I hate that I sprung an entire week on him without a word. Tristan is a junior, so we never have class together. The first time we spoke was when we both sat down with Mr. Lee during our interview for this job. Mr. Lee said he was impressed with our knowledge of books and chose us specifically for the genres we read most. He noticed I'm well-read in young adult and literary fiction, and praised Tristan's expertise in science fiction and fantasy. We later learned we were the only ones who even applied.

"I still feel guilty," I say.

"You shouldn't," Tristan says, shaking his head. "You should take off however much time as you need. I like being here. So don't feel bad."

The wind chimes jingle, letting us know a customer has come in. Tristan looks over his shoulder, and runs a hand through his hair. He whispers, somewhat carefully, "So how are you doing, by the way? I've been wanting to reach out, but I wasn't sure if it was too soon, you know? I'm sorry about what happened to Sam. Things must be hard right now . . ."

I stare at the floor, wondering what to say. Ever since Sam picked up, it's as if the whole world flipped again, and I'm no longer sure how to respond to these questions. How do you bridge grief and hopefulness, without having someone take it the wrong way? Without hinting at your secret? "I'm just taking it one day at a time . . ."

Tristan nods. "That makes sense . . ."

The wind chime jingles again. I use this momentary distraction to change the subject. I run a hand along the shelves. "Anyway, how's the store been?"

"Pretty good," Tristan says, understanding. "Actually, you should see this." He takes my arm, pulling me to another section of the store. A woman and her son are perusing some used books by the front window. Tristan smiles at them. "Let me know if you guys need anything," he says.

We arrive at science fiction, his favorite section.

"Look—the entire Space Ninja series, collector's edition," Tristan says, showing me the shelf he's been working on. "They only have fifty of them in the world."

"Oh, wow."

Tristan opens up the book with careful hands. "It has a holographic map of the entire NexPod Galaxy. Isn't that cool?" He turns the page. "Here's a picture of Captain Mega Claws—also holographic. If you tilt it a little, his claw moves."

"It's beautiful." I touch the holographic paper as it glimmers. "Looks expensive, though."

"It's already sold."

"Oh—so why is it still here?"

"I still have to ship it," he explains. "Someone bought it on-line."

"We're online?"

"Only since last week," Tristan says. "We have an online store now and everything. It's really expanding our customer base."

"That's amazing. And Mr. Lee is okay with it?"

"Of course. He even asked me to update our Facebook page. And we have a Twitter now, by the way."

"Do people still use that?"

"You'd be surprised."

"Interesting."

Tristan returns the book to the shelf. "I also reached out to the author, Steve Anders. I asked him to come do a signing here and got a response."

"Oh my god. When's he coming?"

"He's not," Tristan says, frowning. "His publicist said they've never even heard of Ellensburg."

"Most people haven't," I say with a sigh. "At least you tried."

"Yeah. That's what Mr. Lee said."

The wind chimes jingle again, bringing in another customer. It's always great to see people come into the store, even if they don't buy anything. After a quiet moment, I catch the scent of sage and tea leaves. A calm energy embraces the store. I turn to see the back room's door propped open, and Mr. Lee standing beside Tristan, a hand on his shoulder. He has that tendency to appear as if from nowhere.

"Good afternoon, Julie."

"Mr. Lee . . ." is all I get out. I was hoping he would be here today. I feel a pang of guilt in my chest for not reaching out sooner, but I know he understands. No one knows this, but Mr. Lee was with me the day I found out Sam died. In fact, it was right here in this store when I got that phone call from Mika in the morning. Mr. Lee picked me up off the floor, closed down the bookstore early, drove me to the hospital, and waited to bring me home. He always loved having Sam around.

Mr. Lee said he "brought in good luck."

"What did I bring in?" I once asked him.

"You brought in Sam."

"The books missed you," Mr. Lee says with a lift of a hand. While someone else might find his words strange, I've grown accustomed to how he imbues personalities into the books of the store, bringing them to life. For instance, when a new book would come in, he'd say, "We'll need to find this one a home." It always makes me smile.

"I've kept them in my mind," I say.

He nods. "I had a feeling you were stopping by," he says. "Perfect timing. There's something I would like you to see."

We leave Tristan with the customers as we head to the back office. The room is behind a secret bookcase that isn't really a secret. Every time I step through it and follow the blinking string of lights and paper ornaments along the ceiling, I feel like Alice stepping through the looking glass.

The room is filled with stacks of brown boxes, each filled with various books we either don't have a place for yet or just haven't sorted through. Mr. Lee asks me to wait here while he disappears inside the little office in the corner. When he returns, he's holding a book I don't recognize right away.

"I found this in last week's donation box. Take a look—" He hands it to me.

I run my hand over the cover. It is a beautiful brown cloth-bound, soft to the touch, with embroidered floral patterns that appear dusted with gold with nothing written on top. Maybe the book sleeve is missing. I skim through some pages in search of the title. But everything's blank.

"It's a notebook," Mr. Lee says. "Quite a beautiful one, don't you agree?"

"It is . . ." I whisper, admiring the quality of the pages. "I can't believe someone gave this away. It hasn't even been used yet."

"I immediately thought of you," he says, and points to the old computer on the back table. "I've noticed you stealing paper from the printer to write on. So I figured you might appreciate this gift. Who knows . . . maybe if you change the medium in which you wrote, it might inspire something."

"I was only borrowing the paper," I say.

Mr. Lee chuckles and waves it off.

I look down at the notebook. "I can have this?"

"As long as you make good use of it," Mr. Lee says with a nod. "I think of it as an investment."

"How so?"

"You see—once you finish your book, we can put it on the shelves, right in the front of the store," he explains. "And I can tell customers she wrote it here, you know? In the journal I gave her."

I smile as I hold the journal close to me. Mr. Lee is always encouraging me to write more. *"Use your time at the store. Talk with the books for inspiration. They're full of ideas."* Sometimes I share my stories with him to get his thoughts. Unlike my English teachers at school, Mr. Lee is well versed in the world of literature and always finds beauty in my words. He understands what it is I'm trying to say even when I'm not sure myself. "I don't know if I could write a whole book, though," I admit. "I'm having trouble just thinking lately. I'm not sure what to write about anymore."

"What have you been thinking about?" he asks.

I run my hand along the spine of the journal. "Everything, I guess. My life. What's happening in it." *And Sam, of course.*

"Then write it down. Write down what's happening."

I look at him. "Mr. Lee, nobody wants to read about my life."

"Who are you writing for again?" Mr. Lee asks, arching a brow. He has asked me this before. I know the answer he wants to hear. *I write for myself.* I'm not sure what this really means, though. I can't help caring about what people think, especially about my writing. "We have too many voices inside our heads. You have to pick out the ones that mean something to you. What story do *you* want to tell?"

I stare down at the journal, thinking about this. "I'll try, Mr. Lee. Thank you for this. And I'm also sorry for not letting you know I was gone—"

Mr. Lee holds up a finger to stop me. "No apologies necessary." He opens the bookcase door and gestures toward the store. "The books welcome you back."

I always feel at home when I'm in the store. I could spend hours and hours in here. There's a comfort in being surrounded by walls of books. But as nice as it is to be back, Sam is waiting for me. We planned to make another call today. But this time, he asked me to meet him somewhere new for us to talk. He said he wanted to show me something.

I had just made it out of the bookstore when the wind chimes went off again, followed by the sound of Tristan's voice.

"Julie! Wait!"

I spin around to see him with his hand extended, holding my phone.

"You forgot something."

A gasp escapes me. *"Oh my god—"* I grab the phone and

press it tight against my chest. My heart is pounding as thoughts of *what if* flash through my head. *What if I lost it? What if I couldn't call Sam back? How could I be so careless? How could I forgive myself?* I make a promise to never do this again. *"Thank you so much,"* I say breathlessly.

"No problem," Tristan says. "You left it on the front counter."

"You're such a lifesaver."

Tristan laughs. "What would we do without our phones, right?"

"You honestly have no idea, Tristan."

I breathe relief and smile as I wait for him to head back inside. But he doesn't. He just stands there, a bit awkwardly.

"Was there something else?"

Tristan scratches the back of his head. "Sort of. I mean . . . I forgot to mention something earlier."

"What is it?"

"It's about the film festival. Spring Flick? My film was accepted. I wanted to tell you," he says.

"That's incredible, Tristan! Congratulations. I knew it would be."

Spring Flick is part of the annual Ellensburg Film Festival that takes place at the university. It's one of the biggest events in town. Tristan and his friends submitted a short film in the high school category. They spent the last six months filming a documentary on Mark Lanegan, the alternative-rock musician from Ellensburg. Sam was a huge fan.

"It's next month, a few weeks before graduation," Tristan goes on, running a hand through his hair. "I have an extra ticket. You mentioned you wanted to go last time, if the film was accepted. Did you still want to?"

The word *graduation* catches me off guard, and I nearly panic.

Is it really only two months away? I haven't even heard from colleges yet. And I'm so behind on school, what if I don't catch up in time? I become so lost in thought, I forget what Tristan even asked me. I must take too long to respond, because his face flushes, and his voice stammers. "I'm so sorry. I shouldn't have brought this up this soon. You probably have a lot on your mind right now. I should go back in—" He turns toward the store.

"*Wait,*" I call him back. "Of course. I'll go."

"Really?" he asks, suddenly beaming. "I mean, okay. Okay, great. Cool. I'll tell you more about it soon. And, you know, let me know if you change your mind. That's cool, too."

"I'll be there, Tristan," I say as I turn to go.

Tristan stands at the door, waving, as I cross the street and disappear around the corner.

Cherry blossoms fall at my shoes as the bus drops me off at the university entrance. The brick tower of Barge Hall rises behind the trees as I look around. The paths throughout campus are covered with pink and white petals. There is a stream of water that runs beside the library. I cross a bridge to get to the other side. As I cut across the grass, branches drop petals on my hair and shoulders. A small breeze twirls them in the air as I keep walking. When the trees blossom in the spring, central Washington feels like a place from a dream.

The Sakura festival happens once a year, and people from all over Washington come to see it. Sam and I would take the bus here all the time when the weather was warm. It is a beautiful stroll along the university paths. This is the first I'm seeing them this year. I breathe in the scent, and remember the two of us walking together, Sam's hand in mine.

Sam stops to sniff the air. "This really takes me back . . ."

"Is it close?" I ask.

He looks at me. "To what?"

"To the cherry blossoms in Japan."

Sam takes a good look around. "That's like comparing a lake to the ocean. You know what I mean? It's not close at all." He just returned from a trip to Kyoto to visit his grandparents and attend the Sakura festival there. He said it was a family trip . . .

I fold my arms. "Thanks again for the invitation."

"I told you." He laughs as he takes my hands. "We'll go this summer after graduation. I promise. You're gonna love it there. It'll be like nothing you've ever seen."

"Nothing like Ellensburg?"

"Different worlds."

I smile and kiss his cheek. "I can't wait."

"So how are the blossoms this year?" Sam's voice over the phone pulls me back.

I called as soon as the paths cleared and it's only us out here.

"They're beautiful," I say. I look up at the trees that line the paths, listening to the stream of water running somewhere up ahead. "But nothing like the ocean, right?" Sam doesn't answer, but I sense him smiling on the line. "Why did you ask me to come here again?"

"It's our tradition," Sam says. "To walk through here every spring, remember? I realized we never got to see them this year.

And it made me a little sad. I didn't want you to think I forgot. So I figured I'd bring you here one more time, while I still can."

"But you're not here," I remind him.

"I know." Sam sighs. "But pretend I am. Just for a second. Right there, beside you, like before . . ."

I close my eyes and try to imagine this. A breeze moves across my face but nothing changes. *You should have let me come with you last time. This can't make up for it.* "It's not the same, Sam. Not at all . . ."

"I know. But it's the best I could do right now."

A couple holding hands walks past me, reminding me of what's missing. *The touch of a hand. The warmth of skin. The sense of him beside me.* Even though I'm connected to Sam again, he's not really here, is he? I squeeze the phone tight and push this thought out of my mind and keep walking. I was worried about being out in the open like this and running into someone. Sam told me I shouldn't tell anyone about our calls because he doesn't know what might happen. I don't want to take any risks, so I promised to keep our connection a secret for now. When the campus has cleared a little, I find an empty bench away from the path and sit down.

"So what's it like at school?" Sam asks. "Is everything . . . different?"

"You mean, without you there?"

"Yeah."

"I guess so," I say. "I've only been back a few days. But I hate that you're not there anymore. I don't like sitting beside an empty chair, you know?"

"Are people talking about me?"

I think about this. "I don't know. I don't really talk to anyone."

"Oh . . . Okay."

There's something in his voice. A note of sadness? "I'm sure people still think about you, though," I add. "They have photos of you in the front office and in some of the hallways. I always see them when I come in. People haven't forgotten you, if that's what you're wondering."

Sam says nothing. I wish I knew what he was thinking. As I sit there in silence, thinking about people from school, a question comes to me. "Are you talking to anyone else, Sam?"

"What do you mean?"

"I mean, on the phone. Like this."

"No. Only you."

"How come?"

Sam takes a moment. "You're the only one who called me."

I consider this. "Does that mean if someone else had called you, you would have picked up for them, too?"

"I don't think so."

"Why is that?"

"Because our connection is different," he says. "And maybe I was waiting for your call. In a way."

"Could it be something else?" I ask.

"Like what?"

"I don't know," I say, suddenly thinking about it. "Maybe there's something you're supposed to tell me. Or maybe there's something you need me to do . . ."

"Or maybe I wanted to pick up, and make sure you were okay," Sam says. "Is that so hard to believe?"

I lean back against the bench and take this in. "How long do we have this for?"

"It won't be forever. If that's what you're asking."

I was afraid he would tell me this. I swallow hard. "So that means one day, you won't pick up anymore?"

"Don't worry. We would say good-bye first, okay? We'll know when it's going to happen before it does."

"You won't just leave again?"

"I promise, Julie. I'll stay as long as I can."

I shut my eyes for a moment and try to find comfort in this. I don't ask Sam any more questions. I don't want it to ruin this beautiful day. A breeze stirs petals along the grass. When I open my eyes, I look up through the branches and catch the sun glimmering like silver coins through the cherry blossoms.

"I wish you were here with me," I whisper.

"I wish I were there, too."

The sun has set by the time I get home. I was on the phone with Sam for so long, I lost track of the day. I wanted to call again once I got back to my room, but he said we should wait until tomorrow. This is probably for the best. Even though school is the last thing on my mind, I have so much work to catch up on. I'm so behind on all my readings, they've piled up on my desk. It's a struggle to focus. I barely get through one chapter of my history book when a *crack* at the window jolts my head up. A second later, there's another *crack* as a rock comes flying into the room, bouncing across the floor. I rush to the window and look out.

A tall figure moves across the driveway. A familiar one.

"Oliver? Is that you?"

Down below, Oliver stands in his letterman jacket, waving up at me.

"Hey—what's up?"

I give him a look. "What are you doing here?"

"Oh, you know, just passing by," he says, shrugging casually. "Thought I'd say hi. Hope I'm not bothering you."

"Oliver—you threw a *rock* at my window."

"Right, my bad, that was totally rude of me . . ." he says, holding both hands in the air as if surrendering to something. He doesn't seem to be going anywhere.

"Do you *need* something?" I ask.

He shakes his head. "No. Not at all. I mean, maybe. Sort of . . . Yes? I mean no. I mean—"

"Just spit it out."

Oliver drops his shoulders and sighs. "I wanted to ask if you wanted to go on a walk or something."

"Right now?"

"I mean, unless you're busy."

"Kind of."

"Oh . . ."

I don't think that was the answer he was expecting. He looks around in the dark, a bit flustered.

"I'm sorry," I say.

Oliver shrugs. "No, it's okay. I guess I'll head on home then . . ." He half turns, facing the street as if he's about to head off. But he doesn't. Instead, he just stands there frozen in this pose that looks like he's about to leave. I wait a bit longer but nothing happens.

"You're not leaving, are you?"

He drops his head, looking miserable. "I really need someone to talk to," he says.

I glance at the schoolwork on my desk and then back at Oliver. "Okay, fine. I'll be right down. Just don't make any more noise."

Oliver covers his mouth and holds up an OK sign.

A few minutes later, I find Oliver waiting for me on the porch steps, his hands in his pockets. It's dark out. The moment I step into the porch light, Oliver's eyes widen.

"Oh—uh, your shirt . . ." He stammers a little, and steps back.

It's a bit chilly tonight, so I threw on Sam's plaid shirt before I left my room without thinking about it. I wasn't sure if he'd notice.

"I couldn't find my jacket," I say. I roll up the sleeves and cross my arms, trying not to bring attention to it. The two of us stand in silence for a while. "So where are we walking?" I ask.

"Nowhere really," Oliver says. "Is that okay?"

"Sure."

He smiles a little. In the porch light, I see him better. Dark brown hair curls across his pale forehead, not a strand out of place. I've always been envious of Oliver's hair. The curls can't be natural.

Oliver motions me down the steps. "After you."

We walk along the lamplit sidewalks in silence. The only sounds are our footsteps on the concrete and the occasional passing car. Oliver stares straight ahead, his eyes distant. I don't know where we're heading or if that matters.

After a while, I decide to say something. "Are we going to talk at all?"

"Sure," he says. "What'd you want to talk about?"

I stop walking. "Oliver . . . you asked *me* to come out tonight."

Oliver pauses on the sidewalk without looking back. "True." He glances up and down the street for cars. "This way," he says and crosses the road. I follow him reluctantly. As we leave the neighborhood, I get the sense he's leading us somewhere.

Oliver doesn't look at me. He keeps walking. After a while of this, he finally asks me something. "Do you still think about him?"

I don't need to ask who. "Of course I do."

"How often would you say?"

"All of the time."

Oliver nods. "Same."

We cross the street again, avoiding the lights from town. Oliver drifts onto a gravel road I'm not sure we should be walking on. I follow him anyway, checking back and forth for cars.

"Have you checked Sam's Facebook lately?" Oliver continues.

"No, I deleted mine recently. Why?"

"It's really weird," he says. "People are still writing on it. On his wall. As if he can still read it or something."

"What are they saying?"

"Exactly what you'd expect them to say," Oliver says, his jaw tense. "I can't stand it. No one even uses Facebook anymore, you know? I don't remember the last time I wrote on someone's wall. Suddenly, he's dead, and it's flooded? I read through them all. It's like they're not even writing to him. It's like they're writing to each other. Trying to see who can grieve the most, you know?"

I'm not sure what to say. "People cope in different ways sometimes. You shouldn't let it get to you."

"It's not different if everyone's doing it." He points across the road. "This way."

It's getting late but I don't say anything. The town is somewhere behind us now, and I've lost track of how long we've been walking. I usually wouldn't go this far out, especially at night. But Oliver's with me. And I can tell he doesn't want to be alone.

The temperature drops a little and I see my breath in front of me. But for some reason, I don't feel cold. I keep my arms crossed and focus on the sound of the gravel crunching beneath my shoes, until Oliver suddenly stops and I almost bump into him. Then I look up and see the sign. Even in the dark, the bold white letters reflect the words.

LEAVING ELLENSBURG

We are standing at the edge of the city limits. A field of grass stretches out from the line of gravel that divides Ellensburg from the rest of the world. The air is still, the stars just beginning to show themselves. I look left and see the moon hanging low over the trees, lighting the tips of the grass that are slightly frosted from the cold, making it glitter like moonlight on water.

Oliver touches the line with his foot as I stand near his side, watching. He stares out into the distance for a while, hands deep in his pockets.

"Sam and I would come here a lot," he says, almost wistfully. "I mean, we used to, anyway." He looks at me. "Before he met you."

I don't say anything.

Oliver looks away. "You know . . . for a long time, I was mad at you."

"For what?"

"For stealing my best friend from me," he says. "I was always a little jealous, if you wanna know the truth. How he'd always leave me to go see you. And whenever we hung out, you were all he talked about."

I look back at him, a flutter of laughter inside me. "That's funny. Because I was always jealous of you for the same thing."

Oliver smiles, and then stares out again. "Me and Sam made a lot of plans together, you know. To leave Ellensburg eventually. Whenever we got sick of this place, or one of us was having a bad day, we'd walk all the way here, and step over the line," he says as he does it. "We always talked about finishing college at Central, and where we would go after. But that was before he made new plans with you."

"And that's why you always ignored me?"

"I'm sorry about that."

"It's okay," I say, and cross the line, too. "Maybe I wasn't the nicest to you, either."

After a moment, Oliver lets out a breath, his eyes glinting. "It really kills me, you know. That he never made it out of here. That this was it. That this line was as far as he got." He shakes his head.

I swallow hard. "It hurts me, too."

"I'm glad he met you, though," Oliver says without looking at me. "I could tell you made him happy. The times you were together. At least he had that." When I don't say anything, he adds, "Don't listen to any of them, by the way. The others who blame you. They don't know anything." I look away as he continues, "Sam really loved you, you know? If they knew him at all, they'd know how much he'd hate the things they're saying. I'll try to stop it if I hear anything."

I don't know what else to say. "Thank you."

The two of us stare out at the grass in silence for a while. Then out of nowhere, Oliver says something, almost to himself or the moon. "I wish I could tell him one last thing." Then he turns to me. "Do you think about that? About what you would say to Sam, if you had one more chance?"

I look down. He doesn't know that I already have that chance. That I still have Sam. But I can't tell him this. "Yeah, I've thought about it."

"Me, too."

It's getting late. But we stand there in silence, just thinking and staring out at the other side of the world for a few more minutes longer before we finally have to head back.

Once we reach my house, Oliver walks me to the front door. Before I head inside, I have to ask him, "So what would you say to him?"

Oliver stares at me, somewhat confused.

"I mean, to Sam. If you had the chance?"

"Oh, well, I—" he stammers. His mouth opens and closes, as if he's forgotten how to speak. As if something is stopping him. Seeing him struggle like this, I touch his shoulder.

"You don't have to tell me," I say.

Oliver breathes relief. "Maybe another time," he says.

I smile and unlock the door.

"Do you think we can do this again?" Oliver asks.

"Go on another walk, you mean?"

"Yeah," he says, nodding. "Or you know, hang out or something."

I think about this. "I'd like that. But just knock next time. Or a text will do."

"I'll try to remember that," he says. "Although I did text you. But you never responded."

"When?"

"Earlier today. And yesterday, too."

"You mean—more than once? That can't be right." I check my messages again to be sure. There's not a single text from Oliver. Now that I think about it, there aren't any new texts from anyone. Are they not coming through anymore? I've noticed this has been happening since I started talking to Sam a few days ago. "It might be my phone. It's been acting strange lately."

"That's a relief," Oliver says. "I thought you were ignoring me."

"So you decided to show up and throw rocks at my window?"

Oliver holds back a grin. "What can I say . . . I'm annoying."

"Maybe a little bit. Anyway, I should go inside."

But before I do, Oliver leans in without a word and wraps his arms around me again. It's a longer embrace than last time, but I let it happen. "Your shirt," he whispers near my ear. "It still smells like him."

"It does."

We say good night. I close the door behind me and listen to Oliver linger on the porch before he eventually makes his way down the steps. As I get ready for bed, I keep wondering what Oliver would say to Sam if he had the chance. I wonder if he will ever trust me enough to share it. Or maybe it's something I might have already known.

CHAPTER

SIX

There is this song I listen to whenever I sit down to write. It's called "Fields of Gold," the beautiful live version by the singer Eva Cassidy. The song opens with a distant guitar and a sad voice that sounds like a wolf whimpering or a songbird crying. Every time it plays, I close my eyes and see myself there, standing in a field of golden barley, a cool breeze blowing my hair, and the warm sun setting against my back. No one is ever with me, only the endless rolling fields and the sound of a guitar coming from somewhere I can't see.

Sam learned to play the song for me after he tapped my shoulder in class and asked what I was listening to. I remember one day while we were lying out on the grass, I asked him to sing it for me, even though I knew he was sometimes embarrassed of his voice, and he said *"Someday."* I've asked him many times after, and he always had an excuse, like he hadn't warmed up yet, or he was feeling a bit hoarse, or he needed some more practice. Maybe he was afraid he would ruin the song for me, because he knew how much I loved it. He's only hummed it to me on a few rare occasions, like the night he sat with me on the porch after I helped my father move his things out of the house and watched him drive away.

As I listen to the song alone in my room, I suddenly realize I will never hear Sam sing it for me, and that "*Someday*" never came.

The next morning is filled with Sam's music. I find one of his old CDs in my mom's car and sit alone in the parking lot, listening to it before school. It's a playlist Sam made me of live recordings he mixed in his bedroom, each song tugging me with beautiful acoustic guitar riffs he played over popular ballads that he made his own. He has an old taste in music he gets from his dad. Elton John, Air Supply, Hall & Oates. Even though no one really listens to CDs anymore, Sam always made them for me anyway, because he knows I prefer physical copies over digital counterparts. Just like with books, I like something real to hold in my hands. Sam recorded dozens of them over the years, each one longer and more thoughtful than the last, personalized to how he felt about me at the time—something I learned later. He loved a good slow song, something we had in common. One of his favorites was Fleetwood Mac's "Landslide." It was one of his go-tos when someone asked him to play something on the guitar. The music scene in Ellensburg isn't the best, but he made the most of it. He performed at school talent shows, weddings, in a few coffee shops that allowed him to, and a hundred times only for us. I always told him this place wasn't big enough for him. He told me the same thing.

I realize this is the only CD I have left from him after I threw everything out. On the front, written in blue ink, is my name in his handwriting. Before I get out of the car, I put the CD carefully back in its sleeve and keep it inside my bag.

School hasn't changed since I returned. Heads turn the other way and no one says a word to me. I really don't mind being ignored anymore. There's some peace in being left alone. I was looking forward to art history class today, because it's the only class Mika and I have together. But she didn't show up again. I haven't seen her in a while. I finally texted her this morning but she hasn't responded yet. I'm not sure if I should be worried. I hope everything's okay. Maybe she's not getting my texts?

I find Jay waiting for me when I get out of third period. He's wearing a sky-blue dress shirt, casually unbuttoned, with the sleeves rolled up. He styled his hair differently today, letting soft wisps fall above his brows, making him look like a pop star. It's almost criminal how this school doesn't appreciate his style. When I compliment him on it, he smiles, bringing out his cheekbones.

"Remind me, did you model back home in Thailand?" I ask.

Jay angles his face toward the ceiling light, eyes smoldering. "Is it obvious?"

"*Your cheekbones.*"

We planned to meet Yuki outside for lunch today. Rachel won't be joining us. She's been trying to help start an Asian Student Club with some friends, and they need twenty-five signatures by next week. Jay told me they're having a tough time getting people to join.

There's a table set up at the end of the hallway. Rachel is

sitting with her friend Konomi, talking with a few seniors who have crowded around them. When I notice Taylor and Liam are there, my skin prickles.

Liam picks up one of the flyers. "So none of us can sign up? Says here Asian students only."

"It doesn't say that," Rachel says.

Taylor tilts her head a little, pretending to look interested. "So what are the requirements?"

"We don't have requirements," Rachel answers. "Anyone can join."

"Then why call it the *Asian* Student Club?" Taylor says, pointing at the table sign. "That doesn't sound very inclusive. What do you guys even do?"

"Probably wasting school money to watch anime." Liam laughs.

My cheeks burn. Sam would speak up if he was around. But he isn't anymore. Would he want me to say something? Stand up for Rachel? As I stand there, wondering what to do, Jay walks right up to the table.

"What's the problem?"

Liam shoots him a look. "Who said we had a problem?"

"If you're not interested in the club, you don't have to join," Jay says. "No need to make fun of it."

Taylor folds her arms. "Ever heard of a joke?"

"No one was even talking to you," Liam says. He straightens himself, as if to intimidate Jay into backing up. But Jay just stands there, keeping his cool. Before this can escalate further, I finally appear between them, hoping to defuse this.

"You know, your jokes aren't that funny," I say to Liam. "Why don't you guys leave them alone? Stop wasting everyone's time."

Liam exchanges a look with Taylor before he turns back to

me. "Are we bothering your friends? The only ones at school who talk to you? At least they speak English, so that's something."

"You're an asshole," I nearly shout.

His eyes narrow at me. "At least I showed up to my friend's funeral. Then again, I didn't have anything to do with his death."

A chill goes through me. I don't even know what to say back. I just stand there, trying not to let the shock show on my face. Taylor shakes her head before turning away. Before they walk off, Liam grabs a handful of candy from a bowl on the table and stuffs it in his pocket.

"Later."

Once they're down the hall I let out a heavy breath and turn to the table.

"You alright, Rachel?" I ask.

"No worries." Rachel smiles as if nothing's really wrong, as if what they said didn't bother her. It's a smile I'll never be able to understand. "What about you?" she asks me back. "Are you alright?"

I don't have an answer for her. I take the signup sheet and write my name down.

The day doesn't get better. I can't seem to pay attention in any of my classes. Every time I stare at the clock, I think it stops, making the day feel longer. I scribble on notebook paper and stare out the window to get time moving again but it doesn't work. Nobody takes the seat beside me. I pretend not to notice. My teachers drone on, and I don't hear a word they're saying. All I can think about is Sam. I wish I could talk to him right now. But we made plans not to call until later tonight, so I'll have to wait. As I'm sitting in the back of English class, something occurs to me. I wonder why I haven't thought of it before. I take my phone out and send him a text, telling him I miss him.

The message fails.

I try to send another one, which also can't be delivered. That's strange. I'll have to ask him about this later.

The bell rings, relieving me from a long lecture on *Oliver Twist*. As the class begins packing up, Mr. Gill, our English teacher, says something that makes my body jolt.

". . . and remember, if you haven't already—make sure you hand in your papers to me before you leave."

Papers? A cold douse of shock pours over me as I remember the comparative assignment between *Hamlet* and *Gatsby* that I haven't thought about in weeks. It was due last Wednesday, but Mr. Gill gave the class extra time to get it done because of what happened. Because of Sam. He sent us several email reminders about it, yet somehow I still forgot. To Mr. Gill, turning in late work is an offensive crime that could lead to failing the class.

As everybody files out, I don't know what to do but approach his desk, even though I have no words prepared. So I cut out the small talk and jump to the point.

"Mr. Gill, I'm so sorry, I actually don't have the paper right now," I say.

"And why is that?"

"I don't really have an excuse. I've just been distracted with everything."

He picks up the stack of papers and evens it out on the desk in front of me. "You're right. That isn't an excuse."

"I know, I'm really sorry. I'm behind on a lot of things." I don't know what else to say. "Is it possible for me to give it to you to-morrow or something?"

"Julie, I already gave you extra time on this." Mr. Gill rises from his seat, carrying the stack of papers.

"I know . . . I've been having a real tough couple of weeks," I say, following him around the desk. "I haven't really been able to think straight."

"And I understand. Which is why I gave everybody an extension," he repeats as if that's enough, as if I should be grateful or something. "I can't simply give you an extra day, because that would be unfair to the rest of the class."

"*Please*, Mr. Gill . . ." I say more desperately. "Can't I just turn it in late and get marked down?"

"I'm sorry, Julie. I can't accept a late paper. It's in the syllabus."

"But why not? Why can't you mark me down or something?" We only have four papers for the semester. One zero could bring me close to failing, and I won't be able to graduate. And if I can't graduate, then I won't be able to leave this stupid town and move to Portland to go to Reed College and get into their writing program, even though I haven't heard back from them yet.

"Because I'm preparing you for the real world." Mr. Gill points vaguely out the window. "And out there, life doesn't give you extensions. Even during the hardest times. So let this be a valuable lesson for you. You'll thank me later."

He puts a hand up to end our conversation. This isn't the first time he's said something like this. He truly believes he's doing me a great favor by being strict. *But this isn't the real world,* I want to tell him. *It's high school. And as much as I don't want to care about it, failing this stupid class might affect the rest of my life.*

I don't say anything else because there's no point. I storm out of his class before I say something I'll regret. As much as I hate to admit it, maybe he's right. I should prepare myself for a world where nobody is on your side or willing to help you out even when it costs them nothing at all.

I need to go home and talk to Sam. He'll understand me. I rush to my locker to grab a few things before I head out. But there's someone waiting in front of it.

"Oh—Mika."

She doesn't say anything. She just looks at me. Her face is pale and there are dark rings under her eyes. I wonder if she's sick.

"Are you okay?"

"Yeah, I'm fine."

"I haven't seen you around. I texted you a few times."

"I've been at home."

Her hair is a bit of a mess. I move some of it out of her face. I whisper, "You seem tired."

"I get it, I look terrible," she says, leaning back against the lockers.

"I didn't say that."

"I've had a lot of stuff to deal with." She looks around us. "And I don't like being back here."

"You mean, at school?"

She lowers her gaze.

"Is there anything I can do?"

Mika looks at me. "There's a vigil tonight. It would be nice if you came, too."

"There's another one?"

"It's a candlelight vigil," she says. "The school asked my family to put it together. Everyone is supposed to meet in town later tonight. I could really use some help."

Sam and I have another call planned tonight. I don't want to keep him waiting on me, wondering where I am. But I can't tell Mika this. What should I say to her? "I don't know if I can yet . . ."

Mika gives me a look. "So you're gonna miss this one, too?"

"Mika—" I start.

"I don't know why I asked," she says, picking her bag up from the floor. "I knew you wouldn't go. I'll see you later."

A pang of guilt stabs me as I stand there, unsure of what to say. If only she knew my reasons. I can't leave things like this between us. As Mika walks off, I grab her arm.

"I'll come! I'll come to the vigil."

"You don't have to," she says, taking her arm back.

"I *want* to. I mean it. I want to be there this time."

Mika studies my face, reading me like she always does. "It's at eight o'clock, if you want to meet at my house. We can go together."

I'm supposed to call Sam around that time. But I'm sure I can call him right after. He'll understand. I don't want to disappoint Mika again. I hate seeing her this way.

"I'll be there. I promise."

"Tonight," she says to make sure.

"Tonight."

I throw my bag on the floor the second I get home. The house is quiet—my mother must still be at work. As I open the door to my room, a breeze blows through the window, sending papers flying off my desk. I hurry over to shut it, but the frame is stuck again. I give it a few good hits but it doesn't budge, so I leave it alone. I don't even bother to pick up the papers. I just walk around them, leaving them where they are. I was planning to write in my new journal once I got home, work on my writing sample, but I've lost the motivation. Today was draining. There's an ache in my left temple that's hard to ignore. I keep thinking about Liam and Taylor and Mr. Gill and that stupid paper I forgot to turn in.

I wish I could talk to Sam right now. I miss having him around. I miss being in the same room with him, my head on his chest, talking through whatever was bothering me. He was always there to listen. Even when he didn't know what to say back. I check my phone. Our next call isn't until later tonight. I know I should wait, but I've had such a terrible day, and am so desperate to hear from him. His shirt still hangs on the back of the chair. I stare at it for a long time before I decide to take the chance and call him anyway.

The phone rings longer than usual. But eventually he answers. His voice is warm in my ear. *"Hey . . ."*

"Sam."

"I wasn't expecting to hear from you so soon," he says. "Is everything's alright?"

"I couldn't wait to call you," I say. "I hope that's okay."

"Of course it is. You can always call me, Jules. Whenever you need."

I breathe a sigh of relief. *"Okay.* That's good to know."

"Are you sure you're alright? You sound a bit tense." He could always read my voice. It was one of the things I loved most about him. I could never hide what I was feeling.

"I had a rough day. That's all."

"What happened?"

"Just some school stuff," I say, sparing him the details. "It's nothing really." I sit on the edge of the bed and let out a deep breath to release some tension. Now that I have Sam on the line, I don't want to ruin our call with talks of an English paper I forgot to turn in. "We don't have to talk about it . . ."

Sam laughs a little. "Is this the real Julie?"

"What do you mean?"

"I mean, you once complained to me for four hours about an overdue library book, remember?" he says. "You can tell me anything. Pretend it's just like before. Let me know what's wrong."

I sigh. "I'm just behind on everything. And I forgot to turn in a paper."

"For Mr. Gill's class?"

"Yes, but it's not that big of a deal," I say. "We have one more coming up, and if I get a good score on that, I should be okay." I glance up at the calendar that's pinned above my desk. "And graduation isn't too far away. I just have to push through a little longer, you know? I'll be fine." For the first time, I want Sam to know I'll be okay. Even if I'm not so sure.

"Graduation . . ." Sam repeats the word, almost to himself. "I forget about that for a second. Must be really nice to have something to look forward to . . ."

My throat thickens at this. I'm not sure what to say back. "I guess so . . ." I say. Suddenly the image of me walking in a cap and gown doesn't seem appealing anymore. Especially if Sam won't be there. Maybe I should skip it altogether . . .

"Have you figured out what your plan is? After graduation, I mean."

"Uh—" I go quiet, unsure of how to answer him. Because Sam and I used to stay up all night, thinking about this. Mapping out a future together. Where we would live, the jobs we wished for, things we wanted to do. Now he's gone and I'm left with a bunch of plans that have been ripped in half. "I don't know yet. I'm still figuring it out."

"You haven't heard from Reed yet?" Sam asks.

"No . . . not yet."

"I'm sure you'll get in. Things will work out."

"I hope so."

Truth is I should have heard back by now. I've been checking the mail every morning for a letter from them. Reed is a realistic choice for me, given my grades. Honestly, I'm tired of reading books where the protagonists only apply to Ivy League colleges, and somehow always get in. I don't quite have the résumé for that. I like Reed's quieter reputation that goes under the radar.

But I don't feel like talking about the future right now. Not like this. Not when Sam doesn't have a future of his own to plan out. So I change the subject. "I saw Mika today at school," I say. "They're holding a candlelight vigil for you tonight. She asked me to go with her. I think a lot of people will be there."

"Mika . . ." Sam's voice brightens at her name. "How is she?"

"She's been better. She really misses you."

"I really miss her, too," Sam says. "I think about her a lot. Sometimes, I wish I could talk to her, you know?"

I move the phone to the other ear. "Why don't you? That would mean so much to her." Sam and Mika grew up in the same house together. You would guess they were siblings from how close they were.

Sam lets out a sigh. "If I could, I would, Jules."

From the open window, the sound of a car coming up the driveway lets me know my mother's home. I go to make sure my door's locked in case she tries to come in, which she does occasionally.

"Can I ask you something?" Sam asks after some silence.

"Of course. Anything."

"Since I'm not there anymore, can you look out for Mika for me? Make sure she's okay and everything, I mean."

"Of course I will, Sam." I feel a pang of guilt that he needed to ask me this. I make a mental note to reach out to her as soon as we end the call. "I'll make sure she's okay. I promise."

"Thank you," Sam says. "I'm sure she could use a friend right now. Even if she won't say it. So please don't forget, okay?"

"I won't forget. So don't worry."

"I know you won't. Because you always remember. And that means a lot to me." We don't say much more about this. The conversation continues for a little longer until my mother comes up the stairs, calling me to help bring in groceries. "Anyway, I should probably let you go now," Sam says. "I'm sure you have a lot of work to catch up on. Don't want to distract you from the world."

"You've never been a distraction."

Sam laughs. "I'll talk to you tomorrow, okay?"

"Wait . . ." I say before he hangs up. "One last thing." There's something I've been afraid to bring up. It's been burning in the back of my mind since I returned to school. But I don't even know how to ask him this. It takes a while for the words to come out.

"What is it?" Sam asks.

I hesitate. "Are you . . . mad at me?"

"Mad about what?"

"About what happened that night."

"I'm not sure what you mean, Julie . . ."

I swallow hard, wondering how to say this. "I mean, what I'm asking is . . . do you blame me for it? Do you blame me for what happened to you?"

A long silence.

"Oh . . ." Sam's voice deepens, finally understanding. "Julie—why would you even ask me that? Of course I don't blame you. I could never blame you for what happened," he says. "None of it's your fault, alright? But . . ." He stops there.

"But what?"

Sam takes some time to answer. "To be honest, I don't know what else to say . . . I don't know how I'm supposed to answer that question. I don't really wanna blame anyone. Because it won't change anything, you know? Nothing can change what happened. It's hard enough to accept that . . ." For the first time, there's pain in his voice, like something sharp is caught in his throat.

"I'm sorry. I shouldn't have asked—" I start.

"*It's okay*, Jules. Really," he says to ease me. "Where did the question come from anyway? I hope that's not what you've been thinking."

"I didn't at first. But I've heard some people talking at school."

Sam's voice sharpens. "Forget them. They don't know what they're talking about. They weren't there when it happened, okay? Don't let them get into your head."

"I'll try not to."

"I'm sorry you have to deal with all this right now," he says.

"And I'm sorry you died."

Neither of us says anything else. After we hang up the phone, I pick the papers up from the floor and sit down at my desk. It's hard to focus after that conversation. I spend more than an hour trying to start a history paper, but barely get two sentences down. I keep thinking about calling Sam back, but I need to get some work done. The words inside the textbook blur and rearrange themselves, and I forget what it is I'm reading about. I must have dozed off at some point, because when I open my eyes, I'm no longer in my room.

A fog moves across my shoes, and when I look up, I find myself standing at a bus station. It's dark out. I can't see anything past the curtain of fog, not even the sky. I glance around to find someone but it's only me out here. The only thing is the suitcase I borrowed from my dad when I last visited him. There's a buzzing in my pocket. I reach inside and pull out my phone.

I turn on the screen.

Nine missed calls from Sam. Twelve texts I haven't opened. It's 11:48 p.m.

Out of nowhere, the sound of a truck rumbles like thunder, but I can't see it. It is this sound, and the exact time of the clock, that brings me back to that night from nearly two weeks ago.

This is the night Sam died. And this is where I stood.

The phone rings again, even louder this time.

It's Sam. I didn't bother to pick up last time because how could I know? This time I do, just to see if the ending changes.

The line crackles in my ear but I don't hear anything.

"Sam! *Sam*—are you there?"

Nothing but white noise, like someone crinkling paper. I angle the phone, and turn in circles, until a voice finally comes through the line. But I can barely understand it.

"Julie? Who's there? Hello?"

"Sam, it's *me*! It's Julie!"

"*Where are you? I can't find you. Julie?*"

The phone keeps crackling. I don't think he can hear me.

"Sam—I'm coming! Don't worry—just wait right there!"

"*Julie? Where are you—*"

The phone crackles again before it sparks in my hand, and I yank it from my ear. Smoke pours from the screen as I'm shouting Sam's name, filling the air like fog until I can no longer see what's in front of me except vanishing streaks of red and white sparks.

A horn goes off, followed by the sound of guitar strings breaking, and I wake up at my desk. The smoke is gone.

I don't bother to check the time or see if it's dark out. Instead I hurry downstairs, grab the car keys, and head out the door. I back the car out of the driveway before my mother comes out, and head up route 10, following the railway, leaving Ellensburg.

This might sound ridiculous, but Sam might be out there waiting for me. I have to go find him. My headlights are the only things shining on the barren highway for miles. I keep looking out the window to see if Sam's walking along the side of the road. I can't help thinking back to that night.

Sam was at a bonfire by the river with some friends. It was the same night I was returning from my trip to Seattle to visit my dad. Sam had promised to pick me up, like he always did. But when I called him from outside of the station, he was still at the bonfire, more than an hour away. He kept apologizing, but I was so upset he forgot, I hung up and stopped answering his calls. I told him I would walk home. How could I know that would be the last thing I ever said to him?

I guess Sam thought I must have been testing him, which in

hindsight, maybe I was. Because he left the bonfire to find me. It was somewhere between eleven thirty and midnight while Sam was driving down route 10 when a truck swerved into his lane. I imagine Sam must have honked for his life. I wonder if he tried to dodge out of the way.

But Sam didn't die in the wreck that flipped his car. Not only did he manage to stay conscious, he freed himself from the seat, crawled out onto the road, and began walking. Somehow, he made it more than a mile down the road before collapsing. An officer said it was a testament to how strong he was. I think it was a testament to how much he wanted to live. It took hours before someone finally found him. It was too late by then. Sam had lost too much blood and died from exhaustion. No one likes to say it, but maybe it would have been easier for him if he'd died there in the crash. But his will to live on was too stubborn. Just like him.

They found Sam's phone near the crash site, covered in glass and dirt. Maybe if I had called at just the right time, he might have heard it and picked up, and I could have sent for help. Maybe if I hadn't been so angry with him, he might not have left the bonfire so quickly and might have missed the truck entirely. Maybe if the stars were aligned differently, or the wind blew the other direction, or it suddenly started raining, or something else, Sam would still be alive, and I wouldn't be driving out here in the middle of the night looking for him.

There's something up ahead. My headlights illuminate the dark road in front of me as I slow the car. Along the side of the road, the rails have been tied up with dozens of white ribbons. I put the car in park and get out. I follow the line of ribbons until I reach it. There beside a wreath of flowers and burnt candles is a portrait of Sam nailed to the rail. I kneel down in the dirt beside it. He's wearing his denim jacket, the one I threw out the other day. A breeze sends some ribbons fluttering. I touch the picture frame with my fingers.

"I'm sorry, Sam," I whisper.

After all this time, I finally found him. But I'm too late.

CHAPTER SEVEN

BEFORE

The drive-in is crowded for a Tuesday night. There are a few tables outside, each packed with teenagers sharing fries beneath long strings of light. It takes a while before some seats open up for us. I am sitting beside Mika, while Sam leaves to grab our drinks. This is the first time the three of us have hung out together. I've only met Mika once, at a party a few weeks ago. I wasn't planning to go out tonight. But Sam texted me an hour ago, asking me if I wanted to grab something to eat. He didn't tell me his cousin was coming, too.

Mika and I barely speak to each other. I wish Sam hadn't left us alone like this. Maybe I should have offered to pick up our order instead. I wonder what's taking him so long. Then out of the blue, without even turning to me, Mika asks something completely inappropriate.

"So you're in love with Sam, right?"

"What—" I was too thrown off to string a sentence together. Something gets caught in my throat. "I mean, *excuse me?*"

Mika runs a calm hand through her smooth black hair, unbothered by my reaction. "I'm just saying, he seems to be really into you."

My eyes widen, shocked by her nonchalance. "Should you be telling me that?"

Mika gives me a look. "Don't pretend you didn't already guess. It's so obvious. The whole school knows."

My mouth moves but no words come out. *What's taking Sam so long? Why did he leave me with her?*

"You should compliment his hair," Mika continues.

"What—why?"

"It's only a suggestion," she says, and leans closer to me. "Do you like Sons of Seymour? The band, I mean."

"I think I've heard of them," I say vaguely.

"They're playing downtown this weekend. Sam's *obsessed* with their newest album. You should suggest we go. He already bought his ticket."

"Then why would I need to suggest—"

She holds up a hand. "Just do it."

A second later, Sam reappears through the crowd, holding milkshakes. Mika whispers, "He's coming back. Act natural."

Sam sets the tray down between us. "So they ran out of straws . . ." he says, reaching into his jacket. "Had to fight a guy for the last two." He hands one to each of us. "I guess I'll wait for mine to melt so I can sip it."

"That's gross," Mika says.

Sam looks at me. "Straws are bad for the environment anyway. I hear they're trying to ban them in Seattle."

"Are you trying to impress us, or make us feel bad?" Mika asks.

"Feel free to ignore her," Sam says with an eye roll. He takes off his jacket, then removes his hat.

"Oh—" I notice his new haircut. "I like your hair."

"Really?" he says, suddenly blushing. "I was worried they cut it too short."

"No, it's nice."

We smile awkwardly at each other. I take a sip from my milkshake as Sam sits across from me. I watch as he stares into his strawless cup, waiting for it to melt.

"So there's no school this Friday," Mika says to stir up conversation. "Isn't that a relief?"

"Yeah . . . finally a three-day weekend," Sam says. He looks at both of us. "Do you guys have any plans?"

Mika nudges me with her foot.

"Oh—uh, well, I hear there's a concert this weekend," I think she wants me to say. "Sons of Seymour is playing."

Sam leans into the table, his eyes bright with excitement. "Oh my god, I just bought my ticket to that. I didn't know you listen to Sons of Seymour."

"Yeah, I didn't know you did, either." I take a sip of my drink, trying to be casual.

"*Of course!* I've been obsessed. What's your favorite song from them?" Sam asks.

"Oh—" I pretend to think about it. "Uh, I like the entire album. The new one, I mean."

"It's *so* good."

"Right?"

"Maybe we can go together," Sam says. "I'm sure they'll sell tickets at the door."

"I'd love that."

"Cool."

I glance at Mika. She smiles to herself as she sips her milkshake, appearing very pleased.

It was at this moment that I decided to like her. I started looking forward to those days she would tag along with us. I especially loved it when she'd send Sam on random fetch quests to give us a moment to chat—often about him. Like that time we were at the Wenatchee Valley Museum, looking at the Ice Age exhibit, and she made Sam go get her jacket from the car.

Mika leans her nose to the glass case, examining a mammoth bone. "How was your weekend in Seattle?"

"It was fun. It rained most of the time, though. What about yours?"

"Sam and I rewatched *Avatar: The Last Airbender*," she says. "One of his favorite shows. He asked me about you."

"Oh?"

She taps the glass, even though we're not supposed to. "About what I thought about you, that is," she says.

"And what did you say? If you don't mind me asking . . ."

"I said I liked you better than other girls at school," Mika says. "Which, frankly, isn't saying too much, considering where we live."

"I'll still take that as a compliment."

"As you should," Mika says, nodding. "My approval is very important to Sam. He knows I have very good intuition. Especially about people." She looks at me. "I hope I'm right."

Eventually Sam returns from the car.

"You never brought a jacket," he says.

Mika slaps her forehead. "I totally forgot." She checks her watch. "Anyway, I'm late for work. I should really go."

"What do you mean *work*?" Sam asks. "It was your idea to come here."

"It slipped my mind," Mika says. "You two can finish the exhibit without me."

"How are you getting back?" I ask.

"My mom's picking me up. She should be here any second now." Mika checks her phone. "Gotta go. Have fun, you two."

This isn't the first time she's done this. Makes plans for the three of us to hang out, then finds a way to leave us alone.

Sam and I turn back to the mammoth bones. It's my favorite thing in here.

"Sorry about Mika," Sam says with a sigh. "She tends to . . . get involved." I hold back a knowing laugh. "Just to be clear. I'm not behind this."

I turn to him. "Does that mean you don't want to be here?"

"What? No! I only meant—" Sam stops, takes a deep breath, then calmly starts over. "What I mean is, as much as I love Mika . . . I don't need anyone's help to ask you out."

"That's fair," I say.

We turn back to the glass. After a moment, Sam's phone chimes. A second later, mine does, too. We look at our messages.

I look at him. "Is yours also from Mika?"

"Yeah."

"What does your text say?"

"She says I should nix the exhibit and ask you to dinner." He looks at me. "What about yours?"

"She says I should say yes."

It's impossible not to smile. Especially for Sam. "Shall we, then?"

Sam holds out his arm. I link mine with his. And we leave the Ice Age and mammoth bones behind us.

Eventually he finds the courage to invite me out more often. And so do I. While we start spending more and more time together, Mika is never out of the picture. I learned you can't get to know one without getting to know the other. They were like siblings that way. We drive to school together, have lunch at the same table, share a group chat, and go on the occasional road trip. The most memorable road trip we took was to Spokane, where we snuck into a pub to see a battle of the bands contest. It also happened to be our worst.

The music is so loud I can't hear anything. I stand in the back near the bar, holding my water. Sam's friend Spencer is supposed to be going up any minute now. Their band is called the Fighting Poets. I asked them earlier if it was a reference to Emily Dickinson, but they said *"No!"*

Sam has been chatting for a while with some guys we met earlier. I look around for Mika, but it's too crowded here. Maybe there's a line at the bathroom. I should have gone with her. Now I'm just standing here, keeping to myself, trying to block out the obscenely loud music.

And then it happens.

A man comes up behind me. His hands slither around my waist.

Shock moves through me and I feel sick to my stomach. I spin around.

"Don't touch me."

He's younger than I thought he would be. Probably in college.

He has this nasty smirk on his face I want to slap off. I can't tell if he's drunk but that doesn't matter.

Sam appears.

"What's going on here? Are you bothering her?"

"Is that your girl?" the guy slurs. "Why don't you tell her to chill out."

Sam instinctively shoves him away from me. But I wish he hadn't. We're seventeen and not allowed to be in here. I don't want to cause a scene.

The guy finds his balance. He shoves Sam back with double the force, and Sam goes stumbling back into some stools and falls over. Everyone around us has turned to see what's going on. Sam picks himself up and comes back for more, this time more furious.

I grab his arm.

"Sam. Don't."

This is when Mika shows up. She must have seen everything from a distance, because she's shouting at the guy, telling him to apologize.

I'll never forget what happens next.

The guy throws a punch at Sam, but Mika *catches* his arm like an arrow. She holds a strong grip on the guy's wrist, which seems to surprise everyone—especially him. This is the night I learned Mika helps teach a women's self-defense class at the YMCA. Mika twists his hand to the point of breaking it, sending him to his knees.

"So you like harassing girls," Mika shouts. "Apologize!"

"Alright! Sorry! Now let go!"

But it didn't matter whether he apologized or not. Mika lifts her other hand and delivers a final blow, sending him to the floor.

I remember everyone around us cheering. Mika taught me that same move a few weeks later.

There are so many moments I wish I could relive again. Especially the smaller ones. The quieter ones that we often don't think about. Those are the moments I look back and miss the most. Us sitting on the floor in Sam's room doing homework together, or watching movie musicals in Mika's living room on the weekends. Or that time we decided to grab blankets and bring them to the backyard to watch the sunrise together, for no reason. We stayed up all night, talking about what we wanted to do ten years from now, waiting to see that burning red glow curve along a dark sky, oblivious to the significance of seeing another day. And oblivious to a future when one of us would be gone.

CHAPTER
EIGHT

NOW

I wake up the next morning to a text from Mika.

Hey. I'm outside.

I rub my eyes and blink away sleepiness. What's she doing here so early? As I think about this, a gasp escapes me as I remember. *The candlelight vigil!* I was supposed to meet her last night and help out. But I fell asleep and completely forgot. She probably came here to talk face-to-face. I need to respond.

Okay. Be right down.

I brush my teeth, get dressed fast, and skip breakfast. When I come outside, I find Mika sitting alone on the porch step with her back facing me. Her head leans against the porch rail as she stares out at the lawn. She doesn't say anything when I step out.

"I didn't know you were coming . . ." I say.

No response.

"Are you okay?"

Mika doesn't turn around. She doesn't look at me.

I take a seat on the porch beside her. An air of silence hovers between us. She must be angry with me. "I'm really sorry about last night. I completely forgot we were supposed to meet. I feel so terrible, Mika."

"I really thought you'd show up," she says. "I was waiting for you. I made everyone wait."

"I'm so sorry . . ." I don't know what else to say.

"I tried calling you. Why didn't you answer?"

I think back to last night. I'm not sure what came over me. I must have left my phone at home when I drove up and down route 10, looking for Sam. And I remember falling asleep as soon as I got back. But I can't tell Mika any of this. She'll think I'm crazy.

"It wasn't on purpose," I say. "I just fell asleep early. I don't have an excuse. I'm sorry."

"If you didn't care about going, you should have said so."

"Mika, I really did—"

"No you didn't," she cuts me off. Then she looks at me, her voice sharp. "If you really cared, you would have gone to everything else. But you didn't. I don't know why I keep expecting you to." She leans her head back against the rail, sending a pain through me. "It doesn't even matter anyway. You were right all along."

"What do you mean? Right about what?"

"How none of this really matters," she says. "Like the vigil last night. It doesn't change anything. He's still gone."

I think back to our conversation at the diner. I never thought it would stick with her this way. I suddenly wish I could take back what I said. I wish I could explain myself. Sam asked me to make sure Mika is okay, and I only made things worse between us. I'm not sure how to fix this. "That wasn't what I meant," I say.

"It's exactly what you said."

"It's different now. I don't believe it anymore. I wanted to be there this time."

"So did I. But it's too late now."

Mika looks away again, staring at the lawn. We're silent for a while. When she readjusts her hands, I notice something in her lap. A piece of paper.

"What are you holding?"

Mika lets out a breath. Without a word, she hands it to me.

I unfold the paper and read the first line. "An admissions letter?"

"It's a rejection," Mika says. "From the University of Washington. They emailed me the other day. I got the official letter this morning."

I read the letter. UW is a hard school to get into, but not for someone with grades like Mika's. She should have been a shoo-in. "I can't believe this. This must be a mistake."

"Well, it isn't," Mika says back. "Joining a bunch of clubs and good grades don't guarantee you anything, I guess."

I touch her shoulder. "I'm so sorry, Mika . . ." I whisper, unsure of what else to say. I can't imagine how she's feeling, especially with everything else happening around us. We worked on our applications together, so I know how much time she put in. While I applied to two colleges, Mika applied to nine. She spent months tailoring each application, strategically framing herself with different aspirations and traits based on her research of each school. UW was her top choice. Out of everyone I know who applied, she should have gotten it. Nothing's fair. "It's gonna be okay. You're still waiting to hear from other schools. There's going to be good news coming, I know it. This is their loss, Mika."

"This isn't my first rejection," Mika says, almost with a laugh. "I was too embarrassed to tell anyone. There aren't many letters left that I'm waiting on." She shakes her head. "I don't know why I put in all this work. For what? At least Sam will never know how much of a failure I am."

"Don't say that," I say, taking her hand. "You haven't failed anything. It's still only March. You're going to get in somewhere."

Mika pulls her hand away. "I don't even care anymore. It was all a waste of my time."

"Mika . . ." I start.

But she rises abruptly. "Forget it. I have to go."

"Wait—why don't we walk together?"

"I'm not going to school today," Mika says as she steps off the porch.

"Where are you going?"

"Don't worry about me," she says without looking back. "Worry about yourself."

I go quiet, letting Mika disappear down the block without following after her. It hurts to have her think this way about me. If only she knew Sam and I have been reconnected, and I can speak to him again, she'd understand things are different now. *I'm* different. This is all my fault for not being there with Mika through any of this. I need to find a way to fix things between us. There's only two months until graduation, and I can't leave us this way. Especially after I made a promise to Sam. I don't want to lose her, too.

It's hard to focus at school. I keep thinking about how I should explain myself to Mika without lying to her. How can I show her I still care about Sam, when I have to keep things a secret? At lunch, I sit with Jay, Rachel, and Yuki at a table in the middle of the cafeteria. It's teriyaki meatloaf day so everyone brings their own lunches. Jay cuts his fruit sandwich with a plastic knife to share with me. It's almost too beautiful to eat, which is true about most of the food he brings. Rachel is looking over forms for the Asian Student Club they're trying to start. She wants to host a movie screening by the end of the semester.

"We still need seven signatures," Rachel tells us. She reaches into her bag and hands me a few flyers she made by hand. "Julie, do you think you can ask some of your friends to join us?"

"Oh—" I guess she doesn't realize my only friends are sitting at this table. And the three of them have already signed up. I take the form anyway. "I suppose I can ask around."

"Great!"

There's some ruckus a few tables down from us. I look across the cafeteria. Liam and his friend are throwing fries at each other, while Taylor sits on top of the table with her hair tossed back. I notice Oliver is with them. After we hung out the other night, I thought he might at least come say hi. But he hasn't spoken to me since. He doesn't even bother to glance our way. It was the same thing from him yesterday. Maybe he doesn't want to get caught associating with me in front of everyone. I actually thought things would be different between us.

Yuki notices me looking over. "Is something wrong, Julie?"

I turn back around. "No. Just some guys being loud."

"Ignore them," Jay whispers.

I nod and try to eat.

After a moment, Yuki says turns to me again. "We missed you last night. At the vigil."

I look at her. "I didn't know you guys were going."

"A lot of people from school did," Rachel says. "The street was filled up. Cars couldn't drive through."

I lower my gaze to the table, ashamed to hold eye contact. Because I should have been there, too.

"Sam's family came as well," Yuki says. "His mom asked about you."

Sam's mom. I look up again. "What did she ask?"

"She wanted to know if I heard from you," Yuki tells me. "She wonders where you've been, that's all. She said she hopes you might come over for dinner someday. It would mean a lot to her."

My chest tightens. I haven't spoken to Sam's mom or his family since he died. I realize how terrible this is of me, especially after I think about how often I used to come over and have dinner with them. Sam said his mom always had a place set for me at the table just in case. Whenever she made Sam lunch for school, she made sure there was something for me, too. I thought she would hate me after I missed the funeral. After she noticed not a single flower was sent from me. And now the vigil, too. Shame washes over me, making me lose my appetite. What would Sam think of me if he knew this? If he knew I wasn't the same person he fell in love with?

I can't even look at my food. I push the tray away from me. "I know, I should have come last night. I should have showed up this time."

Jay places a hand on my shoulder. "It's okay. Don't be so hard on yourself."

"But it isn't okay," I say to the table. "Because I skipped all of it, everything you guys did for Sam. And now even Mika hates me for it." I didn't even mean to miss the vigil this time. After I got off the phone with Sam, I fell asleep at my desk, and had that strange dream, and the next thing I knew I was out looking for him. It's easy to forget that everyone is mourning for Sam when I've been speaking to him every day. The worst part is I can't even explain myself. I promised Sam I wouldn't tell, because it might affect our connection, and I can't risk that. My eyes start watering, and I don't know what else to do. The others at the table are kind enough not to say anything else.

At the end of lunch, the three of them walk me to my next class. Before I head in, Yuki says something. "You know, maybe we can do something else for Sam. Something special to honor him by."

"That's a great idea," Rachel says, nodding. "And we can bring Mika, too. The five of us, together."

I think about this. *Something special for Sam. To honor him by.* "Like what?" I ask.

They all glance at each other, looking uncertain.

"We'll think of something," Jay promises.

I smile at them. "Thank you. I don't know what I would do without you guys."

It's the end of school. I need to hurry home without running into anyone. But it's difficult to avoid people when you can't even get to your locker without bumping into a dozen shoulders. As I'm packing up my books, someone taps me on my arm.

It's Oliver. *Again.*

"Hey. Whatcha up to?" he asks me.

"I'm about to leave."

"Cool—where?"

"*Home.*"

"Oh."

I shut my locker and walk toward the front doors without another word.

"Hold up—" Oliver says as he follows me down the hall. "I was gonna ask you if you wanted to do something."

"Sorry, I'm busy."

"It doesn't have to be too long," he says. "Maybe we can grab some ice cream."

"I told you, *I'm busy,*" I say without looking at him. "Why don't you hang out with your other friends?"

"Did I do something wrong?" Oliver asks, scratching his forehead.

I don't feel like explaining it to him. I shouldn't have to. "I'm just not in the mood, okay?"

"For ice cream?"

I turn to him. "For anything."

"Just two scoops," he insists.

"Oliver. I said *no.*"

"One scoop."

It's like he can't hear me. I walk off again, leaving him standing there.

"*C'mon!*" he shouts down the hall. "*Pretty please!*" His voice is loud and desperate. "*It's on me!*"

Maybe it's the empathy from being a writer that makes me stop walking. Or maybe it's Sam's voice inside my head. Reluctantly, I take a deep breath and turn around.

I narrow my eyes. "It's on you?"

"I'll have three scoops of pistachio, hot fudge, some marshmallows, whipped cream on top, rainbow sprinkles, and don't go easy on it," I say to the man behind the glass. I turn to Oliver. "What are you having?"

"Uh, one rocky road, please . . ."

We find a pink table in the corner of the ice cream shop. The place is a little empty. Oliver hangs his jacket behind his chair before sitting down. Both of us picked cups instead of cones. Oliver eats slowly, swirling the whipped cream with his spoon.

"Thanks for coming," he says after a while.

"What made you want ice cream?" I ask.

"It's Thursday."

"What about it?"

Oliver points at the window behind me. There's a poster of a crudely drawn cow with discounts painted over cartoon udders. THURSDAY: FREE TOPPINGS! The image is a bit disturbing, if you ask me. I turn back around and try to erase it from my mind.

I take another bite of ice cream.

"Sam used to get pistachio," Oliver says.

"I know."

"Except he preferred a cone."

"I know that, too."

Oliver doesn't say anything. He stares at his spoon, looking sad all of a sudden. Maybe I should be more sensitive.

"Just so you know, I'm not mad at you," I decide to tell him. "It's your friends I don't care for."

Oliver nods. "That's fair. They kinda suck."

"Then why do you hang out with them?"

"I don't know if you noticed," he says, leaning back in his chair. "But my best friend's dead."

My face turns to stone.

"I'm sorry," he says immediately, shaking his head. "I shouldn't have said that. I don't know what's wrong with me. I don't—" He swallows.

I reach out a hand to calm him, and say, "No it's alright, Oliver. Really."

He takes a deep breath and lets it out.

I pick up my spoon and we resume eating ice cream. Although neither of us is in the mood anymore.

"Sorry to bring him up," Oliver says again, some guilt in his voice. "I didn't mean to make this depressing."

"It's okay . . . I don't mind talking about Sam."

"That's good to know."

A half hour passes and we finish our ice cream. I check the time. It's a quarter past four. "I should probably get going."

"Already?"

"Yeah, I'm a bit tired," I say as I rise from the table.

"You don't want to, I don't know, see a movie or something?" Oliver asks out of nowhere.

"I really shouldn't."

"Sam told me you like musicals," he says randomly. "It's iconic musical month at the theater. It's right down the street."

"I don't know, Oliver . . ." I say, trying to let him down easy. "What are they even playing?"

"It changes every week," Oliver says. He checks his phone. "Tonight is . . . *Little Shop of Horrors*. Have you heard of it?"

"Of course I have. It's one of my favorite musicals."

"Mine too."

"I've seen it a dozen times."

"Same."

"You know, I even tried making Sam watch it with me," I say, sitting down again. "But he wouldn't. He said it sounded scary."

Oliver laughs. "It's not supposed to be scary!"

I lean into the table. "I know! But you know Sam. He doesn't like musicals."

"Oh my god—that was *so* annoying about him," Oliver says with an eye roll.

"It really was!"

For a moment, it's like we forgot what happened. Then Oliver stops smiling as we both remember again. Things turn quiet. I try to bring us back to the conversation. "Is there even a showing right now?" I ask.

Oliver checks his phone again. "There's one in ten minutes . . ." He looks at me with puppy dog eyes.

I tap my fingers on the table, trying to decide.

After a moment or so, Oliver says, "I'll take that as a yes."

The ticket booth manager scowls as we burst out of the theater in song. The ushers had basically kicked us out for disrupting the lobby with all our laughter. The movie was as wonderful as I remembered! Maybe it's because I've heard it a million times, but I'm singing it in my head as we're leaving. I never thought I'd have so much fun with Oliver. He kept throwing popcorn at the screen and singing along to the musical numbers. Thankfully we were the only ones in there watching. I'm so glad I decided to see it again with him. Then I remember Sam. There's an ache of guilt in my chest. He always wanted Oliver and me to be friends someday. He should have been here to enjoy the movie with us, even if he hated musicals. *The three of us, finally together.*

It's already dark out. The neon lights of the marquee illuminate the streets as we begin our walk home. I see the songs are stuck in Oliver's head, too. He grabs a streetlamp and swings around it like Don Lockwood in *Singin' in the Rain,* as he sings out loud.

"*Suddenly Seymour, is standing beside you . . .*"

Another time I might be embarrassed, but I can't help smiling as Oliver keeps singing.

"*You don't need no makeup, don't have to pretend . . .*"

At one point I join in, too, as we continue our walk.

"Wow," Oliver says. "It never gets old, you know?"

"I know. It's really, what's the word—" I pause. "Timeless."

"Was it just me, or did the man-eating plant look bigger than I remember?"

"It might have been the screen."

"That makes sense," Oliver says, nodding. "Man, but don't you love *the ending*? It's so perfect, right? How Audrey finally gets everything she dreamed of. A quiet life, a house in the suburbs, a toaster . . . and *Seymour*! She never asked for too much, you know? That's the thing. It really makes you feel good."

"It really does," I agree. "But did you know that wasn't the original ending? They actually had to go back and refilm it."

"What do you mean?"

"In the original version, Audrey gets eaten by the plant."

Oliver looks at me, eyes wide. "You mean, Audrey *dies*?"

"Yeah. She does."

Oliver stops walking. "Why would they do that?"

"Because that's what actually happens in the play," I explain. "But when they showed the film to audiences, it made a lot of people upset. Because everyone loved Audrey too much. So they rewrote it and changed the ending."

"I'm glad they changed it!" he says, a edge in his voice. "It would have ruined the entire movie."

"I agree with you. I'm only saying that another ending exists."

"But it *shouldn't*," he says. "It doesn't matter what they filmed before. Because Audrey lives."

"Maybe in the movie. But in the play, she doesn't."

"Well then I won't watch the play—" He walks off.

I follow beside him. I didn't mean to ruin the film. "You know, I don't think it's that big of a deal. Having different versions of something. At the end of the day, you get to decide what happened. So both can be true."

Oliver turns to me. "*That's wrong.* There can't be two different versions of the same thing."

"Why not?"

"Because one is the original, and the other is a copy. Something can feel the same or sound the same, but it isn't the same at all. It's inherently something else. So in order to have two different endings, you need two different Audreys."

I think about this. "What exactly are you talking about?"

"I'm saying there's only one of him, and that's the one I knew. You can't clone him or make different versions of him, and try to write a new him. You can't make changes. Because there's only *one* Sam."

We are no longer talking about Audrey.

"Maybe you're right. It was only a thought."

We reach the corner that splits our path home. A hedge of white roses peeks over a fence beside us.

"Sorry to kill the mood again," Oliver says.

"It's alright. I get it."

"Thanks for seeing the movie with me."

"I'm glad I went."

Before we part ways, Oliver notices the roses. He leans forward to touch one.

"Careful," I say. "It might bite."

He smiles as he plucks a rose from the hedge. For a second, I think he might give it to me. But he doesn't. He just holds on to it.

"Heading home then?" I ask.

"Eventually," he says. "Have to make a stop somewhere first."

"Where?"

"Nowhere special."

We say our good-byes. Back at home, I get started on schoolwork. I do as much as I can for the rest of the night, but it's hard to focus. I can't stop thinking about what Oliver said. About how you can't have two endings to something. About how you could have multiple versions of someone, but only one can be the original. Maybe Oliver's right. I don't want a different version of Sam. I want the one I lost. The one I'm still somehow connected to, even though it's only his voice over the phone.

I wish I could call Sam right now, but I know I shouldn't. As much as I miss talking to him, I have a hundred things to focus on—schoolwork, graduation, getting my life back together. We have a phone call planned for tomorrow. He said he has another surprise for me. I fall asleep late, wondering where we're going to meet next.

CHAPTER

NINE

Sam's voice comes to me in my sleep. It fills the crevices of my mind.

"Where are you, Julie . . .

. . . why can't I find you?"

A lamp above me flickers on. I'm standing in a soft glow of light, surrounded by darkness. I can't see anything around me. I can't hear anything, except the buzzing of the lamp above my head. There's a suitcase beside me. When mist moves across my shoes, I realize I'm dreaming again. A part of me is trying to wake up. The other part is curious to see a different ending.

And then my phone rings, as expected.

I feel around my pockets, but nothing's there. I don't know where my phone is. How am I supposed to answer?

The phone keeps ringing. I can't tell where it's coming from. I feel around the floor in case I dropped it.

Where is it? I'm running out of time.

Suddenly, a surge of light zooms through the darkness, blasting cold air at me, and my heart jolts. I rise up in time to see taillights, the sputter of smoke from a muffler, and the vanishing silhouette of a truck.

My throat closes as I stand there, watching. I know exactly where it's heading. And I need to get there first. I have to get to Sam before it's too late.

The suitcase falls over as I rush into the darkness, racing after the taillights. But it's too fast for me. I'll never reach it in time. Then I notice something. A rope tied to the back of the truck. I seize it at once, grabbing hold of it tight.

It's a guitar string! I pull it with all my strength, digging my feet into the ground. The string tenses in my grip as the truck stalls in the distance, honking furiously, its taillights flashing violently. This isn't superhuman strength. It's the strength born out of fear and desperation.

When I feel the ground softening beneath me, I glance down and see water rising up to my knees. But I keep on pulling with everything I have until water reaches my waist, and my feet feel like they're about to slip. The truck keeps honking, and I keep *pulling* and *pulling* the guitar string—until finally it *breaks*, and I go crashing back into my bed.

I wake up crying in the middle of the night. Since I can't go back to sleep, I call Sam, hoping he picks up. As soon as he does, I ask if that was him trying to reach me in my dream. If it was him trying to send me a message.

"I'm sorry, Jules . . . but that wasn't me. It was only a dream."

"Are you sure?" I say hopefully. "Maybe my dreams are another place we can find each other."

"I wish that could be true. But I think we're connected only through our phones."

Only through our phones.

My lip trembles. "It felt so real, though, Sam. It felt like . . . I had another chance, you know?"

"Another chance at what?"

I don't answer this. I'm afraid to know what he'll think. I'm afraid he'll tell me what I don't want to hear. Not right now.

Sam exhales. "It's just a dream, Jules. You should try to get some rest, okay? We'll talk tomorrow. I have another surprise for you."

"Okay. I'll try."

Whenever I call Sam out of the blue, our conversation doesn't last long. It always takes him a while to pick up, and when he does, his voice sometimes fades in and out, like he's moving around, searching for a signal. I'm not sure why this is. If we want to keep a strong connection, I've learned we have to plan out our calls and make them at the right time and place. Even though I'm allowed to call whenever I need him, Sam says I have to be cautious about how often I make the calls. I think about this. Is there a limited number of calls we have left? Are we running out? I wish I knew how this all worked.

It's hard to pay attention in school. In class, I keep taking my phone out to make sure it's there. It brings me some comfort when everyone is ignoring me. I can't stop thinking about how Sam and I are connected again. About how we got this second chance. I've started keeping a log of all our phone calls in my notebook. The time of day, where it took place, how long the call lasted. I also write down the things we talk about, along with questions I still have that need answering. Questions like . . . *Why were we given this second chance?* And *How much longer do we have this for?* Sam told me doesn't have the answers to these things. I wonder if I should bring them up again.

Mika shows up to class today. She comes in a little late, and takes a seat on the other side of the room, several rows away from me. Her clothes are wrinkled, her hair is unbrushed, and she brought no books with her. She hasn't responded to any of my texts since we spoke on my porch yesterday morning. I want to talk to her after class, but as soon as the bell rings, she grabs her bag and rushes out the door before I get my chance. I wish she would speak to me, give me a chance to explain why I've been ignoring her. I think about writing a note and sticking it in her locker. But what would it even say?

Dear Mika,
I'm sorry for missing the vigil the other night. I've been talking to Sam these past few days. I think it's interfering with incoming calls and texts, and causing things to slip my mind. Yes, our Sam. He's still dead, but he can pick up the phone when I call him. It's hard to explain because he hasn't given me any answers on how any of this is happening. Anyway, I hope this helps you understand things now, and we can be friends again.

Julie

She'd probably turn it in to the counseling office to get me checked, and understandably so. I decide to hold off on the letter and wait for another chance to see her. It will give me time to figure out what to say.

Lunch is the only part of the school day I look forward to. Jay, Rachel, and Yuki always manage to brighten my mood. It's Pizza Friday—Jay's favorite day of the week.

"It's America's favorite pie," he says, enjoying a second slice of pepperoni.

"Isn't that *apple* pie?" Rachel asks.

Jay shakes his head. "Really? I thought it was pepperoni."

"I don't think pizzas are considered pies," Yuki chimes in.

I take out the journal Mr. Lee gave me and open it on the table. I've been thinking about what he said the other day. *What story do I want to tell? Who am I writing for?* The questions bounce around in my head as I stare at the blank page. I wish I could say I write for myself. But maybe that's not the truth. Maybe I'm always writing for someone else. Like the English professors at Reed who might read this as my writing sample and decide if it's good enough. What will they think of it? What if none of them care what I have to say? *What do I have to say?* And what if it's insignificant to the rest of the world? I guess that shouldn't matter, as long as it matters to me, right? It's harder than it sounds, though. *To write for yourself.* Maybe that's what Mr. Lee meant when he said we have too many voices in our heads. I wish I could mute them all so I could find my own. I tap the back of my pen against the table and keep thinking.

"That's a beautiful notebook," Yuki says. "Where did you get it?"

"Mr. Lee gave it to me." I close the journal to show her the cover. The embroidered flowers reflect like jewels in the cafeteria light. "Someone donated it to the store last week."

Rachel leans in to get a closer look. "It's *so* pretty. Can I hold it?"

"I know, it's almost too pretty to write in," I say, handing Rachel the notebook. "Feels like I'm wasting pages."

"What are you writing about?" Yuki asks me.

I stare at my hands in my lap, unsure. Then it comes to me, almost like memory. As if I always had the answer. "Sam. I'm gonna write about Sam. About us."

Yuki smiles at this. "I would love to read it someday. If you ever want to share it."

I smile back at her as someone approaches the table.

"Mind if I sit here?"

I look up at Oliver. He's holding a plate of cheese pizza and a chocolate milk. I glance over at the other table with Taylor and Liam, and see them glancing over their shoulders, watching him.

"Yeah," I say. "Of course you can."

"Awesome."

Oliver pulls a chair up right beside me, forcing Jay to scoot over.

"*Hey Yukes,*" he says, nodding at her from across the table. "How's choir going? Any new solos?"

Yuki blots her mouth with a napkin. "Hopefully I'll get one soon. We just had auditions for our next concert."

"I'm sure you blew them out of the water," Oliver says, opening his chocolate milk. "Remember that time you and Sam killed it at that karaoke room? Classic."

I almost forget Oliver and Yuki know each other through Sam.

"We'll see," Yuki says, blushing a little.

"I'll be there regardless," Oliver says. Then he turns to Jay, resting an arm on the back of his chair. "I don't think we've met. I'm Oliver."

"Oh—I'm Jay."

Oliver rubs his chin. "Where do I know you from?"

"You came to one of the meetings for the environmental club," Jay says. "But you never came back."

"Oh, *that's right*," Oliver says, as if remembering it fondly. "You guys were talking about beach cleanups or something. It sounded a little lame, if I'm being honest."

I nudge his arm. "*Oliver.* Jay is the treasurer of the club. The beach cleanup was his idea."

"I'm only teasing," Oliver says, waving me away. "I'm very impressed with his work."

Rachel reaches across me and taps Oliver's shoulder. "Do you want to join our club?" she asks, handing him the form. "We still need six signatures."

"Of course. What club is it?"

She takes my pen and hands it to him. "The Asian Student Club. We're hoping to host a movie screening at some point."

Oliver signs his name without question. "I hope you guys are watching *Akira*," he says. "That's a classic."

"I can put it on the list," Rachel says. "We plan to have a vote."

"How democratic." Oliver nods as he hands back the form. "Will there be a vote on snacks, too?"

The table bursts with laughter as we talk about the club. I didn't expect Oliver to sit down with us, let alone get along with everyone so quickly. There's something different about him today. A softer side I'm still not used to seeing. Maybe things are better between us now. Maybe there's a chance we'll be friends after all. I'm glad he decided to finally join us.

The bell rings. As I'm packing up, Yuki turns to me. "Have you decided if you're meeting us later?"

"For what?" I ask.

"We're going somewhere after school to think of ideas for Sam," she says. "I sent you a text last night."

I look around the table, a little confused. "I never got your text," I say. "I didn't know we were supposed to be meeting." I take out my phone to double check. I've had it with me the entire day. Why do I keep losing messages? "When did you send it?"

"It was pretty late," Yuki says. "You might have been asleep."

I think back to last night. Maybe the calls are blocking them. I remind myself to check the log of phone calls I've been keeping later.

Jay appears beside me. "You should come," he says. "You know Sam better than all of us."

"What about Sam?" Oliver asks, looking curious.

"We want to do something special for him," Rachel says. "With Julie."

"Like what?"

"We're still deciding."

"Oh . . ." Oliver leans forward, his lips pressed. "Can I . . . be part of it?"

Everyone turns at me.

"Of course you can," I say. I look at Yuki. "But I can't meet you guys after school today. I'm really sorry. I already made plans with someone." I don't mention that that someone is Sam.

Yuki touches my hand. "Don't worry. We'll get together again. We'll plan something great for him."

Although I smile at this, I can't help feeling a little left out of the group. It's been a while since I spent time with the three of them outside of school. We used to go over to Sam's house regularly, listening to music together. Since it's my last year here, I don't know when I'll see them all again.

As soon as school gets out, I head straight into town. Instead of stopping by work like I normally would, I wait at the corner stop for the three o'clock bus out of Ellensburg. I won't be going too far. Only until the mountain ridges rise into view and the roads become nothing but trees and sagebrush. This is Sam's idea. He said he had a surprise for me when we last spoke. I'm supposed to call him as soon as I get off the bus.

The bus drops me off near the footpaths where there's a crowd of hikers, but I wander off the main trail toward the line of trees. I've never gone this far off the path before. All around me is nothing but endless woods and mountainsides. I cut through fields of wildflowers, letting my fingers brush along the tops of purple-and-yellow asters. Sam's voice guides me like a hand over the phone, leading me through a sunlit clearing in the middle of the wood. His voice swells with excitement. It's the first time I've heard him this way since that first phone call.

"I've been waiting to show you this forever," he says.

"But what *is* it?" I keep asking.

"I told you, it's a surprise," he says with a laugh. "You're almost there. Keep going."

Tree trunks thicken as the path he guides me through becomes more wooded and narrower. Rods of sunlight shine at different angles through the high branches. Wildflowers color the ground purple and gold. A breeze blows the low-hanging branches, making their leaves brush gently over my shoulders as I pass beneath them.

"There should be a small creek up ahead," Sam says. "Once you find this million-year-old log, cross over it and then turn right."

I can't believe he can recall all these details. It's as if he can see it, too.

I glance around me. "How will I find my way back?" Town is miles and miles away from where I am. Even though I have him on the phone, it's only me out here.

"Don't worry," Sam says. "I'm right there with you."

Sunlight shimmers at the end of the wood as I head toward it. Once I break through the trees and reach the other side, I brush my hair back and take in the view that emerges before me. A field of gold stretches from my shoes, spreading out toward the sky. A breeze comes up from behind me, bending the tops of the grasses, sending them rolling like ocean waves. In the distance, a single tree stands in the middle like a boat stranded in a golden lake. I take a few more steps out, letting my hand glide along the foxtails as soft as feathers. It doesn't take me too long to realize why he brought me here.

"Barley . . ." Sam whispers in my year. "Just like from the song."

A breath escapes me. "*Sam* . . ." is all I get out.

I close my eyes and breathe it all in. If I listen closely, I can almost hear the hum of his guitar playing somewhere in the distance. "How did you find this place?"

"I wandered off the trail and found it one day," Sam says. "It reminded me of the song I always play for you. The one you listen to when you write. I know you've been having some trouble thinking lately. I thought that, maybe if you saw it in person . . . the *fields of gold* . . . it would inspire you to write again."

A breeze blows strands of hair across my face and I leave it. "Why didn't you bring me here sooner?"

"I was waiting for the right moment to show it to you. I had it all planned out. It was supposed to be special. I didn't know I would run out of time."

A pain goes through me.

"Is it how you imagined it in the story?" he asks.

My throat swells, making it hard to speak. "It's so much more," I say. "Thank you for this."

"I wish I could see it again," Sam goes on. "I wish I was there with you. I wish I could see the look on your face . . ."

Tears form behind my eyes as I stare out at the golden fields, the endless barley, and the sun that's beginning to set, trying to hold on to every single detail so I will always remember this. So I won't forget. And then I hear something I never thought I would hear again. Sam's voice on the phone, singing the song "Fields of Gold," just like he promised me he would someday . . .

> "I never made promises lightly
> And there have been some that I've broken
> But I swear in the days still left
> We'll walk in fields of gold
> We'll walk in fields of gold . . ."

We watch the sunset together, just like Sam had planned for us. I find a spot in the grass to lie down, and place the phone beside me with the speaker on. We talk for hours, about everything, laughing like old times as the sky changes colors above us, and I swear it's like he's here with me. Sam's right, it's even more magical out here at night. The stars feel so close you could reach out and touch them. I look for constellations and tell Sam which ones I think I know. For a long moment, I can *feel* him lying there besides me. If I turn my head to look, I'd see him with his arms tucked behind his head, wearing his plaid shirt, his eyes opened wide at the sky, his beautiful dark hair, that handsome smile on his face. But I don't dare to look, because I'm scared no one will be there. So I just stare straight up at the stars, and allow myself to keep pretending.

I close my eyes for moment. "Thank you for bringing me here. I didn't realize how much I needed to be away from everything."

"Feels like a different world, doesn't it?" Sam whispers next to me. "Like Ellensburg is a million miles away."

"Do you miss it, Sam? Ellensburg, I mean."

"Yeah I do . . . I miss everything about it."

I open my eyes back up to the stars. "I think I'll miss it, too."

"So you're still leaving?"

"That was always the plan," I remind him. "To finally get out of here, you know? Move to a big city, go to college or something, become a writer."

"You don't sound too excited," Sam says.

"Well, I didn't want to do it alone."

There's a long silence before Sam speaks again. "You're gonna be okay, Julie. Wherever it is you go, whoever you end up with. You'll figure things out."

"There's no one else I want to end up with. You're still here, Sam. And that's all that matters right now. Nothing else."

"Julie," Sam says, somewhat tensely. "Don't do this."

"Do what?"

"Hold on to us," he says. "As if we still have forever."

"Why do you keep saying that?"

"Because it won't always be like this. It can't. I need you to remember that."

"But *why* can't it be?"

"It just *can't—*" His voice cracks a little. "Think about it. You're not going to live the rest of your life talking to your dead boyfriend on the phone, while everyone else is out there living their lives, meeting new people, moving on with the rest of the world. You can't live this way forever."

"I don't see what's so wrong about this," I say back. "You're making it sound worse than it is." I can't think of anything I want more in the world right now, other than having him be alive again. "As if I care what other people think of me. As long as I have *you*. And if we can still be together, we should make it work. Even if it isn't exactly like we planned—"

"*Stop it*, Julie," he interrupts me. "You and I can't do this forever. That's just not possible."

"But you said I could take as long as I need to say good-bye," I remind him. "What if I don't? What if I refuse to say it?"

Sam lets out a breath. "So is that what you decided to do . . . to never say good-bye to me?"

"That was *always it*, Sam. Since the day I met you . . .'"

I think of the day when he will no longer pick up when I call and I can barely breathe. I finally heard him sing; what if I forget his voice? I can't imagine losing him all over again.

Neither of us say anything for a long time. I stare at the sky as some clouds part, revealing the moon. Out of nowhere, a glitter of white light streaks across the sky, vanishing behind the mountain line.

"A *shooting star.*" I point at the sky, as if Sam could see it, too.

"I'm surprised you've only seen one out there," he says. "Did you make a wish?"

"You know I don't believe in stuff like that."

"Why not?"

"Think about it. Have you ever heard of one coming true?"

"Doesn't mean you shouldn't give it a shot. You could wish for the other bookend back."

"You're a real dreamer," I say.

Sam laughs. "Alright then. What would you wish for, if you could have anything?"

"Anything?"

"Anything at all."

"No limits?"

"No limits."

I hesitate. "Do you really want to know?"

"I wouldn't be asking if I didn't," Sam says.

I close my eyes and take in a deep breath. I don't have to think long because I already know the answer. "I wish you were here," I say. "I wish you were lying right next to me. I wish I could look over and see you smiling back. I wish I could run a hand through your hair, and know you're *real*. I wish we could finish school and graduate together. So we can finally leave this place like we always planned, and find an apartment somewhere, and figure out the rest of our lives together so I don't have to do it alone. I wish you were *alive* again . . . and I wish I had picked up the phone that night, so that all this would be different, and everything would go back to before . . ."

There is a long silence as Sam takes this in. He doesn't say anything during or after but I feel him there on the phone, *listening*. I'm surprised he even let me say all of this. I don't know if that was what he expected to hear, but he asked for the truth.

The rest of the night is like this. I lie there in the fields, on the phone with him for what feels like forever. We don't say anything else. We just quietly live in this imaginary world where everything I wish for is still a beautiful possibility.

CHAPTER

TEN

When I wake up in the morning, something is different. I sense the warmth of someone beside me. But when my hand moves across the sheets to find them, no one is there. It's only me again. I rub my eyes until the walls of my bedroom come into focus. Streaks of light glimmer across the ceiling like sunlight on water. If it wasn't for the thin window curtain, I wouldn't know it was daylight out. It's one of those mornings where you don't know how much time has passed since you fell asleep. Hours or days, I'm not sure. I have to check the clock on my phone to orient myself for the day. It's Saturday. 9:14 in the morning. None of this seems right, but there's no point in arguing with it.

I sit up on the bed, and glance around the room. The chair at my desk is turned to face me, Sam's shirt still hanging behind it. Sometimes, I like to pretend he's in the bathroom, or grabbing some water downstairs, and is about to come back. *Anytime now.*

It makes me feel less alone when we're not on the phone together. I stretch my arms toward the ceiling. Sometimes my hair gets tangled in my sleep, so I run my fingers through to straighten it out. The smell of barley comes through, and I remember. *The golden fields.* Was that really last night? If I close my eyes, I can see it again. It's strange to be back in my room with nothing but the memory of it. Like waking up from a dream, and having no one there to talk about it with.

Another world, another life, another thing to keep to myself.

I couldn't sleep well. I had the same dream where I'm back at the bus station, looking for Sam again. It wasn't quite as bad this time, but I'm still a bit shaken from it. I wish I could talk to someone about the dreams. Someone besides Sam, I mean. After everything I said to him last night, I don't want to give him more to worry about. There are things I should probably keep inside.

I stay curled in bed until a third alarm goes off, reminding me to start the day. My mother left me half a pot of coffee downstairs. I finish two cups and a bowl of cereal. An hour later, I meet Oliver outside on the porch. He texted me this morning, inviting me on another walk. But we have a different destination this time. It's Oliver's idea. I wasn't sure about it at first, but I said yes anyway. We're on our way to Sam's grave.

The clouds are out this afternoon. Oliver and I take the long route to avoid the crowds in town. When I tell him I've never visited Sam's grave before, he doesn't judge me. Maybe he already guessed this. Maybe he understands why I'm afraid to see it. As memorial hill rises into view, my stomach turns to knots. A few steps before we reach the iron gates, something stops me. Just like before . . .

Oliver looks back. "You alright there?"

"I just need a second—" I don't know what else to say. I stare at the iron bars of the opened gate, wondering if this is a mistake. *Don't be scared, Julie. That's not Sam up there. He's still with you. You haven't lost him yet.*

"It'll be okay. Here . . ." Oliver holds out a hand. "We're going in together."

I take a deep breath, squeezing his hand tight. Together we pass under the gates, and make our way up the hill. Oliver leads me through grass lined with grave markers and pinwheels. I step around them carefully, out of respect. I would have never been able to find Sam's grave on my own. The grass seems to go on forever, spreading in every direction. It isn't until Oliver stops and releases my hand that I realize we're here. He steps around the stone marker, letting me see it better.

SAMUEL OBAYASHI

My body goes still. I read it to myself a few times.

He never liked the name Samuel. He would have wanted it to say Sam.

Sunflowers bloom from the vase in the center of the stone. They look fresh and beautiful, as if someone recently brought them here. A petal has fallen over his name, so I kneel down to brush it off. Then I notice something else in the vase.

A single white rose sticks out of the sunflowers. I touch it gently. It takes me a second to remember. "Is this one from you?" I ask Oliver.

"Yeah . . ."

My mind flashes back to that night we saw the movie together. "So this is where you went after . . ."

"I stopped by."

I look at him. "How often do you come here? If you don't mind me asking."

Oliver shrugs. "Maybe too often."

I take a few steps back and stare at the grass. *The space beneath the gravestone. Is that where Sam is supposed to be?* I imagine him sleeping peacefully down there, because I can't picture him dead. *This is surreal. I was just on the phone with him.* I swallow hard and look at Oliver. "Should I . . . say something? I don't know what I'm supposed to do . . ."

"You don't have to. We can just hang out here for a little while."

We sit on the grass together. The air feels eerily still, as if the wind doesn't reach this place. I haven't felt a single breeze since we entered. The trees around us are as inanimate as if they're made of stone. I keep glancing over my shoulder. We seem to be the only two out here this afternoon.

Some time passes. Oliver picks at the grass in silence. He hasn't said anything in a while. I wonder what he's thinking about. "Do you usually come here alone?" I ask him.

"Usually."

"And you just sit here like this?"

"Sometimes I change the water in the vase."

I stare at his rose again. I wonder how many flowers he's given Sam. "You really miss him, don't you?"

"Probably no more than you."

We both look at each other. Then he looks away, and things go quiet again.

"I think Sam would be happy to know you visit him," I say after a while. "I think it would mean a lot to him."

Oliver looks up. "You think so?"

"I do."

After a moment, he lets out a tense breath. "I just don't want him to feel alone, you know?" he says. "Like, what if he needs some company? I want him to know that someone's here."

A pain shoots through me. I wish I could call Sam and let him hear this. I wish I could tell Oliver about our calls, just to give him some sort of peace. What would he even think? Would he believe me?

In almost a whisper, Oliver asks a bit nervously, "Can I tell you something?"

"Of course."

"Sometimes . . . I talk to him."

"To Sam?"

Oliver nods.

"What do you mean?"

"I mean, right here," he says, gesturing at the grass where we sit. "Out loud, I guess. About normal things. Like stuff we used to talk about, you know?" Then he looks away, shaking his head. "It's stupid, I know."

If only he knew the truth. If only I could just tell him. "No, it isn't," I say to ease him. "I get it. If it makes you feel better, I tried calling him."

"You mean, on the phone?"

"Yeah."

For a second, I think he might ask me more about this, but he doesn't. Though a part of me wishes he did. I wonder what my answer would have been. I watch Oliver pick at the grass again and feel a pang of guilt. Guilt for getting to talk with Sam, and not being able to tell anyone about it. Maybe I should. Just to know what happens next. Or for him to tell me *this is real.* Without looking up, Oliver asks me another question. "Can I tell you something else?"

I lean forward and listen.

"Remember what I asked you that one night? About what you'd say to Sam, if you had one more chance?"

"I do."

"Do you want to know mine?"

"Only if you want to tell me."

Oliver takes a deep breath and lets it out. His mouth opens and closes, as if something inside is stopping him. But eventually, he lets it out, like he's been holding his breath for a long time.

"I would tell Sam I love him. That I always have."

"I'm sure Sam loved you, too," I say.

He looks at me. "But not the way he loved you."

A silence.

"It doesn't matter anyway," Oliver says, shaking his head. "It's better that I never told him. Maybe we'd stop being friends if I did."

"Why would you say that?" I ask him. "You know Sam would be your friend no matter what."

Oliver looks away again. "I always thought he might have felt the same way, too. That maybe there was something more between us, you know? Between me and Sam. Before you came here, I mean." He drops his head. "I guess we'll never know . . ." He goes quiet for a long time. When he wipes his eyes, and tears pour down, I realize he's crying. Seeing him like this, my eyes start watering, too. I come behind, and put my arms around him. I rest my head on his back, and feel a pulse or heartbeat or I'm not sure what, but it's someone else's and not mine. Something I haven't felt in a while.

"I wish he was still here," Oliver says through tears.

"I know. I do, too."

"You really think he'd still be my friend if I told him?"

"My honest answer?"

I feel him nod.

"I think Sam already knew."

Judging from his silence, maybe he always wondered this. Maybe I've always wondered, too. About Oliver. Maybe this was the reason why he and I could never get close. Because of Sam. Because we both loved him in the same way. It's the one thing we share now after he's gone.

Out of nowhere, a breeze rolls through us and down the hill, sending pinwheels spinning as tree branches stretch to life for the first time since we got here. Oliver and I look up the hill as if expecting to see someone standing there, watching. But no one's there. The sound of a hundred pinwheels turning is all we hear. Somehow, each one plays a different note, like wineglasses filled with water when you move your finger along the rim.

"Do you think that could be Sam?" Oliver whispers.

"It could be . . ." I move my ear in the direction of the wind, *listening*. "The song. It sounds familiar."

Oliver tilts his head and listens, too. The two of us sit there in the grass in silence for a long time, trying to see if one of us can recognize the melody.

I walk Oliver home after we leave memorial hill. I wanted to make sure he was okay before heading to work. It's my first shift since Sam died. I knew Tristan needed some time off, so I offered to come in this weekend. Since things are slow at the bookstore, there's usually no need for the two of us to be here, so we rarely get a chance to work together. The only times we see each other are the moments we come in to switch shifts. It makes it hard to start our local book group we've been planning to promote at the store. We haven't even decided on a first book yet. Tristan has been pushing *The Hitchhiker's Guide to the Galaxy*, but I said everyone's already read it. "It's a book you have to read at least twice," he keeps saying.

Behind the counter, there's a pin board where Tristan and I leave notes for each other, laying out which tasks have been taken care of, along with what needs to be done next. Sometimes, we leave personal messages. I find a blue note card pinned over the checklist.

> *Hope you're feeling better.*
> *Left your ticket in the first drawer.*
> *—Tristan*

I check the drawer. Inside a gold envelope, I find my ticket to the film festival next month. *I almost forgot about this.* Tristan has been working on this documentary for months. It's his second time submitting something to the festival, so it's wonderful to see things finally come together. A part of me is a little envious of him. He's not even a senior yet but his creative work is being recognized. Meanwhile I haven't even started my writing sample yet. I try not to think of things this way, and compare myself to others, but sometimes it's hard not to.

I find a pen and write a message back to him.

> *Thanks again for filling in.*
> *And can't wait to see your film!*
> *—Julie*

It's starting to rain outside, so there are fewer customers than usual. At least our online store seems to be doing better. Tristan gave me a list of book titles to find and package. Mr. Lee will pick them up on Monday and ship them off to new homes. I finish my tasks early, and even find time to sweep the store. Once the place is empty, I grab my journal and sit at my spot by the window. The sound of rain always puts me in a mood to write. Something about it that drowns out the rest of the world, clearing my mind. I think back to the lunch table yesterday, when Yuki asked me what I was writing about. I told her I was writing about Sam. But I'm not sure what it is I want to say yet. What do I want to tell the world about him? I imagine what some people might expect from me. *Write about his death. About what happened. About what it meant to lose him.* But that's not something I want to focus on. Because I don't want to remember Sam as a tragedy. I don't want that to be his story. When people think about Sam, I want them to think of his best moments. I want them to remember him as a musician, staying up late on a school night, writing music on his guitar. I want them to know him as an older brother, building giant forts in his room. And I want them to remember us, and the last three years we spent together. How me met, our first kiss, all the reasons I fell in love with him. I want them to fall in love with Sam, too. Maybe that's what I'll do. *Write down the memories of him. Memories of us. Tell our story.* Once I decide this, moments from over the years flash across my mind. I spend the next hour jotting down the ones that mean the most to me. I keep writing until I completely lose track of time.

The wind chime jingles above the door, making me look up. I shut my journal as someone comes into the store.

"Yuki! What are you doing here?"

Yuki holds a lilac umbrella, folded down. Her hair is tied back with a blue ribbon. She looks around the store. "I remembered you were working today. I hope it's okay I stopped by."

"Of course. Let me take your umbrella—" I grab it from her and set it against the wall. "I'm so glad you're here. It was starting to get lonely."

Yuki smiles. "Then I'm glad I came." There's something in her other hand. A small plastic pouch dangles at her side, carrying a whiff of something savory.

"What do you have there?" I ask.

Yuki looks down at the bag, a little surprised. "I hope you don't mind," she says through a smile. "I brought us lunch."

We finish our pickled cucumber and pork sandwiches by the window. I make hot water in the back room, and bring Yuki some tea. It's still drizzling out, so she stays at the store with me to wait out the rain. A bus passes by the window. On the other side of the street, kids in raincoats are racing down the sidewalk, puddles splashing under their boots. I stare at my reflection in the window for a long time, until Yuki's voice wakes me from my thoughts.

"Is something on your mind? You seem distracted."

"I'm a bit tired, that's all," I say. "Haven't been able to sleep much."

"What's wrong?"

"My dreams have been keeping me up lately."

"May I ask what they're about?"

I look at her. "Sam."

Yuki nods knowingly. "I see. They must be bad dreams then, if they're keeping you awake."

"It's the same dream," I say. "Over and over again. I mean, they're slightly different, but they always start in the same place."

"And where is that?"

"At the bus station. The night Sam died."

"And do they end the same?" she asks.

I look down at my hands. "I haven't gotten there yet . . ."

Yuki takes this in. "I see."

"I know," I say. I lean my head against the window glass. "I just wish I knew what they meant . . ."

Yuki stares into her tea in thought. "You know . . . when my grandma passed away a few years ago, I had dreams about her, too. And they were all a bit similar," she says. "In one of them, I dropped her favorite teapot and tried to put the pieces back together before she came in. In another one, I remember hiding my test scores from her. But she always found out. I remember the look on her face and how sad I kept making her. I didn't want to go back to sleep. I didn't want to upset her all over again . . ."

"Did the dreams eventually stop?" I ask.

Yuki nods. "Once I finally told my mom. She said something that helped me understand what they meant."

I lean forward. "What did she say?"

Yuki takes a sip of her tea. "She said that, sometimes, dreams mean the opposite of what they show us. That we shouldn't understand them exactly as they are. It can mean something in our life is out of balance. Or maybe we're holding in too much. Especially when we lose someone, dreams show us the opposite of what it is we need to find balance again."

"And what was that for you?"

"It took me a while to figure it out . . ." Yuki says into her tea. "I guess, all my life, I was worried about disappointing her. I just needed to remember how much she loved me. That she always had, no matter what happened." She looks at me. "Maybe you need to seek the opposite, too. Figure out how to bring balance into your life."

I think about this. "And how do I do that? Find the opposite . . ."

"I'm not really sure," Yuki says regretfully. "It's different for everyone."

I stare out the window again, unsure of myself.

Yuki touches my shoulder. "But sometimes they're just dreams," she says. "And they might mean nothing at all. So don't worry too much, alright?"

"Maybe you're right," I say. "I just wish I could get a regular night's sleep . . ."

Yuki looks away in thought. "You know, I might have something that could help," she says, setting down her tea. "Come . . ."

I follow Yuki to the counter where she left her bag. She opens it, searching through the pockets. When she finds what she's looking for, she turns around and places something in the palm of my hand.

"Here . . ."

"What's this?" I say, turning it in my hand. "A crystal?"

Pristine white, pearly, and translucent, it almost glows from within, giving off its own light.

"It's selenite," Yuki says. "My mother gave it to me. It's supposed to bring you luck and protection. It also wards away negative energy. Maybe it can protect you from bad dreams."

I run my fingers over it. "How does it work?"

"You just carry it with you," she says softly. "It's named after the moon goddess, you know. You see"—she turns the crystal over in my hand, revealing its sides—"selenite is said to hold a drop of light that dates back to the beginning of the universe. People believe it's connected to something outside of our world . . ."

I study the faces of the crystal. It feels warm in my hand, glinting back at me like moonlight. "You really believe in it?"

"I like to think it's protected me," Yuki says, nodding. "Now it's yours, though. It's also a bit fragile, so be careful."

I hold the crystal close to me.

"Thank you," I whisper.

"I hope this brings you some peace," Yuki says. "I have a feeling you'll need it."

It's still raining by the time Yuki leaves the store. I haven't seen a customer in hours, so I decide to close the place up early. At home, I help my mom make dinner. There's this Parmesan from a specialty store an hour away that she buys, and it pairs well with mushroom and spinach pasta. High-quality cheese is one of the few luxuries allowed in our household. My mom always says, "It's an investment." I never argue with her on this.

I set the table as my mother pulls the breadsticks from the air fryer. The news is playing in the living room with the sound muted. My mother likes to leave the TV on throughout the day. She says it makes the house feel less empty. Usually during dinner, my mother likes to share strange theories her students come up with in her classes. Like the one where we're all living in a video game controlled by a twelve-year-old girl on her brother's computer. But tonight is quieter than usual. Like we both have something on our minds. "You got a letter in the mail today," she says after a while. "I left it on the counter."

"I saw it," I say. It's an acceptance letter from Central Washington University. I already got the email a few days ago.

"Well what did it say?"

"I was accepted."

My mother stares at me, beaming. "Julie, why didn't you tell me? We should celebrate."

"It's not that big of a deal," I say, twirling the pasta with my fork. "Everyone gets in there." Central is not the most competitive. As long as you have decent enough grades, you get in. It's the decision from Reed I'm still waiting on.

My mother watches me pick at my plate. "I know it isn't your first choice, Julie . . ." she says. "But you should still be proud. Central Washington is a perfectly good school, even if you might not think so. I mean, I teach there, after all. Don't write it off so fast."

I look at her. "You're right. I didn't mean it like that. It's just . . ." I sigh. "I don't know if I want to spend another four years in Ellensburg. That wasn't my original plan. That's all."

"That wasn't any of our plans," my mother says, maybe more to herself. The table goes quiet again. "But I get it . . . Things haven't been so great around here. Especially recently. Especially for you." She stares at the table for a moment, as if in thought. "Maybe it's a bit selfish of me, wanting to have you around a little longer. I know you're not going to be here forever, Julie. But . . . I was hoping we'd at least spend some time together before you graduated. Before you left."

"I haven't gone anywhere yet," I say. "I'm still here."

"I know . . ." she says, releasing a breath. "But I don't get to see you too much. I know it isn't your fault . . . but you've been hard to reach lately. This is the first time you and I sat down for dinner in two weeks. I just feel a little less . . . connected to you. But maybe that's just me."

I stare at my phone on the table, then back at my mom. Has it really been that long since we had dinner together? After Sam died, I brought my meals up to my room. And since we've been connected again, I been spending all my time with him. I was gone all day yesterday. And the day before. A wave of guilt hits me as I think of what to say. I used to talk to her about everything. But I can't open up about Sam. I can't tell her what's happening. "I'm sorry," is all I can say. "I didn't mean to ignore you."

"That's alright," my mother says, smiling a little. "We're spending time together now. Thank you . . . for having dinner with me."

I stare at my plate again, making a mental note to do this with her more often.

After dinner, I help clear the table and head upstairs. As much as I want to call Sam, I should catch up on schoolwork. I make some progress on an essay for Gill's class that isn't due until next week, and finish an art history assignment. My mind seems to have cleared up, and I find it easier to focus. *Maybe it's the crystal.* Yuki said to always keep it with me, so I set it near Sam's bookend I keep on my desk as I work. I like to look at it from time to time. It makes me feel protected.

Sam told me I could call him sometime tonight. Since we spent an entire day on the phone yesterday, tonight's call can't be too long. I don't mind this. I want to hear his voice again, even if it's only for a few minutes.

Since my mother is in one of her intense vacuuming modes, I decide to make the call outside on the porch. The rain sounds like tiny pebbles hitting the roof. During past rainstorms, Sam and I used to sit out here together, watching for lightning. From the looks of it, there might be some tonight. It's a bit chilly out, so I put on his plaid shirt. I dial Sam's number.

Every time his voice comes through the line, it's as if time stops, just for us. "That sound . . ." He pauses to listen. "Where are you calling from?"

"Outside. On the porch step."

"Missing the fresh air?"

I recall the fields from yesterday, and smile to myself. "Among other things," I say. "And I just needed a break from my desk. Thought I would call you. *I miss you.*"

"*I miss you, too. I miss you infinity.*"

Sam's voice is warm against my ear. I wish things could stay like this. I wish we could talk forever.

"Tell me about your day," he says. "How are things at the bookstore? How's Mr. Lee?"

"It was nice to be back. Feels like home, you know?" I say. "And Mr. Lee is fine. He gave me this journal the other day. I forgot to tell you. It's almost too beautiful to write in."

"So you're writing again?"

"I'm starting to. Today, at least." *That was why he brought me to the fields. To inspire me again.* I wanted to surprise him with this, but I'm no good at holding things in. "Actually, I'm writing about you."

"*Me?*"

"Yes, *you.*"

Sam laughs. "What's it about?"

"You know, I'm still figuring that out," I admit. "I just started! But I'm really enjoying it. It's been a while since I've gotten into that rhythm of writing, you know? I want it to be about us, though. *Our story,* I mean. I started writing down some of our memories. Little vignettes. I just have to figure out how to stitch them together. Into something meaningful."

"I'm glad you found your rhythm. And glad I made it into one of your stories. *Finally.*" He laughs. "What's this for again?"

I let out a breath. "I'm not sure yet. I was just getting into the practice of things, you know? But if it turns out well, I might use it as my writing sample for Reed. Apparently, they need to look at one before I'm allowed into their creative writing classes. Not that I've been *accepted* yet, but I don't want to get into that right now. Anyway, who knows? If it ends up being really good, maybe I can try to get it published or something. It's something to work toward, you know? Get one of my stories out there. Like Tristan."

"What about Tristan?"

"I forgot to mention. His documentary was accepted to the film festival."

"Oh."

"He invited me to the premiere."

A silence.

"That's nice . . . For both of you."

I turn my head to the side, trying to read his tone. "Both of us? I haven't accomplished anything. I barely have an idea for a story."

"You still have time, though. To write it. And leave something behind. I wish I did."

"What do you mean?"

"I mean, I wish I had time to finish things, too, you know? Leave on mark on the world or something . . ."

"What did you want to finish?"

Sam lets out a breath. "It doesn't really matter anymore, Jules . . . There's no point in talking about it."

"But Sam—"

"Please. I shouldn't have said anything."

An ache of guilt goes through me. I thought sharing this would make him happy. *I'm writing a story about us, after all.* I didn't expect this to bring up feelings he won't even talk about. So I change the subject, just as he asked.

"I saw Oliver today. He really misses you."

"Oliver?" Sam's voice brightens at the name. "I've been thinking about him lately. How has he been?"

"He brings you flowers," I tell him. "I found out he sits by your grave sometimes, to keep you company. He really is a great friend."

"We were best friends. Since forever."

"He said he loves you . . ." I say.

"I love him, too. He knows that."

For a second, I think about asking him what he means. Ask whether or not there was something more to them than I knew. But I decide not to, because maybe it shouldn't matter. At least, not anymore.

Sam asks, "Is this the first time you've seen him since?"

"No," I say. "We've seen each other a few times, actually. We even saw a movie the other day. It was a musical. It happened out of the blue."

"I always told you. You guys have a lot more in common than you know."

"I'm realizing that. Guess I should have listened sooner."

"Does that mean you're friends now?"

"I think so. At least, I'm hopeful about it."

"I'm glad you guys finally gave each other a chance," Sam says.

I'm glad we did, too. If only it didn't take losing you for it to happen.

Rain continues to tap against the patio roof. I'll have to head back inside soon. Before I do, there's a question I want to ask. Something that's been burning in my mind for the past few days.

"What is it?" Sam asks.

"It's about our calls. About having to keep this a secret. I was wondering, what would happen if I told someone?"

"If I'm honest, Julie," Sam says. "I'm not completely sure. But I have this feeling it might affect our connection."

I think about this. "Is there a chance nothing would happen?"

"Maybe," he says. "I guess we won't know until it does. But there's a chance it could break our connection forever. I'm not sure if we should risk it."

I swallow hard. The thought of this sends a chill through me.

"Then I won't tell anyone. I'll keep this a secret. I don't want to lose you. Not this soon."

"I don't want to lose you, either."

A bright light flashes in the sky, followed by the sound of a distant rumble.

"What was that?" Sam asks.

"I think a storm is coming."

"Lightning?"

"Sounds like it."

When you live along the Cascade Range, occasional lightning storms are the only things that bring some life to the sleeping towns.

"I wish I could see," Sam says.

"They sound far away."

Another flash of lightning goes off, rupturing the sky for a split second.

"Remind me what they look like?" he asks.

"Like little cracks in the universe. And another world is peeking through."

"Maybe that's exactly what they are."

"And maybe you're on the other side."

Another flash, another rumble.

"Can I listen?" Sam asks.

I put the phone on speaker and hold it up.

We listen to the storm for a long time.

Another flash, another rumble.

"You're right," he says, "It does sound far away."

I stay there with him, on the phone, all the way until the storm ends.

CHAPTER

ELEVEN

A few days pass without any bad dreams, but I still wake up with the same empty feeling. Like there's a hole in my chest. I don't know what's wrong or how to explain it. The feeling seems to come whenever I get off the phone with Sam and find myself alone again. It's like this void inside me that I can't seem to fill up. I wish I could send Sam a text, or see our call history on the phone, so I can remind myself it's real. Because sometimes I'm still not sure. Maybe that's where the hole is coming from.

Whenever this feeling comes, I reach for Sam's things, because they're the only things that seem to make sense. His shirt on the back of the chair, the other bookend on my desk, the other things in my drawer—I still have everything. But his smell on them is beginning to fade, and I'm finding it harder to distinguish this bookend from the one I threw out.

I wish I could talk to someone else about this, or even show them his things, so they can tell me I'm not out of my mind. But Sam said it might harm our connection, and I'm scared to risk that—losing him all over again. I can't stop thinking about it, though. About the chance that nothing bad would happen at all if I tell someone about our calls, but I don't want to bring this up to Sam again. At least, not right now.

My phone buzzes. It's a text from Oliver, telling me to meet him outside in fifteen minutes. A second message from him says, Don't forget. I cannot be late to Spanish again. I get ready quickly, but when I come outside, he isn't even here yet. I check my phone. There's another message from him. Omw. Someone was walking their dog. Had to stop for a pic. He even sends me the photo.

For the past few days, Oliver and I have been walking to school together. His house is a couple blocks from mine, so he usually sends me his estimated time of arrival, which I'm learning is never accurate. We've been spending a lot more time together, talking about films and musicals and Sam. I can't believe it took three years and both of us losing someone we loved to get to this point. We made plans to visit his grave again soon. I'm going to bring flowers next time. *White blossoms.* Oliver has become a rock during a time when it feels like everything is blowing away from me. It makes me feel guilty about keeping secrets from him, especially knowing how much he loved Sam, too. I wish there was something else I could do for him. It takes me a while, but I finally think of something. A gesture to commemorate our new friendship.

Oliver tugs the straps of his backpack. "Ready to go?"

"One second," I call from inside the house.

The front door is propped open. Oliver sticks his head in. "We're gonna be late!"

"That's because you stopped to take photos with a dog."

"It was a beagle. His name was Arthur."

A few seconds later, I'm outside, holding something behind my back.

There's a pause between us.

Oliver arches a brow. "What do you have there?"

"Something I want to give you."

"For what?"

"Just because."

"Give it."

I hand it over. Oliver blinks at me. "This is . . . Sam's shirt . . ."

"Yes. And I want you to have it."

"Why?"

"It doesn't fit me. And I figure it'll look better on you."

Oliver stares at the shirt for a long time. "I don't think I can take this," he says.

"What do you mean? Of course you can."

He hands it back to me. "No, I can't."

I push his hands away. "Don't be ridiculous. It's only a shirt."

"It's *Sam's* shirt."

"And I'm giving it to you."

"I'm not taking this—" Oliver tries forcing the shirt back in my hands, but I push it away again. We do this back-and-forth game until I'm annoyed.

I slap his wrist. *"Why are you being like this?"*

Oliver sighs. "Because Sam obviously wanted you to have it," he says. "Not me."

"You don't know that. So just take it, okay?"

Oliver stares at me, and then back at the shirt. "I don't get it. Don't you want to keep it?"

"I have plenty of his things. Don't worry."

Oliver runs a hand over the shirt. Then he holds it tight. "Thank you."

I smile at him. "Just don't lose it, okay?"

"You know I won't."

I slide my backpack on and head down the steps, ready to go. For some reason, Oliver remains on the porch, unmoving.

"What's the matter?" I ask. "Not changing your mind, are you?"

"No," he says, sliding off his letterman's jacket. "I feel like I should give you something now." He steps off the porch, and places it over my shoulders.

"You're giving me your letterman's jacket?"

"I'm letting you *borrow* it. Until graduation."

"I'm honored."

We begin our walk to school. There's a slight chill this morning, so the jacket feels nice around me.

"Remind me, Oliver, what sport did you play again?"

"I never played one," he says. "I bought it off a senior who graduated last year."

"So it's all for looks?"

"Precisely."

"I admire that."

I nudge him on the shoulder and we both laugh.

Columns of red and white balloons are pillared along the walls, and aluminum stars hang from the ceiling as I enter the hallway. Things are returning to normal at school again. People are wearing bright colored T-shirts, playing music in the bathrooms, and throwing paper balls across the lockers. Any lingering sentiments of Sam's death have been replaced with school spirit. There used to be a picture of him on the wall by the bulletin board. I don't know if it fell down, or if someone removed it, but it's gone now. There's a stack of student newspapers in each class, and for the first time in weeks, Sam isn't mentioned. It's like everyone has moved on from him. Somehow, this doesn't surprise me. I see pep rallies, soccer games, and graduation are what's trending.

My French test goes better than I expected. I spent all night studying for it, so I'm glad it paid off. I surprise myself on the oral portion of the test. According to Madame Lia, I've always been a natural at pronunciation. In English, Mr. Gill is out sick for the day (an answered prayer), so our substitute, a squat gray-haired man who squints when someone asks a question, tells us to read *Animal Farm* silently to ourselves. I work on my essay instead because I left my copy of the book at home. I love the topic I chose. How Octavia E. Butler's sci-fi novels are better at teaching history because of their emotional appeal to the readers. It's about the power of storytelling that humans have been primed for since the Stone Age when they carved pictures on cave walls. I draft three pages before the bell rings. I've been much more focused this week. *I think it's the crystal.* I make sure to carry it with me for peace and luck.

"How did your test go?" Jay asks me at lunch.

"Pretty good, I think. Did you finish your group project?"

"My group has two lacrosse players . . . " he says, ripping a sandwich in half. "So no."

"It could be worse."

"How?"

"Three lacrosse players."

We laugh as Jay hands me half the sandwich. A second later,

Oliver shows up. He places his tray on the table, and squeezes a chair right next to me, forcing Jay to move over.

"Love the earth shirt, Jay," Oliver says, stealing one of his fries.

Jay is wearing one of the shirts he designed for his environmental club, the one of a sick globe with a thermometer sticking out of its mouth. "Thanks. I made it myself."

"And how come I never got one?"

"Well, if you actually came to our meetings, you would have."

"I came to the first one," Oliver reminds him, then whispers to the rest of us, "and it was a *long* one."

Jay gives him a look. "You know I can hear you."

"What—we didn't say anything," Oliver says, then winks at me and the others.

"Enough, guys—" Rachel interrupts them, and rises from her chair. "There's a club emergency. The form is due tomorrow, and we still need five more signatures."

"Can't you just, you know, *make them up*?" Oliver suggests.

Rachel's eyes widen with hope. "Will that work?" she whispers.

"*No*," I say.

We all glance at each other, trying to think of ideas that won't get us into trouble.

"Do you really need a school club to host a movie?" Yuki asks. "We can always get together informally."

"No, but if we get approval, the school gives us a hundred-dollar budget for snacks," Rachel explains.

Oliver smacks the table. "Then we need these signatures!" he says, and everyone laughs.

"Since you're popular, Oliver, do you think you can help us?" Rachel asks, handing him the form again.

"On the condition I get final say on what we eat."

"Deal."

Oliver holds up his hand. They high-five each other.

"Hey, it's Mika—" Jay points behind me.

I look up and see her walking this way. She hasn't made an appearance at lunch in a while. "Mika!" I call her name but she hurries pasts us without looking at me, and disappears through hallway doors.

Yuki frowns. "Is she okay?"

"She doesn't look too good," Oliver notes. He turns to me. "Have you spoken to her lately?"

"I've tried to . . . But she keeps avoiding me."

"Is she mad at you?"

"I guess so." I look down at my tray, feeling guilty for letting things get this way. "I missed the vigil after I promised her I'd go. I missed a lot of things. So she doesn't think much of me right now."

"I ran into her in the restroom yesterday," Rachel says. "She was crying."

Oliver leans back in his chair. "That's rough. I wish there was something we could do."

"Me, too," I say.

The table goes quiet for a while. No one really touches their food. Especially me. I can't seem to eat at all. *How can I after promising Sam I'd make sure Mika's okay?* I could have reached out to her more. It's like I'm failing him. Failing the three of us. After all, it's my fault she isn't talking to me. I wish I could just tell her about Sam. Maybe it would fix everything, and we would understand each other again.

After a long silence, Rachel looks up at us. "I have an idea. We should invite her to release the lanterns with us. It might help her, too."

I look at her. "Lanterns?"

"It's the idea we came up with," Yuki says, nodding. "To honor Sam, we're going to release lanterns for him. They're called memory lanterns. It lets you whisper something to a person you lost, and the lantern will carry the message to them in the sky."

"Like little hot-air balloons," Rachel explains. She uses her hands to cup something invisible. "You put a candle inside and watch them float away." She raises her hands, as if releasing something.

"It's a long tradition across different many cultures," Yuki goes on. "People have been doing it for thousands of years. All over the world, for many kinds of ceremonies. It brings peace and good luck."

The image of lanterns skimming the air floats across my mind. "It sounds beautiful . . ." I say.

Rachel leans forward. "That means you like our idea?"

I can't help smiling. "It's perfect."

She claps her hands together. "I'm so excited. I've seen it in movies. And I've always wanted to do it."

"There is one problem," Yuki says, sharing a look with Jay. "We are having some trouble finding a place to release them. It has to be away from town, somewhere like an open field."

I think about this. "I know a place. A field, I mean. I can bring us there."

"Perfect!" Rachel says.

Smiles are exchanged around the table as we continue our conversation about the lanterns. A few days ago, I wasn't sure if anything would ever come to fruition. But listening to everyone sharing ideas to make this happen brings me a sense of joy. I realize this isn't about me anymore. Especially if Mika and

Oliver are there, too. This is something beautiful for us to share together. And it will all be for Sam.

At the end of lunch, before we all pack up to go, I say one last thing to the table. "Thanks again for all of this. I think Sam would truly love your idea if he was here."

Yuki touches my shoulder. "We'll let you know when we have it ready. It's going to be something special. We promise."

The school day goes by quickly. Oliver and I are supposed to walk home together, but he texted me last period, saying he has to stay after class to discuss his grade. I left his jacket in my locker, so I go to grab it along with some books. The hallway is packed as I'm heading out. I bump into someone's trombone case and drop my things. As I bend down to pick them up, someone murmurs something.

"*Nice jacket.*"

I look up to find the voice.

Taylor stares down at me as I gather the rest of my things and straighten up. A group of her friends stand beside her, watching. "Is that Oliver's?" she asks.

Of course it is. She knows this. What does she expect me to say? "He's just letting me borrow it."

"When did you two become so close?"

"What do you mean? We've always been friends."

She gives me a look. "You know that isn't true. Oliver doesn't even like you. We used to talk about you behind your back. He didn't mention that?"

I clench the jacket tight, unsure of how to respond to this. I should walk away. *Who cares what Oliver used to say? Things are different now. Why does she want to ruin it?* "Why are you telling me this?"

Out of nowhere, Taylor rips the jacket from my hands. "You think we all just forgot what you did? Just because Oliver's being *friendly* to you?"

"What's wrong with you?" I shout, my cheeks burning. I reach for the jacket. "Give me that back—"

Taylor throws out her arm, almost hitting me. "What's wrong with *us*?" she says back. "We're not the ones who moved here to ruin everyone's life."

"What are you talking about?"

Taylor's eyes narrow at me. Her voice sharpens. "Don't play stupid, Julie. It's your fault he's dead."

A chill goes through me as people around us stop to listen. I knew she would confront me with this one day. But I didn't expect it to be in front of everyone at school. I swallow hard, trying to keep my voice steady. "Don't you blame me for that. You don't—"

"Don't *you* pin this on anyone else," Taylor cuts me off. She presses her finger to my collarbone, forcing me to step back. "You made him drive an hour away to pick you up. Sam was only trying to spend time with his friends. It was the first night all of us were together since *you* came here. But you wouldn't even let him have that. We were all there, Julie. You made him leave and ruined everything."

"That's not true," I say. "He was the one texting me. I told him he didn't have to go. I said I would walk home."

Taylor shoves another finger at my chest. "You're such a liar. I was talking to him before he left. He told me everything you were saying. And you *guilted* him into leaving. And that *killed* him. Because of *you*."

My stomach hardens. "You're wrong. You don't know the whole conversation. Sam wouldn't—"

"You don't know what Sam thinks," Taylor cuts me off again.

"And you don't know what happened. You didn't read our texts."

"Then show me them."

"I can't . . ."

"Why not?"

"Because I deleted them."

"That's what I thought."

This is the last conversation I want to have. I want to run away, but too many people have stopped to listen, so I have to defuse this before it turns into something worse. I take a deep breath and force myself to say something. "Even if I made him go, it wasn't me who was driving the truck. It wasn't me who swerved into his car. How can you seriously blame me for that? I'm about as responsible for his death as whoever planned the bonfire, which was *you*."

Taylor presses another finger into my chest, even harder this time. "So you're trying to blame this on me now?"

I clench my fists. "I'm not blaming anyone. It's you who's blaming me."

"If this isn't your fault, why didn't you show up to his *funeral*?" Taylor asks me. "Was it because you felt guilty or you just didn't give a shit?"

It's like the wind gets knocked out of me. I open my mouth to say something, but nothing comes out. But suddenly I don't need to. Because Mika appears from nowhere, stepping in front of me.

"This is none of your business," Mika says to Taylor. "She doesn't have to explain anything to *you*."

"Why don't *you*—" Taylor starts.

But Mika doesn't let her finish that sentence.

I hear the slap across Taylor's face before the scene processes. The hallway echoes with a collective gasp and then falls silent again. I cover my mouth, unsure of what's about to play out. Only a few people know about Mika's self-defense classes, or the story about her fight at the bar in Spokane. When Taylor tries to strike back, I know she isn't one of them. Mika swiftly smacks away her arm and throws Taylor against the locker! A crowd swarms around them, some pulling out their phones. Suddenly Liam breaks through the crowd. He grabs Mika by the back of the shirt like he's about to fling her across the room.

"*Hey*—" Liam shouts.

But Mika elbows him right in the gut, and he falls to the floor, wheezing.

The crowd erupts. The noise attracts more people into the hall, including a few teachers who arrive to break up the fight. One of them, Mr. Lang from biology, brings two fingers to his lips and blows them like a whistle. Everyone glances around before the crowd quickly disperses.

Someone touches my arm.

"*Julie—we should go.*"

Yuki appears at my side, beckoning me to follow the crowd outside.

"What about Mika?" I say, searching through the crowd for her. There she is with Mr. Lang. He has one hand on her shoulder, and the other clenching Liam's arm.

"I'm not sure if there's anything we can do," Yuki says. And as much as I want to do something, I know she's right.

❀

I've been waiting outside school for more than an hour. Yuki stayed with me for a while, but they were taking so long in there, I told her she should go home without me. I think Mr. Lang took everyone into his office. *What's going on in there?* I hope Mika isn't in too much trouble.

A half hour later, Mika finally comes out the front doors. She holds an ice pack over her left eye.

"Mika—are you okay?" I reach out to inspect it, but Mika turns the other way.

"It's nothing," she says.

"What happened in there?"

"I'm suspended."

"That's terrible. This is all my fault. Let me go in and tell Mr. Lang—"

"Just forget it. I have to go—" she says abruptly, then hurries off, leaving me standing there.

"Mika! Wait!" I call after her a few times, but she doesn't look back.

I almost run after her. But something inside me says she wants to be left alone. At least, for now. So I just stand there, watching her disappear down the block. I wish she would let me help her, after everything she's done for me. But I don't know what I'm supposed to do. I don't know how to get through to her. I stare down at the pavement, wondering how I'm going to fix this . . .

When I get home, I call Sam right away and tell him everything. I tell him about Oliver, his jacket, and the things Taylor said. Then I tell him about Mika and the fight that broke out between them.

"She won't talk to me," I say. "I'm don't know what to do."

"Have you tried texting her?" Sam asks.

I check my phone again. "I asked her if she made it home earlier. But she never responded. I feel terrible."

"Taylor should feel terrible," Sam says, a strain in his voice. "I can't believe she said those things to you. I'm sorry, Julie. I wish I was there. I wish I could do something about all this."

"I wish you were here, too."

He lets out a long breath. "It feels like this is all my fault."

"Sam—you can't blame yourself for any of this."

"But it's hard not to," he says, sounding frustrated. "Mika wouldn't be feeling this way, and getting into fights, and no one would be saying those things about you if I hadn't . . . If only . . ." His voice trails off.

"*Stop it*," I say. "That isn't your fault, Sam. None of this is. And I don't care what people say about me, okay?"

A long silence.

"I feel so useless, though. Not being able to do anything," he says. "Not even for Mika. I can't imagine how I'd feel if I lost her, you know? At least you can talk to her, though. Maybe you can go over there, see her in person."

"I don't know if she would even listen," I say.

"You think you could you try again?"

"You know I want to," I say. "But every time we talk, I always have to hide something from her, and I think she can sense it. . . . It's like this wall between us now."

"So what are you thinking?"

I hesitate to answer this. I'm afraid of what he'll say. "I want to tell her about you. I think it would fix things between us. I think she'd understand."

Sam goes quiet.

"Do you think I shouldn't?"

"I don't know, Jules," he says. "I don't want something bad to happen to our connection."

"But you said there's also a chance nothing will happen," I remind him.

"I mean, maybe nothing will. It's still a big risk, you know?"

"So you're saying this is a bad idea?"

Sam goes quiet again, considering this. "I'll let this be your call."

I stare out the window, wondering what to do. "I wish you gave me clearer answers sometimes."

"I'm sorry. I wish I had them."

CHAPTER TWELVE

I couldn't wait another day to see Mika. I couldn't leave things the way they were. The guilt was eating me up, making it hard to focus. The sun casts shadows along the driveway as I reach the front door to her house. The van is parked outside the garage, so her parents must be home, too. I hope it'll be her mom who answers when I ring the doorbell. Whenever there was bickering between us, she was the peacemaker.

The sound of footsteps lets me know someone's coming. Mika's front door has multiple chains and locks. I listen from the other side as somebody undoes them, one after the other. The door cracks open.

Mika peeks at me through the length of a chain. "What are you doing here?"

"I was hoping we could talk," I say.

"About what?"

"Anything."

Mika says nothing. She just stares at me through the doorway.

"Can I come in?" I ask.

Mika considers this. Then she shuts the door on me, and I think the answer is no. But the last chain unlocks from inside, and the door opens again. Mika looks at me without a word before turning back inside. I take off my shoes and follow her into the hall.

Steam rises from the kettle as Mika goes to shut off the stove. I hang beneath the archway of the kitchen as she grabs a few things from the cupboards. I sense something different about the house. I sniff the air. *Incense?* It's coming from the other room. Since Mika seems busy at the moment, I decide to follow the smell.

There is a wooden cabinet in the living room. On the middle shelf, whiffs of smoke rise from a silver bowl where the incense is burning. A beautiful bowl of fruit sits beside it. I noticed the cabinet the first time I came over to Mika's house a few years ago. It's always full of photographs. Portraits of people in Mika's family whom I've never met. She once told me they were pictures of ancestors. She said it is a symbol of respect for the dead.

And then I see it. A picture of Sam that wasn't there before. He's smiling in his plaid shirt, a blue sky behind him. Something cold moves down my back, sending a shiver through me. I keep forgetting that to the rest of the world, he's dead.

"It's the best one I could find."

I turn around. Mika is holding a tea tray.

"The picture," she says. "My mom and I picked it. She said he looked handsome."

I can't seem to find words. I just stand there, staring at his photo.

Mika sets the tray down on the coffee table. "I was making tea before you got here," she says.

We sit on the couch together. Mika lifts the teapot and pours me a cup without asking. I notice her left eye. It's a little bruised. But not as bad as I'd expected.

"It's chrysanthemum," Mika says.

"Thank you."

I blow on my tea. I can see Sam's picture from where we're sitting. It's like he's watching over us. I notice Mika looking at it, too.

"I wished they asked me for his picture," she says.

"Who?"

"The school. I didn't like the one they used in the paper. They should have asked me."

I remember the article. It was his school photo. Sam would have hated it, too.

"The one you picked is perfect," I tell her.

Mika nods. She takes a sip of tea.

"I'm sorry about your eye. How did that happen?"

"One of Taylor's friends threw a purse at me when I wasn't looking," she says.

"I'm so sorry, Mika."

"It was a cheap shot. But I'm okay."

"I forgot to thank you earlier," I say. "For sticking up for me."

"I wasn't doing it for you. I did it for Sam."

I lower my gaze, unsure of what to say.

Mika blows on her tea and takes another sip. After a long silence, she says, "When I saw Taylor talk to you like that . . . I thought of him. I thought of what Sam would have done if he was there. He's always better with his words than me, you know? That's why everyone liked him better.

"Even though he's gone . . ." she continues. "I keep expecting to see him again. Whenever someone comes through the door, I wonder if it's going to be him. *If it's Sam.* It's those moments when I forget he's gone and remember again, that I feel the most sad." She stares into her tea. "I know you don't like to talk about Sam, but I really miss him. I don't know how people can let go so fast."

"I haven't let go," I say.

"But you're trying to."

I shake my head. "That's not true anymore." *That was me two weeks ago. Everything's different now that I'm connected to Sam again. If only she knew this.*

"It doesn't matter anymore if you do," Mika says, looking at Sam's portrait again. "Sometimes, I wish I stopped thinking about him, too. I don't care about the vigil. I don't even care that you missed it. But you were so busy trying to forget him that you were willing to forget *me*. You forget there were three of us. It wasn't just you and Sam. I was a part of that, too . . ." She pauses, and looks at her phone on the edge of the coffee table. "I know this will sound stupid, but I still read through our group messages. *Between the three of us.* I thought about sending something the other day, just to keep it alive, you know? So that it wouldn't just end . . . But I couldn't. Because I was scared neither of you would answer. And I don't want to be alone in there—" Her voice breaks, sending a pain to my chest. *I deleted our group chat.* It never once occurred to me that I was deleting Mika, too. I want to say something to fix this, but I know there are no words good enough.

Mika stares deep into her tea again, and continues in almost a whisper. "The other day . . . my mom was looking for pictures of me and Sam together for a photo album. But she said it was hard to find one without you in it, too. So instead, she made it about the three of us." She wipes her eyes with back of her sleeve, trying to keep herself composed. "You know, when it happened . . . When Sam died . . . I remember thinking, how are you and I going to get through this? *What are we going to do,* you know? I kept waiting for you to text back, return my calls, and show up at the door. But you never did. *You didn't even want to see me—*" her voice gives out, as if she's holding back tears. "It was like when I lost Sam, I lost you, too."

She wipes her eyes with her sleeve, and goes on. "His family came over a few days ago. I guess his mom still wakes up to the shock that he's gone. For the first few days, she kept checking his room to see if he might be there. Like it was a dream or something. She called my dad to come over to help move Sam's things out, but then she changed her mind again. They're just sitting in boxes in his room. Like she's keeping it for him . . . in case he comes back or something."

My eyes are watering at this point. *I should have been there with her at the beginning. I should have shared some of this pain.* I take her hand. "Mika, I'm sorry. I shouldn't have left you alone like that, okay? I promise I never forgot about you and Sam. I still love him, and I think about him every day."

Mika pulls her hand away. "It doesn't look that way to me," she says through tears. "Seems like you've moved on with your life. I see you with your new group of friends. All of you at lunch, laughing like nothing's wrong. Like Sam was never even here." She wipes her eyes again. "Did you even cry once when he died?"

The question stabs me. I hate that she thinks of me this way. *"Of course I have,"* I answer. Had she asked me this back at the diner, I might have said otherwise. But I'm not the person I was then. *Because I found Sam again.* If only I could just tell her this. "I know it might not seem like I care about him, but I do. Of course I do, Mika. But it's complicated. You have to understand—"

"I know when you're not being completely honest, Julie," Mika says. "I know when you're keeping things from me, too. I also know you *meant* what you said at the diner that morning. How am I supposed to believe you changed your mind since then? Just like that—"

"Because something strange happened since then," I tell her. "I wish I could tell you, but I cant. I'm sorry. You have to believe me, though."

Mika dismisses this with a shake of her head. "I can't do this, Julie. I'm tired of all these nonanswers," she says. "And I can't take being ignored anymore."

"What do you mean?"

"I've called you a dozen times since he died," Mika says. "And you never picked up. I know you didn't want to talk to me. When I needed you. And yet you expect me to sit here and listen to this?"

Mika's been calling me? I stare at my phone again, trying to remember when. *It's Sam's calls, isn't it?* When I'm on the phone with him, nothing else comes through. That's why I keep losing text messages, calls, and I don't know what else. It's like our connection is blocking me from everyone else. It's keeping me from Mika, the person Sam asked me to make sure is okay. And I can't even explain myself to her. *"It's my phone . . ."* is all I can say. "Something's wrong with it."

What else am I supposed to say? How do I fix this without telling the truth?

"Maybe it's time you go," Mika says abruptly. She looks away, letting me know she doesn't want to hear more. Like she's about to get up, ending our conversation. I wish I could tell her everything. So she will understand why I've been acting the way I have, and know I haven't let go of Sam because I never needed to. *Because he never left me.* But I don't want to risk our connection. My hands clench and unclench as I hesitate on the couch, deciding . . . After all, Sam left it up to me, didn't he? And there's still a chance nothing bad will happen if I tell her. I can't keep letting Mika think this way. I can see how much she's hurting. I need to be there for her, like I promised him. I can't let her go through this alone anymore. *And I can't lose her, too.* I want to break down this wall that's building between us. I don't even know if she's going to believe me, but I swallow my breath and tell her anyway.

"*Mika, listen—*" I take her hands before she gets up. "The reason I'm not getting your calls . . . or why I'm not grieving over Sam, is because we're still connected. *Me and Sam,* I mean. He isn't gone yet."

"What are you talking about?"

"This is going to sound strange . . ." I start to explain, carefully choosing my next words. "But I can talk to Sam. On the phone. I can call him and he picks up."

"Our Sam?"

"*Yes.*"

Mika gives me a look. "What do you mean, you can *talk* to him?"

"I mean, he answers me. Through the phone," I say. "I can tell him something, and he responds. We've been talking for hours, almost every day, like old times again. And it's really him, Mika. It isn't anyone else, or some sort of prank. It's *Sam.*" My heart pounds inside my chest. *I don't know what else to say.*

Mika takes this in. "Are you sure about this?"

I lean forward, squeezing her hands. "I *promise* it is. It's his voice, Mika. It's him, it's *Sam*. You have to trust me."

Mika squeezes my hands back, nodding slowly. "I believe you. I'm trying to."

I've been waiting so long to hear her say this. But there's something in her voice that doesn't give me the relief I expected. There's something in her eyes that makes me second-guess myself.

"And when did you start talking to him?" she asks carefully.

"The week after he died."

"Only through the phone?"

"It's the only way to reach him."

"Can you show me the calls?" she asks.

I hesitate. "I can't do that . . ."

"Why not?"

"Because none of our calls show up on my phone," I explain. "I still don't really understand why. And we can't text, either—only calls."

Mika leans back, her face deep in thought. There's a long silence. My chest tightens. Maybe I shouldn't have told her.

"You think I'm crazy, don't you?" I ask.

"*Of course not,*" she says. "Losing someone is a difficult thing for all of us, Julie. But, do you think there's a chance this might be all in your head?"

"I considered that at the beginning. But it isn't, Mika. It's really Sam. It's really him I've been talking to, *I know it*."

Mika takes in a deep breath. Her voice softens. "Sam is dead, Julie. You remember that, don't you? You know we buried him, right?"

"I *know*, I'm not saying he isn't, but it's hard to explain. It's—"

My voice gives out, because I don't have the answers. "I know this doesn't make sense, okay? But I need you to believe me."

When Mika says nothing, I know she doesn't. My head aches as the room starts to spin. *I'm beginning to lose myself, too.* There's only one way to prove this. One thing that will explain everything. "Here, let me just call him . . ."

"Julie—" Mika starts.

But I've already made the call. And it's ringing.

This doesn't have to be long. Just enough for Mika to hear the sound of Sam's voice, a couple words, maybe a quick conversation to prove it's him—*this will convince her.* My chest tightens with every ring as I wait for Sam to pick up already. I can't believe what I'm doing. *I finally get to share this secret and prove all of this is real.*

But the phone keeps ringing. It rings for so long, I lose track of how many seconds have passed. Mika sits in silence, watching me. The ringing goes on and on, building more pressure in my chest. I don't know what's wrong. *Where are you, Sam?* This isn't like him. He usually picks up right away. My hands are trembling, so I clench the phone tighter. The phone keeps ringing and ringing, and I wonder if he might not pick up this time.

And then it hits me. A terrible thought. Like a bullet to the chest. The missing call history, the texts not going through, the secrets to keep, and the calls themselves. Oh my god. *Has this has all been in my head? Have I imagined it all?* I lower the phone, as the room blurs and everything goes still. A chill moves through me, and the pressure that's been building in my chest *bursts*, leaving a massive hole that makes me want to disappear.

No one picks up this time. So I end the call.

I don't even look at Mika as I rise abruptly from the couch. "I—I have to go." I nearly knock the teapot over as I hurry to leave. I struggle to put my phone back into my stupid pocket, but it won't go in.

"*Julie, wait—*" Mika grabs hold of my arm to stop me, but I pull away.

I force a smile. "I was kidding! It was all a joke. I made it up, okay?" But the trembling in my hands and the petrified pitch of my voice betray me, and Mika isn't laughing things off. She follows me into the hallway as I'm leaving. When I catch the look of worry on her face, I'm so embarrassed, all I can say is, "I'm not crazy, I swear. It was all a joke."

"Julie, I don't think you are. Just wait—"

Something vibrates in my hand, followed by a strange noise that startles us both. I'm so thrown off guard, my phone slips through my hand, bounces off the tip of my shoe, and slides across the rug.

I stare at my phone and see it's *ringing*. This surprises me, because I never have the ringer on. It's always on silent. I glance at the screen, and see the number is unknown.

Mika and I look at each other. She glances at the phone, wondering if I'm going to answer. I hesitate before I slowly pick it up from the floor. *It's still ringing.* I accept the call, bringing the phone to my ear. The sound of my own heart beating is the first thing I hear. "Hello?" I say.

Now, maybe it's because of the frenzy of emotions I was worked up in seconds ago, and the adrenaline that came with it. But I don't remember what is said or why. All I remember is after: me holding the phone out to Mika, saying, "It's . . . for you."

Mika blinks between me and the phone. Then she takes it from me, and holds it to her ear. There's a pause before she speaks.

"Hello? Who is this?"

My heart races as I stand there. I can't hear anything from the other end.

"Sam? Which Sam?" Mika looks at me, her brows arched. "But that doesn't make any sense."

A silence as she listens.

"How am I supposed to believe this?" she says into the phone. "I don't know. This just can't be true . . ." It continues like this for a minute or so. Mika puts a hand over her other ear, as if to hear him better, and wanders off. It's a nervous tic of hers— pacing around—especially when she's on the phone. I follow her into the kitchen, leaving some space between us. I don't want to overwhelm her with this. *A call with Sam.*

"I don't know if I believe this . . . Is this some sort of a joke?" Mika asks. Another silence. Her brows arch and come together. "Ask you what?"

It's strange to only hear one side of a conversation. Like skipping pages in a book, trying to piece the scene together. I wonder what Sam is saying back.

"What kind of a question?" Mika says, sounding confused. "You mean, that only you would know? Let me think then—" She looks at me for a moment, then looks away. She whispers into the phone, "Okay. If you're Sam, tell me . . . the year Julie moved here, after I met her for the first time . . . what did I say about her that I told you never to repeat?"

Mika pauses to listen. The answer must have been right because her eyes widen. She shoots me a look of surprise, and asks, "Did he ever tell you this?"

I shake my head, somewhat confused. *What did she say about me?*

Mika turns away, continuing the call. "Okay, something else? A harder one? Let me see . . ." She pauses to think. "Okay. What about this. When we were seven . . . when Grandpa was dying, you and I went to visit him in his room when we weren't supposed to. Do you remember? He let us play around by his bedside. On his nightstand, there were four things sitting there. We never touched them, and we never even talked about them after. But if you're really Sam, you would be able to recall those things in Grandpa's room, because I can. So what are they?"

I close my eyes, and imagine the nightstand as Mika listens over the phone. As Sam answers, she repeats each object out loud, one by one, as if recalling them herself. *A single white feather. An origami swan, tied to a string. A ceramic bowl, painted with the face of a dragon, filled with incense.*

"And the last thing?" she asks.

I don't get to hear what the last object is, because Mika doesn't repeat it. Instead, she goes silent for a long time. When she turns around to look at me, her eyes are watering, and I know it must have been right.

"It's Sam," she gasps. "It's really him."

A sensation goes through me that I can't explain, one not only of joy, but *relief*. I almost pinch myself to make sure this isn't a dream, that this is all happening, and that Mika is here, too. Telling me it's really Sam on the line. Telling me I'm not imagining it. Telling me this is all real, and has been all along.

Mika stays on the phone with Sam for a while, asking a dozen questions, crying and laughing all at once. She keeps glancing over at me, smiling. She squeezes my hand, and rests her head on my shoulder, maybe to let me know she believes me, or to thank me for this. Even though I've been talking to Sam for a while now, I still can't believe this is happening. That the three of us are connected again.

When the call ends, and we hang up, Mika and I hug each other, both of us crying, neither one able to speak. I can *feel* her trying to grasp how she found herself here. In this impossible alternate world where time moves in another direction, where the fields are endless, and where the ground beneath us has never been more unstable. Although I'm beginning to lose track of which way is up or down, it's a wonderful sense of relief to have someone else here with me. Someone who can *look*, see what I see, and tell me I'm not dreaming. Or maybe we're dreaming together, I'm not sure. But it doesn't matter right now. Neither of us wants to wake up from this.

Later that night, when I'm back home, I call Sam again to talk about everything that happened. He picks up right away this time, like he was expecting me. I thank him for talking with Mika, and for letting me share this connection with someone else.

"I wasn't sure if it would actually work," I say, holding the phone tight. "How come you never mentioned you could call me before?"

"Because I'm not supposed to."

"What do you mean?"

"I didn't want you to know yet. Because if I ever call and you don't pick up, our connection ends right there."

"You mean, forever?"

"Yeah."

A chill goes through me. "How do you know that?"

"It's one of the few things I know for sure," he says. He doesn't explain things further.

I swallow hard, thinking about this. "That scares me, Sam. If that's true, you shouldn't call me again. From now on, I'll only call you, okay?"

"That's for the best," he says.

A breeze blows in through the open window, swaying the curtains. I go over to shut it. Outside, tree branches creep up like fingers, tapping against the glass.

"I'm sorry," Sam says, a bit out of the blue.

"For what?"

"Not picking up earlier. I guess I was nervous. About what might happen."

"But nothing happened," I remind him. "Everything worked out fine. It's even better now! Because Mika knows, and now she understands everything. You guys even got to talk again! Aren't you glad we did this?"

A silence.

"Sam?"

"It's sort of complicated . . ."

Before I can ask what he means by this, the sound of static comes through the line.

"What's that noise?" I ask.

"Noise? I don't hear anything," Sam says, and suddenly, I notice something strange with his voice.

"Sam, you sound like you're moving farther away." Like the receiver is drifting from him. "Is everything okay?"

More static comes through. I stand and tilt my head, adjusting the angle of the phone to try to get a better signal.

"Everything will be okay, Julie," Sam says. "I promise. But I have to go now, okay?"

"Wait—go where?" I ask him. But he doesn't answer this. All he says is, "I'll talk to you soon. I love you."

The call ends abruptly. I stand by the window in silence, wondering if I should call him back. But something cold I can't explain creeps up my spine, telling me not to. That I shouldn't. So I go back to the bed and hold the phone close to me. I stare at the blank screen all night, trying to stay calm.

Did I ruin everything again?

CHAPTER
THIRTEEN

Something's wrong with our connection. Something terrible. I don't know how to fix it, and neither does Sam. It reminds me of when a storm comes, and thunder flickers the lights, throwing off all the electricity in the house, and nothing works. I keep waiting for the clouds to part, for the weather to change, but every time I look out the window the sky is still bruised and purple. It's hard to not let it get to me, because I asked for this, didn't I? This is my fault. I made Sam talk to Mika, and ever since then, our calls are not the same anymore. They have to be spaced further apart and don't last as long. We used to be able to speak for hours, whenever I needed him. Now I have to wait for days to pass before I can call him again, and if our conversation goes longer than ten minutes or so, static comes through the line and it scares me. It hurts that I can't even call him out of the blue anymore, even when I'm desperate to hear his voice.

When I feel like I'm about to fall apart, I have to remind myself I haven't lost him yet—I haven't lost Sam. I know I messed up our connection, but he's still with me. And as long as we plan our calls better, keeping them short, and finding those places where our signal is the strongest, we can make this work. We'll figure it out. Maybe there's a way to fix things.

It's been two weeks since I told Mika everything. Since I let her and Sam speak to each other again. But not all good things come without consequences. During our last call, Sam told me something I refuse to believe. He said there's a chance we only have a few calls left before our connection ends forever. The worst part is Sam warned me this could happen, but I didn't listen. At least he got to speak with Mika one more time. The look in Mika's eyes after their call made the risk worth it. At first, I was desperate to have someone else tell me these past few weeks have been real, that Sam's voice hasn't been all in my head. But once I reconnected Mika and Sam again, it became so much more than that. Mika looks like herself again, and the two of us are spending more time together. I think the call gave her the peace of mind she needed and a new starting point to heal. And now that there are no secrets between us, it feels like we can finally be there for each other.

At least I haven't said good-bye to Sam yet. And as long as I don't, we'll stay connected, right? Isn't that what he promised me? I'm not ready to let him go yet. I hate imagining my life without him. I wish I could hold on to him, keep him with me for as long as I can. I don't know what I'll do when he's gone.

This is all I think about now as I stare at my phone. I do this all day long when I'm not talking to him—on the off chance he calls me and I need to answer right away. So that our connection never breaks again . . .

"Are you expecting a call?"

I look up from the table as the room comes back into focus. Oliver is sitting across from me, waiting for a response. We are at a small table in the back of the café, Sun and Moon. The Moroccan lamps are on, flickering like real flames, even though it's daylight out. At least it isn't crowded this Saturday morning. The two of us have been coming here a lot lately. He always orders the chai latte with extra foam. I tried an Americano for the first time today instead of my usual coffee. I'm not quite sure what the difference is.

"You look like you're waiting for a call or something," Oliver says. "*Earth to Julie.* You there?"

I blink a few times and come back to myself. "Sorry. I was lost in thought for a second. What were we talking about again?"

Oliver lets out a breath. "Graduation."

"Right. What about it?"

"You really weren't listening . . ." he says with a sigh. "It's a few weeks away, remember? Cap and gowns? That one Vitamin C song? Tell me this is happening too soon."

"I guess so. I'm trying not to stress about it."

"Seriously," he says, groaning. "I wish we had another month to figure stuff out, you know? Do you even know what you're doing after, yet?"

I thought I did. I thought I had everything planned out. From the apartment I wanted to live in to the different writing classes I would take. But it's been hard to focus on school since I messed up our connection, so my final grades remain question marks. For some reason, Reed still hasn't sent me my admissions letter. On top of that, I still haven't finished my writing sample, so maybe a writing career isn't even in the cards for me. It seems no matter how much effort I put in, and how much I try to plan things out, nothing ever comes together.

I stare into my cup, which is still steaming. "Not yet."

"I thought you were going to that one school," Oliver says. "Reed, right? You must have heard back from them by now."

He's right, I should have. I don't know why they left me in the dark. What if I submitted my application wrong or something? Or maybe some technical error happened, and it never went through. But Reed would notify me about something like that, wouldn't they? Should I call someone in admissions? I've been checking the mailbox and refreshing my email every morning. But nothing from them. I'm too embarrassed to tell Oliver this. I should have kept these plans private. So I wouldn't need to ex-plain myself when I'm forced to change them.

Why is everyone so caught up on going to college? It's not like an English degree is practical in today's economy, anyway. Why bury myself in loans to write when I can do it on my own? I mean, some of the greatest writers never went to col-lege. Hemingway, Twain, Angelou—I could go on. Admittedly, their circumstances were different from mine, and it was a long time ago. But there is still a point to be made. Of course, my thoughts will probably change once I get accepted. But as I'm learning, you should always plan for the worst. "Actually, I'm thinking about sticking around here," I say casually, and take a sip of coffee.

"Here, as in, *Central Washington?*" Oliver asks, arching his brow. "But you hate this place. More than anyone I know. You always said you'd be the first one to go. I mean, Central isn't a bad school, but it isn't anyone's first choice, I can tell you that. You go because it's next to home." Oliver looks around us, leans into the table a little, and whispers, "Is it because you got," he gulps, "*waitlisted?*"

"What—absolutely not."

His eyes widen. "*Rejected?*"

"No. And it's rude of you to ask," I say defensively. "Maybe I changed my mind. I'm allowed. I mean, you're going to Central, too, aren't you?"

"Yeah, but I'm from here. So it's different. It's what we all do."

"So you stay here, just *because?*"

Oliver shrugs. "Pretty much. It's an Ellensburg thing. You wouldn't get it. You're from"—he makes a long arch in the air with both hands—"*Seattle.*" He takes a sip of his latte and sets it back down. "You're practically an alien to us."

"I feel like one around here."

"Then what's keeping you? It's obvious you can't stand it here, but I don't blame you for that. You always seemed ready to leave. Even if it meant finding a job waiting tables or something. I mean, you even convinced Sam to—" He stops himself.

I drop my gaze. Because I don't want him to look me in the eye and see he might be right. That maybe Sam is one of the reasons I don't want to leave. They were once *our* plans, after all. Moving to Portland together, finding an apartment, and taking whatever part-time jobs we needed to save up money. He'd play his music somewhere, I'd find places to write. But he isn't here anymore. So I have to figure everything out alone.

I stare at the table. "I just need a little more time . . ."

"Yeah, I get it," Oliver says. He reaches across the table for my arm. "Listen, at least you'll have me here. Maybe we can take some classes together. I'll need someone to copy off of."

"You always know the right thing to say."

He leans back, smiling. "I have a way with people."

I take a sip of coffee, ignoring this.

We finish our drinks. At noon, I have to leave for work.

I push in my chair. "Did you want to walk with me?"

Oliver checks his phone. "I would. But I'm meeting someone."

I give him a look. "Oh? Who is it?"

He hesitates. "Jay."

I give him a different look.

"What's that look mean?"

"Nothing."

"Good."

I sniff the air. "Is that why you're wearing cologne?"

"I'll have you know, I wear cologne all the time," Oliver says, folding his arms.

"Yes, but I've been noticing it more recently," I say.

"Aren't you late for work or something?"

I can't help smiling as I leave, but not without whispering, "Is that a new shirt, too?"

"*Please go.*"

I wink at him. "Tell me everything tonight."

I spot Tristan as soon as I enter the bookstore. He's balancing on a ladder, trying to nail down a poster I've never seen before. It's been a while since we worked the same shift. Mr. Lee is out of town for the weekend, so he asked both of us to watch the store together while he's away.

I stare at the poster. "Who is that?"

"It's General Griz from *Space Ninjas,* volume three," Tristan says. "A classic."

"He looks sort of like a bunny."

"A mutated rabbit," he corrects me. "From a lab experiment."

"Gone wrong?"

"Yeah, you've read it?"

"Just a wild guess."

Tristan starts down the ladder, nearly stumbles, and plays it off with a nervous laugh. He runs a hand through his hair and dusts off his shirt.

I set my things on the counter. Beside the register is a tray of streamers, trading cards, stickers, and some name tags. I turn to Tristan. "Are these things for the book club?"

"No actually, it's for the *Space Ninjas* event," he says, gesturing at the other posters around the room. "I'm working to promote it. I just made our store the regional meetup location."

"That's incredible! We must have a ton of people coming."

"Well, only eight people signed up so far," he admits. "And most of them are friends from school."

"That's not so bad. I'm sure more will come."

"I know you're not big on science fiction, but we're having a *Space Ninjas 4* movie release party soon," he says. "You can come, if you want. I can add you to the mailing list."

"Why am I not already on it?"

Tristan blushes. "I'll send you the link."

I tie back my hair, step around the counter, and open the register. There's a box of bookmarks I've never seen before. I go through them. "Tristan, where did these come from?"

Tristan comes and leans over the counter. "Oh—I made them in the photography room at school. It has the store hours and location on it. We're giving them out to customers when they buy something." He points at the illustration. "That's Mr. Lee—see his glasses?"

"Mr. Lee doesn't wear glasses," I say.

"I know. I just think they look cool on him."

We share a laugh as I set the box aside. "You know, you're really transforming the place, Tristan."

"Thanks. That's what the books say. According to Mr. Lee, anyway."

I look around the store, noticing all his personal touches. The posters, the bookmarks, the collectables in the sci-fi section that Mr. Lee moved up a row. Tristan even redesigned the store website, linking all the new social media accounts he's been running. I hate to admit this, but I'm a little jealous of his creativity. He always sees things through. Maybe I should come up with some creative ideas, too. Imbue the store with my own personality, and help out Mr. Lee some more. I think about this as I go back to work.

Tristan hangs around the counter, arranging some things on the tray. When I catch him looking up at me a few times, I get the sense he wants to say something.

After a moment, Tristian coughs to get my attention. "So, uh, are you still coming tomorrow?"

I look at him. "What's happening tomorrow?"

"The film festival."

I hold back a gasp of surprise. "*Oh*—right, of course."

"I also got you a wristband, for the after party," Tristan says, scratching the back of his head. "It's sort of exclusive, they said. Everyone's been texting me about it, but I was only able to get one extra wristband. And I wanted you to have it."

I smile at him. "That's so sweet of you. But don't feel you have to use it on me. Especially if so many people want to go."

"No—I mean, what I meant is, I want to go with you."

"Oh . . ."

"It would mean a lot to me if you came," Tristan says, running a hand through his hair, his cheeks turning red. "There's gonna be food and music and a bunch of people. It's kind of fancy, but you don't have to dress up if you don't want to. I mean, I'll be wearing a suit—because my mom already got it for me—and some of the other filmmakers might be, too, but you can, like, wear whatever you want."

An after party? He never mentioned this before. I thought I would see his film, congratulate him afterward, and head off. Now there's suddenly food and music and people getting dressed up? The way Tristan describes this makes it sound like a bigger commitment than I signed up for. Almost like a date or something. Maybe I'm overthinking this, but I am most certainly not ready for a date. *What would Sam think?* I sense my phone inside my pocket, and imagine how he might feel.

"So you're coming, right?" Tristan asks again.

I bite my lip, unable to meet his eyes. It pains me to do this. But maybe this isn't the right time. "I'm sorry, Tristan. But I don't think I can go anymore."

He blinks at me in surprise. "Oh—oh, that's okay. I totally understand," he says, forcing another smile. "I guess, maybe next time or something."

I stand there as he grabs his tray and takes it to the back room without another word. Maybe I *am* overthinking the festival. I feel terrible for canceling on him at the last minute. But my connection with Sam has already started to crack. So I can't take any more risks.

❁

It's feels like forever since I last spoke to Sam. It's hard to focus or think about anything else except hearing his voice again. When I get home, I play the CD I always keep on hand, and pretend he's there in my room, practicing his guitar. I've been doing this every day, letting his music fill my room like he's alive again. It makes me feel less alone. There are fourteen songs, and I've lost track of how many times I've replayed them. The third track is my favorite. It's one of his originals, a rock ballad, reminiscent of the Nicks era of Fleetwood Mac, and I get to hear Sam's voice humming the melody. There are no words because the song is unfinished. Sam had asked me to help write the lyrics with him. We used to pretend we could be this great songwriting duo someday. Like Carole King and Gerry Goffin. I once asked him what comes first, the lyrics or the melody, and Sam answered, *"Always the melody."* I disagreed with this, but I think that's why our relationship worked. We were two parts of a song. *He was the music. And I was the words.*

I lay on the floor of in his room, looking at the ceiling, notebook paper scattered everywhere. Sam sits cross-legged beside me, his guitar in his lap.

"Play that again . . ." I say.

Sam strums his guitar, filling the room with the melody.

I close my eyes and listen.

The guitar stops. "What are you doing?"

"Shh—I'm trying to get inspired," I say, keeping my eyes shut.

"Sleeping inspires you?"

"I'm not sleeping . . . I'm thinking!"

"Got it—" Sam continues playing as images dance across my mind. Infinite blue skies, a couple holding hands, cherry blossoms falling from the window. I sit up and jot some of these things down.

I look at Sam. "What should the story be about?"

"What do you mean? We're writing a song."

"Every song tells a story, Sam."

He scratches his head. "I just thought it had to rhyme."

"Songs do more than that," I say. "They're supposed to make you feel something. So what's the emotion we're going for? What's this about?"

Sam thinks about this. "Love, I guess?"

"That's too vague, Sam."

"Aren't most songs, though?"

"Not the good ones!"

Sam falls over on the carpet, groaning. "Can't you just come up with it? You're the writer. You're better at this! That's why I asked for help."

I went through my drawers the other day and found my notebook. Inside were a couple verses I had written months ago. After our call on the porch, I spent the rest of the night working on the song again.

Sam and I have another call soon. I want to write as much as I can to surprise him. Especially after our conversation about unfinished things and leaving a mark on the world—maybe this could be it. He's done so much for me, after all. This is my gift back to him. I'm a little anxious when he picks up. When I tell Sam about the song, he asks me to share the lyrics. At one point, I play the track so he can get a sense of how it would sound with music . . .

"Don't judge my voice, okay?"

Sam laughs. "Of course not."

As the CD fills the room with his guitar, strumming a soft ballad, I sing some of it for him, the best I can.

"I see your face, there in the stars . . .
When I close my eyes, you're not too far
Do you feel my hand? It's tied up in yours
I'm keeping you with me, wherever we are . . .
And I still remember, it's sealed in gold
The fields that we run through, I'll never let go
So don't you forget me, those memories we hold
Like water and time
We are written in stone . . ."

I shut off the music and sit back on the floor. "That's all I have so far. *I know*—I don't have the best voice in the world. It'll sound better when you sing it."

"*No, it was great!*" Sam says. "I can't believe you wrote that. It's beautiful, Julie."

"Are you just saying that?" I ask. "You can tell me the truth. I won't be mad."

"It's better than anything I could've written," he says.

"Of course. But that's not what I'm asking."

Sam laughs and says, "I really mean it. It's perfect. The lyrics . . . they're so—what's the word I'm looking for? *Meaningful.* Like there's something more behind it, you know?"

"Anything that needs work? I'm looking for feedback here."

Sam thinks about it. "It might be missing something. Maybe a pre-hook."

I jot down a note on some paper.

Look up the meaning of pre-hook.

"It's only a first draft," I tell him, reading the lyrics over again. "I'm gonna make some changes. But I think we have a hit here, Sam."

"If only that could be true," he says wistfully.

"*Why can't it be?*" I whisper.

A familiar silence before he speaks. "Julie . . . You know why . . ."

I move the phone to the other ear, pretending not to hear this. Instead I imagine our song being put out in the world. "Just think about it," I go on. "We could send it to a radio station, or put it online or something. People would listen to it, Sam. We just have to get it out there. Someone will play it. We can show them all your other music, too. All we need—"

"Julie," Sam stops me. "Listen to yourself . . ."

"What do you mean?"

"Why are you working on my song again?" he asks. His tone is different. Like there's an edge in his voice. "Why are you doing this?"

I stare at the notebook, unsure of what to say. "I don't know . . . I thought you would want me to. A while ago, you said you wanted to finish something. That you wanted to leave something behind. I thought . . . maybe this song could be it. And I can help you write it. Just like I promised."

He sighs. "I told you, Jules . . . I didn't want us to talk about this. About what I never got to finish," he says. "There's no point anymore . . ."

"But what's the big deal? It's just one song. And I don't mind doing this. You have all these beautiful songs lying around. I can help you finish them. I can help put them out into the world, and maybe we can—"

"*Julie, stop!*" he cuts me off again. "*Please.* Don't do this . . ."

"What am I doing?"

Sam lets out a breath, and softens his voice. "Listen . . . I appreciate what you're trying to do for me. I mean that. But you have to let this go, okay? This idea about working on my music and putting it out there for people to listen to—it's too late for me. I've already accepted that. So stop wasting time on this, okay? Please."

"I want to do this, though. I want to help you—"

"*You shouldn't.* You need to focus on your own life, okay? You have to stop thinking about me all the time—"

"I don't think about you *all* the time," I say back. *Why is he talking to me this way?* "I have my own goals and things I need to finish. Like my writing. I think about myself, too."

"Good," Sam says. "I'm glad you do. I'm glad you have other things going on in your life. I'm glad you have a future to think about."

I squeeze the phone tight, speechless. I never expected the conversation to take this turn. I thought I was doing something good. I thought this would make him happy. So what if I think about us sometimes? What's so wrong with that? Why can't we talk like we used to? *Like before?* Before everything was taken away from us. I don't say any of this out loud. I know it's the last thing he wants to hear from me.

There's a long silence between us. I sense our call is running long and I'm not sure how much time we have left. I want to leave us on a better note in case the static comes, so I change the subject. "The film festival is tomorrow night. Tristan invited me again. But I told him I couldn't go."

"How come?"

"I don't know. The way he was talking about it earlier . . . it made it sound sort of like a date," I say. When Sam doesn't say anything to this, I ask him, "What do you think?"

A silence.

"I think you should go," he says.

"Why?"

"It sounds like fun. And Tristan's a nice guy."

"But I could never do that, Sam. I mean, you're still here, and were still connected."

Usually when I say something sentimental like this, I feel him smile on the other end and sense a warmth through the phone. But his voice is a chill in my ear.

"You and I can't be together. You know that."

"I know—" I start.

"It doesn't sound like it."

I say nothing.

"I'm beginning to worry about you," Sam goes on. "I'm worried about our calls and what they're doing. You're supposed to be moving on. And it doesn't feel like you are anymore."

"Sam—I'm *fine*. I promise."

"But you won't even go to a friend's movie premiere. How are you ever going to say good-bye to me?"

"Maybe I don't feel like going out," I say. "And I can say good-bye to you whenever I want."

"Then say it now."

His words hang in the air between us for a long time. *How could he say this to me?* I don't even know how to respond. I hate that I have to prove something to him. A pain goes through me. "I can't right now . . ."

Sam lets out a knowing sigh. "Then when will you?"

There's a long silence between us.

"I think you should go to the festival tomorrow," Sam says. "I think it will be good for both of us."

"What's that supposed to mean?" I ask, trying not to overreact. "Isn't it my choice? What if I just don't want to?"

"I don't see what's the big deal," Sam says. "It's only a few hours. Why are you so against it?"

"I didn't say I was."

"Then prove it. And go."

My voice sharpens. "*Fine.* I'll go! And I'll have a great time."

"Good. I hope you do."

"*I will!*"

We hang up the phone. I text Tristan right away, letting him know I've changed my mind. He responds a second later, words full of excitement, which makes me feel less guilty. But how can Sam ask me to do this to him? To the both of us? I don't understand what he wants me to prove. I try not to let this get to me because it will only show Sam he's right. He doesn't need to worry about me.

I wish our call hadn't ended badly, especially tonight. I get a text from Yuki, telling me everyone's on their way over. It happens to be the night we planned to do something special for Sam. I'm supposed to take us back to the fields to release the lanterns. I think about asking them to postpone it, but they've put in so much effort, I can't let everyone down. I have to collect myself and not let the call bother me. I think about what Sam said earlier. Maybe I am wasting too much time on us. I need to focus on my own life instead.

Jay sits in the front seat with Oliver, and we pick up Mika along the way. This is the first time all of us are together. I am squeezed in the back between Yuki and Rachel. Jay brought some snacks and passes them back to us. I admit, it makes me smile to see everyone jam-packed in the car, eating Pocky sticks. But it doesn't escape me that one person is missing. Jay is navigating with his phone and finds a different path that will cut our walking distance in half.

The sun has vanished by the time we reach the spot, replaced by a vast ocean of a night sky, freckled with stars. I use my memory of that day with Sam to guide our walk through the woods. I'm surprised I remember everything, especially in the dark. Mika has her arm linked through mine for the entire walk. When I see the tips of the barley jumping across the top of the fields like fish, I make us stop.

"We're here."

The others release a collective breath as we stare out at the view in awe.

"How did you know about this place?" Rachel asks.

"Sam brought me here once." I don't tell her when this was.

We move farther down the fields until we find the perfect spot. Jay unzips his backpack as everyone helps prepare the lanterns for the ceremony.

"How do these things work again?" Oliver asks as Rachel comes around, handing out paper lanterns.

"The hot air from the candles will help them rise," Yuki says as she begins lighting tea candles for us. "We just have to let them go."

I watch as my lantern blooms with warmth and light. It's like holding a piece of the sun in my hands.

"These things are *massive*." Oliver laughs, moving his lantern up and down.

I look around at everyone, and see their faces illuminated by the lantern lights, their smiles, the grass swaying at our shoes, the sky starry and endless, and breathe in the beautiful moment we're sharing. I never thought I'd be back here in the fields so soon. Especially with all our friends.

I turn to Yuki. "Is there a significance to this? When you release them for someone, that is."

"It's to let them move on," Yuki explains. "When we release the lanterns—we help release them. The lanterns will guide them to where they need to go."

"But why does Sam need to go?" I ask her. The others look at each other. I realize how strange the question sounds. "I only mean . . . why do they need to be guided?"

"I think they just need to hear from us that it's okay. Sometimes it's hard, even for them," Yuki says. "They need our blessing." She turns, holding the lantern toward the sky. "Remember, these are also memory lanterns. If you have a few last things you wish to tell Sam, whisper them now. The lantern will carry the message to him."

Yuki closes her eyes as if meditating and then whispers into her lantern as the others watch and mirror her. Mika and I share a look the others can't understand. Then she closes her eyes anyway, and whispers something into hers. So I do it, too, even though I haven't lost Sam yet. For now, anyway. I think of something I would say to him right now if I had the chance.

I pull my lantern close to me, and whisper, "Don't go yet, Sam. Just stay with me a little bit longer."

Yuki is the first to let hers go. "*To Sam,*" she says, and the lantern lifts itself from her hands and rises into the air. The others follow, releasing their lanterns one by one, each saying "*To Sam,*" until it's only me left.

I hold my lantern out. "*To Sam,*" I say. And then I let go, too.

But my lantern doesn't move. It hangs in the air, hovering in front of me, its light blinking ever so slightly. I give it a little nudge from the bottom with the palm of my hand, and it rises for a few seconds, then lowers itself as it stays in the air. "Mine won't go," I say as the others look over, watching curiously. "Look." I can't help smiling, and laughing a little at this, because I think

Sam heard me. He heard what I whispered to him, and he wants to stay with me a little longer. And then a breeze comes, and begins to pull the lantern down the fields, keeping it low, letting it almost graze across the grass. I step forward and follow it, trying to keep my hands right beneath to—I don't really know. When the lantern picks up some speed, so do I. And the next thing I know, I'm dashing down the fields with my hands stretched out, chasing after it. Something takes over me. *I need more time. I can't let you go just yet.* But the lantern gains height, like the sail of a ship being blown up from the wind, as I'm stumbling fast toward its light.

"Julie!"

The others are calling my name from behind me, and I realize how far I've run from them, but I can't stop. I think Mika must have chased after me, because her voice is the closest. But my stride becomes too much for her, and my resolve to catch up to the lantern is too strong. Only I remain running further down the fields until the voices calling me sound far away. All I hear are my own heavy breaths and the sound of my heart pounding in my ears.

Another breeze comes and lifts the lantern even higher, moving it past the line of the mountains. And it keeps on going no matter how hard I'm running. But eventually I become so tired and out of breath, I can't run anymore. So I stop and stand there, gazing up, watching it vanish into the sky with all of the others until I can no longer recognize it from the millions of stars.

The lantern is gone. *I lost it. I can't lose you, too. Not again.*

CHAPTER
FOURTEEN

BEFORE

When I close my eyes and everything goes dark, I see him. Sam.
Standing there. Letting his dark hair cut across his forehead at
a soft angle. Wearing a white dress shirt, buttoned up, with a
bow tie. Leaning beside the door of the hotel kitchen as waiters
pop in and out, carrying silver plates. Taking in deep breaths
and tugging at his collar, trying to stay calm. And suddenly I'm
there, too, holding his hand, saying, *"It's gonna be okay, Sam. Just
breathe."*

"Maybe we should leave," he says.

"Don't be ridiculous. You have to go out there soon."

"But I don't know if I can."

"Of course you can. Why are you so nervous?"

Silverware crashes into trays around us. We are standing

behind a curtain that separates the kitchen area from a ballroom full of guests. Sam was hired to perform at his friend Spencer's cousin's wedding in the spring of junior year. They gave Sam a list of songs they wanted him to sing, and he's been practicing for weeks. It's his first paid gig, and I'm not letting him back out.

"I don't know anybody out there," he says.

"You know Spencer. And me. *I'm here.*"

Sam tugs at his collar again, so I help loosen the knot of his bow tie, letting him breathe easier. The first bead of sweat appears on his forehead. I move his hair out of his face.

"What if no one likes it?" He keeps looking around.

"Of course they will. Why else would they have hired you? You're going to do great out there."

"We didn't even have a real sound check . . ."

"You've practiced this a million times. You're going to do great."

Someone with a headset peeks behind the curtain and gives us a thumbs-up. "Let's go, kid."

I squeeze Sam's hand. "Good luck. I'll be right here."

Once he's out there, I peek through the curtain. There is a hardwood dance floor beneath a chandelier, surrounded by silk-lined tables, each crowded with wedding guests. Connected to the dance floor is a stage where the band is set up. Sam appears from the side of the stage, looking nervous. When he steps up to the microphone, and awkwardly adjusts the stand, I hold my breath.

The lights dim, leaving only the stage as everyone goes quiet, turning their chairs to watch. And then the music starts . . .

A live piano fills the ballroom, playing a familiar tune. It takes me a second to recognize it. "Your Song" by Elton John. Sam knows the words like the back of his hand. He's practiced it a hundred times. It's a great choice to start with, perfect for his range.

But then Sam opens his mouth to sing, and there's a tremble in his voice. His hand grips the microphone, as if he's keeping himself steady, while the piano tries to follow him.

There's something off. He's not singing in time with the music. It's like he's a step or two behind. The crowd is noticing this, too. People are looking around, whispering at the tables, wondering what's wrong. This only makes Sam more nervous. When his trembling turns into stuttering, and he starts skipping words, my chest tightens. I can't bear to watch this happen. I wish there was a way to save him. I wish I could move the attention away before this gets worse. *Don't just stand here. Do something, Julie!*

So I take off my heels, and step through the curtain. At one of the tables in the middle of the room, Spencer is sitting beside his brothers. I make my way over and grab his hand.

"Yo, what's up?"

"Come with me."

"*Huh—*"

I pull Spencer out of his chair, leading him onto the empty dance floor as everyone turns to look.

"Uh, what are we doing?!"

"*Dancing!* Just go with it!"

"Oh my god."

My heart is pounding as I place a hand on Spencer's shoulder as we get into position and begin what we hope is a waltz. We have no clue what we're doing or how we look. But everyone is watching us. I don't make eye contact with Sam as we begin our dance. I'm afraid it could make him more nervous. Instead, I lift Spencer's arm and make him twirl me around him to the rhythm of the music.

Our dance is going more smoothly than I expected. At one point in the song, Spencer puts his arms behind my back and *dips* me, making the tables around us cheer. I don't know if it's the piano, Sam's voice, the burst of adrenaline, or the attention of the room, but we suddenly get into this. The lifts, the turns, and our spins across the room come almost naturally as we continue our dance. Maybe we're actually good at this. Or maybe it's all in my head, and to everyone else watching, we look ridiculous. But it doesn't matter. Because I look over at Sam and see him smiling for the first time. His face is glowing in the spotlight as he steps down the center of the stage—as far as his microphone cord allows him—and extends a hand to us as he hits the chorus with a newfound confidence.

I look back to him from across the dance floor as the drums come in, followed by the guitar, and we feel a spark move between us. A crowd of people has formed around the edge of the dance floor. Eventually, a few of them step in and start dancing, too, pulling in others with them. Sam and I look at each other again. *Because we did this.* His voice and my dance with Spencer changed the energy of the room.

When the music begins to fade, I feel the song about to end. I lift my hands one last time and go spinning across the dance floor, as lights swirl around me until the room suddenly vanishes, and I fall straight into Sam's arms, throwing us off the edge of the dock as we go crashing into ice-cold water.

A million bubbles swarm around me as we emerge from the surface of the lake to the sound of fireworks going off in the distance. It's the night before the Fourth of July. The summer after sophomore year. Sam and I made plans to sneak out to meet each other here. *If my mom knew this, she would kill me.*

I shiver in the water. "I can't believe we're doing this!"

Sam laughs and runs a hand over his head, brushing his hair back. His skin is glistening from the water. "You said you wanted to be more spontaneous!"

"I wasn't expecting this!"

More fireworks go off in the distance, lighting the tips of the trees that surround us. Sam flips onto his back and starts swimming backward, showing the bare lines of his chest. I instinctively throw my hands over myself, covering up.

"What if someone sees us?"

"Jules—no one else is out here. It's just you and me."

"I've never done this before."

"Skinny-dipping?"

"I can't believe you dared me!"

"I never thought you'd actually do it."

"*Sam!*"

"Relax—we're not completely naked!"

Fireworks go off again as Sam paddles in circles around me, laughing.

"How did you even come up with this?" I ask.

"I saw it in a movie once," he says. "It seemed really sweet and romantic and everything in my head."

"It's so cliché."

"At least this will be something to remember. And a funny story to tell."

"We can't tell anyone this!"

"Okay—we'll keep it a secret."

Sam swims up to me. And we look at each other. I take in his face illuminated by occasional bursts of light from the sky. He is right about one thing. I don't think I could ever forget the way he's looking at me in this moment.

"Are you mad we did this?" he whispers.

"No. Just a little nervous." I feel a shiver, not from the cold, but from the thrill of being out here with him.

"Me, too."

Sam smiles and moves my hair behind my ear. Then he lifts my chin gently with his other hand, and he kisses me. We close our eyes, listening to fireworks going off around us.

A beam from what could be a flashlight shines through the trees, followed by some voices and the sound of footsteps coming up the path.

"Someone's coming!" I gasp.

"What—"

We dive underwater to hide ourselves. I hold my breath and bubbles swarm and swirl around me as I fall through the water like a stone pulled through space, before emerging onto dry concrete.

It's broad daylight out. The smell of food carts and sulfur fills the air as skyscrapers rise up around me. It's the summer before senior year. I'm standing on the streets of New York City, adjusting a duffel bag that's digging into my shoulder as Sam suddenly appears, dashing past me, pulling along a suitcase.

"No time to stop! *We gotta go!*"

"Hold on!"

Sam is leaving for Japan in an hour and forty-two minutes. The next subway to the airport arrives any minute now, and if he misses it he could miss his flight. He is spending the entire summer in Osaka with his grandparents, so he and I planned a good-bye weekend trip together before he heads off.

Sam glances at his phone for directions. "This way!"

"Just slow down—"

We zigzag through stalled traffic and push through crowds, avoiding steam spouting from manholes and the occasional corner merchant trying to sell me handbags. Once we make it down a narrow stairwell and turn the corner, Sam goes crashing into the metal turnstile and wheezes.

"You have to swipe your MetroCard—" I swipe it once for each of us as we hurry through and head down another set of stairs. When the platform rumbles beneath my feet, I know we made it just in time. I look out and see the train lights shining through the tunnel.

It's time for us to say good-bye. I wish we had a few more days together. I wish I was going with him.

Sam kisses my cheek. "I have to go."

The train doors open behind him, letting people pour onto the platform.

I don't know what to say. I hate good-byes. Especially with him.

"I'll text you soon as I'm there, okay?"

"Don't forget!"

I hand Sam his duffel bag. He kisses me one last time and steps inside.

"I'll be back before you know it."

"Why does it have to be for so long?"

"It's only six weeks. And we'll talk every day."

"Wait . . . " I grab his arm. *"Take me with you."*

He smiles at me. "We can go together next summer. After graduation."

"Promise?"

"Don't worry, we can travel every summer for the rest of our lives, okay? You and me."

"Okay," I say. And then I remember something. "Wait—your jacket!" I take off his denim jacket to hand over before the door closes, but Sam stops me.

"Keep it for me."

I smile and hold the denim close to my chest.

"You better have written a ton by the time I'm back. I can't wait to read it."

"I've barely started anything!"

"Well, now you won't have me as a distraction."

"You're not a distraction—" I start.

But the train doors close between us.

Sam and I look at each other through the window. Then he breathes onto the glass and writes something. I read the letters right before they vanish.

S + J

I smile and place a hand on the window. Sam presses his hand against mine. We look at each other for as long as we have left. I wish I could frame this moment between us.

A voice comes through the intercom, reminding those of us on the platform to stay behind the yellow line. I take a couple steps back as the train begins to move, taking Sam with it. I stand there clenching the jacket, watching the train pick up speed until it becomes a roaring blur of lines, blasting air up from the tracks, blowing back my hair.

And then spots of light appear from behind me, twirling through the subway like fireflies as the ceiling suddenly lifts itself, pulling in a cool breeze. I turn around to find the underground platform has vanished, replaced by an evening sky and carousel lights from the fair.

Gravel crunches beneath my shoes as I look up at the Orbiter, a carnival ride that lifts people into the air and spins them around like a hand mixer.

"What about this one . . ." I ask, pointing at the ride. "Too scary?"

I'm holding hands with James—Sam's little brother. It's just the two of us at the moment. He doesn't answer me. He hasn't been speaking to me all night.

"Do you want some food instead? We can get cotton candy."

James says nothing. He stares at the ground.

I don't know why he's so quiet. I take him to the cotton candy stand, hoping this cheers him up. He's never like this. He and I have always gotten along. It was my idea to bring him here tonight.

A man behind the stand taps impatiently at a sign.

I tap James's arm. "What color would you like?"

No answer.

"I guess we'll take the blue," I say.

James nibbles on his cotton candy as we wander around the fair, looking for Sam. He went to play carnival games with some friends. I thought James and I could use the time to bond. But he refuses to go on any rides with me. As we stop to watch people get tossed around on the Tilt-A-Whirl, I finally ask, "Are you mad at me?"

He stares at the Tilt-A-Whirl without a word.

I frown, unsure how to get through to him. "Whatever it is, James, I'm sorry. It makes me sad that you aren't talking to me. Can you at least tell me what I did wrong?"

James looks at me for the first time. "You're taking Sam from us."

"What do you mean?"

He looks back to the Tilt-A-Whirl. "I heard Sam talking. He said he doesn't want to live with us anymore. He said you guys are leaving somewhere." He looks back at me. "Is that true?"

I'm at a loss for words. Sam mentioned he had an argument the other week with his parents about what he would do after graduation. About moving to Portland with me and pursuing his music instead of going to college. That's probably what this is about.

"I would never take Sam from you," I say.

"So you're not leaving?"

How do I answer this? "Well, I'm going to college. And Sam might go with me. But it doesn't mean either of us is leaving you."

Before I can say more, Sam appears, holding a stuffed animal.

"It's a lizard. Cute, right? Took me forever to get it from that bucket toss game. I'm pretty sure it's rigged." He gives it to me. "I won it for you."

"That's very sweet."

I turn to James, lowering myself to him. "You like lizards, don't you? Here . . ."

James looks at me, at the lizard, at Sam, then back at me. "He gave it to *you*," he says. Then he walks off.

"Don't go too far!" Sam shouts. He turns to me. "Don't worry about him. He's been like that lately. I'll take care of it later, okay?"

"Okay . . ."

"You should cheer up. We're at the fair. Did you want to go on a ride?"

I look around us. All these rides seem too intense for me. "Maybe just once on the Ferris wheel," I say, pointing behind him.

The lights from the Ferris wheel can be seen from anywhere

in town. It stands a hundred feet high, towering over the other rides and almost every building in Ellensburg.

Sam turns around, looking up at it. "Oh. Uh, are you sure you don't want to go on, you know, something else?"

"What's wrong with the Ferris wheel?"

"Nothing. It's just a little high up, that's all."

"Are you afraid of heights?"

"What? Of course not."

"Then let's go."

The Ferris wheel somehow seems taller when you're standing beneath it. We hand someone our tickets and step into our windowless gondola. Sam takes a few deep breaths. He's a bit jittery all of a sudden. When we hear the mechanism coming to life and feel the Ferris wheel begin to move, Sam grabs my hand.

"Are you gonna be okay?" I ask.

"Yeah . . . totally fine . . ." He laughs a bit nervously.

The ground slowly disappears as we move toward the sky.

Sam takes another deep breath. I give his hand a squeeze.

"You know, I used to be afraid of heights, too," I say.

"Really? And how did you get over it?"

The gondola shakes as we make our way back up for the second loop. Sam twitches in his seat.

"You have to close your eyes first," I say, as I do this myself. "Are they closed?"

"Yeah."

"Mine, too."

"Okay. And then what?"

"And then you pretend you're somewhere else," I say. "Anywhere in the world that makes you forget where you are. It doesn't even have to be a real place. It can be somewhere in your imagination."

"Like from a daydream?"

"Exactly."

The Ferris wheel continues to move. But it feels different with your eyes closed.

"So where are you?" I ask.

Sam takes a moment to think. "I'm in a new apartment . . . that you and I just moved into . . . and there's a park right outside the window . . . and we have a record playing in the living room . . . and there are boxes everywhere that need unpacking . . ." He squeezes my hand. "Where are you?"

"I think I'm there, too," I whisper.

I sense him smiling.

"I don't want to open my eyes," Sam says.

But the ride is about to come to its end. *I can feel it.* I squeeze my eyes tighter, hoping to stop time or at least slow it down. Because I don't want to open mine, either. I don't want to lose him. I want to keep them shut and live in this memory of us forever. I don't want to open my eyes and see a world without Sam.

But sometimes you just wake up. No matter how hard you try not to.

CHAPTER FIFTEEN

NOW

The breeze ruffles the blinds whenever a car passes by the house. I'm lying on the living room sofa with the television turned off, staring out the window. I haven't left this spot in I don't know how long. My phone has been buzzing with text messages all day. So I shut it off. It's Sunday evening, the day after we released the lanterns. Everyone's been trying to reach me, but I'm too embarrassed about what happened. I just want to stay wrapped up in my blanket for the rest of the weekend. That shouldn't be too much to ask. Some silence from the world. My mother left me a cup of tea that's gone cold on the coffee table, along with some fruit snacks and a candle that I just blew out. The smell of vanilla was giving me a headache.

"Call me if you need anything," she said before she left the house. "There's some brie in the fridge. Go easy on it."

I finished the brie a few hours ago. I just woke up from a nap, and can't seem to fall asleep again. Outside the window, the sky is a glowing amethyst, like the one my mom keeps on her nightstand. Through the blinds I watch the sky fade to the color of bruised skin as I hear the sound of sprinklers coming on on the lawns. Around six o'clock there's a knock on the door. I wasn't expecting any guests today, so I don't bother answer it. But the knocking continues. I turn on my side, refusing to get up. *Leave me alone.* Then the lock clicks as someone opens the door.

I look up from the arm of the sofa as Mika appears in the living room.

She looks at me. Her voice is soft. "Hey. How have you been?"

I blink at her, wondering how she got in. "When did you get a key?"

"Your mom dropped it off. She said to check in on you at some point. Hope that's okay."

"I guess . . ."

I was hoping not to face her for a few days. I don't want to talk about what came over me last night. Chasing after the lantern, as if it was Sam. *Why can't we pretend it didn't happen? Spare me the intervention.*

There are wrappers all over the coffee table, spilling to the carpet. "I wasn't expecting company. Sorry it's a mess."

"That's alright," Mika says. "I should have called first." She checks her phone and looks at me. "You know, the film festival is about to start soon. Why aren't you dressed yet?"

"Because I'm not going."

"Why not?"

"I'm just not in the mood," I say. I pull the blanket up, hoping she takes the hint.

"You're really gonna do that to Tristan?" Mika asks. She stands there, watching me pretend to sleep. "He's probably waiting for you. Have you even checked your phone?"

"It's not a big deal. He'll understand."

"So you're going to lie on the sofa all night?"

I say nothing.

"I really think you should go. You made a promise."

"I didn't promise Tristan anything."

Mika shakes her head. "Not to Tristan . . ." she says. "To Sam."

We look at each other. My last phone call with him. That's what she's referring to. We haven't had much time to talk about it yet. I could tell Mika wanted to bring it up last night on our way to the fields, but we couldn't find time to ourselves. When I don't respond, Mika comes around the sofa and sits on the coffee table, facing me. She touches my hand. "Julie—I didn't come here to check up on you, okay? I came to make sure you went to the festival."

"Why do you want me to go so much?"

"Because Sam's right. It would be good for you."

Why does everyone think they know what's good for me? What about what I think?

"I told you—I'm not in the mood," I say again. I pull my blanket up and lay my head back down.

Mika kneels down beside me. "Julie, I know you're having a tough time, and I know this is hard for you. But you need to show Sam you'll be okay without him. You need to go to the festival. So I'm not leaving here until you do."

I look into her eyes and see she's serious. Of course she is. This is about Sam.

"And don't forget, I punched someone for you," Mika says. "On more than one occasion. You owe me a favor."

I groan. Because she's right. I do owe her. *"Alright.* I'll go."

A moment later, I'm in my room as Mika helps me get ready. It feels wrong to look through my closet for a dress to wear, so Mika picks one for me. The plain red dress I wore to my aunt's wedding a few years ago. I stare at myself in the desk mirror as she stands behind me, straightening my hair. Neither of us says much. I'm not sure why I need to go to this festival to prove anything, but I decide not to question it. While I'm still upset that Mika's forcing me to do this, watching her brings back some memories.

"Do you remember the last time you did my hair?" I ask.

"Of course I do. It was for that lame dance."

"It was pretty lame."

It was winter formal of junior year. I asked Sam to go this time. The theme was famous couples, but nobody dressed up, including us. A group of drunk seniors kept requesting remixes of country songs, so we left early. The only good memory I have was before the dance when Mika showed up with her makeup bag and curling wand, and pretended she was my fairy god-mother. The three of us ended the night in my living room, eating pizza. Maybe it was a fun night after all, now that I'm remembering it again.

But I know tonight won't end up like that. Because it's all wrong. *Sam isn't here.* I'll be going out with someone else. I don't understand why Mika is forcing me to do this. I stare at her in the mirror. "Why am I the only one who thinks this is weird?" I finally ask.

"You're not the only one," she says without looking at me. "I think it's weird, too."

"Then why are you making me do this?"

Mika runs a brush through my hair. "Because Sam asked for this. It isn't often we get requests from people who've passed away, you know? I think it's important to honor it, if we can."

I never thought of it this way. Maybe because I don't like to think of Sam as dead. The word alone sends chills through me. I don't know how Mika speaks about it so easily. I think back to Sam's picture on her living room cupboard. "Is that a cultural thing? Always honoring the dead like that, I mean."

"You could say that," she says. "It's also a family thing. A cousin thing. I mean, if you could do one last thing for him, why wouldn't you?"

"I suppose . . ."

"But I get it," she says, setting the brush down. "It's a strange request. Especially for you. But it's also a small one. I don't think he's asking for too much."

I think about this. "I guess you're right."

Mika looks at me in the mirror, moving my hair behind my ears. "And after last night, I think you need to do this for yourself." I drop my gaze, unable to meet her eyes. "You can't hold on to Sam forever, Julie," she whispers. "You have to let him move on, too. This isn't good for you. And I don't know if it's good for him, either."

Once Mika finishes up my hair, I check my phone. It's a quarter to seven. If I don't leave the house right now, I might miss Tristan's screening entirely. Mika helps me get dressed, and we hurry downstairs.

"You sure you don't want me to walk you there?" Mika asks as we put our shoes on at the door. Her house is the opposite direction from the university where the festival is being held. I know she wants to make sure I go, but she shouldn't worry. I'm not going to back out this time. I'm going to keep my promise to Sam. After all, this needs to be my decision.

"I'll be fine," I say. "You don't have to wait."

I let Mika go home first so that she doesn't follow me there. After I make sure the candles are blown out, I hurry out of the house. As I'm locking the door, I spot Dan, our next-door neighbor, crossing the lawn toward me, waving something in his hand.

"Some mail got delivered by mistake," he says. He hands me a stack of envelopes. "Stopped by the other day, but no one answered."

"Oh—thank you."

As soon as he goes, I head back inside to leave the stack on the kitchen table for my mom, but then I remember something. I know I should check later, but curiosity gets the best of me. I go through the mail, my heart pounding.

There it is. At the very bottom of the pile. The name REED COLLEGE is printed in red on a white envelope. After all these months of waiting, it's finally in my hands. *Their decision letter.* I know I'm running late, but it's right in front of me and I have to know their answer. My hands are shaking as I tear the letter open, and read what's inside.

Dear Ms. Julie Clarke,

We thank you for your interest in enrolling at Reed College. The Admissions Committee has carefully considered your application and we regret to inform you that we will not be able to offer you admission to the entering class of—

My chest sinks before I finish the sentence.

It's a rejection.

I read the letter again to see if there's some mistake. But there isn't. *They rejected me.* Just like that? After all these months of waiting, that's it? I have to grab the edge of the counter to keep myself from falling. No wonder it arrived so late. I should have already known. People at school who got in found out weeks ago. How could I be so stupid? All this time, I've been making plans for something that was never even an option. Those essays were all a waste of time. And that stupid writing sample I've been working on. Why do I do this to myself? Put so much into things only to have them fall apart. I don't know what to do. I need to talk to someone. I know I'm not supposed to do this, because our next call isn't scheduled for a few days. But I take out my phone and call Sam anyway. It takes a long time for him to pick up. But eventually he does.

I don't have to say anything for him to know something's wrong. He hears it in my breathing. "Julie—what's the matter?"

"*I was rejected!*"

"What do you mean? Rejected from what?"

"From Reed College! I just got the letter."

"Are you sure?"

"Of course I am! It's in my hand."

Sam goes quiet for a moment. "Jules, I'm so sorry . . . I don't know what to say."

My heart races as I pace the room. "What am I supposed to do? I really thought I'd get in, Sam. I wasn't expecting a rejection. I really thought—"

"*Breathe,*" Sam says. "It's alright. This isn't the end of the world. It's just one rejection from one school. Forget about Reed. It's their loss."

"But I really thought I would get in . . ."

"I know," Sam says. "But you're gonna be fine, okay? You don't need Reed's validation. No matter where you go, you're destined to do great things. I know it."

I clench the letter in my hand, struggling to take this in. "It all feels so pointless . . . All that work for nothing, you know? I don't even know what my plans are now. Maybe I'm not as good as I think. Maybe I should just give up."

"You're the most talented person I know, Julie. And you're an incredible writer. If Reed can't recognize that, they don't deserve you," Sam says. "You just have—"

Static comes through the line.

"Sam—what did you say?"

More static.

"Julie?"

"Sam! Can you hear me?"

Nothing but static. And then his voice. Briefly.

"Everything's gonna be okay . . ."

"Sam!"

The call ends.

I stand alone in the kitchen, trying to keep myself together. Because I don't have time to panic. I'm already incredibly late. I still have to get to the festival. I need to go have a good time and prove to everyone, including Sam, that I'm fine, that nothing's wrong with me, and that everything's going to be okay, even though I don't know if any of this is true anymore.

CHAPTER

SIXTEEN

I'm holding back tears when I leave the house. It'll ruin the makeup Mika did for me. And I can't walk into the festival with mascara running down my face, bringing attention to myself. Thank god I decided against heels, because I have to run to get to the university in time. Beams from searchlights cross and uncross in the sky. I follow them until I hear the sound of a crowd, along with live music playing. It doesn't take long to find the festival. You can't miss it. Dozens of white tents rise from the quad, connected by strings of light. A velvet rope blocks me from getting inside. At the entrance, a man in a gold vest asks for my ticket. I hand it to him, and gather myself as I step beyond the ropes and into a sea of brightly lit tuxedos and cocktail dresses.

I'm glad Mika made me dress up tonight. It's like I stepped through a television screen into an award show. Red carpets run between the tents, covering the grass. Someone behind a silk-lined table smiles and hands me a schedule. I skim through it. Main films are showcased in the auditorium, but smaller student-made ones are being shown outside in some of the larger tents. I hurry down the carpet, looking left and right, until I find it—tent number 23. Based on the schedule, Tristan's film should already be twenty minutes in. But when I enter through the slit of the canvas, the screen is off and everyone's sitting around, chatting. When a couple guys in black shirts and headsets brush past me and I find no sign of Tristan, I figure they're having technical difficulties. *Thank goodness.* I wipe my forehead and look around for a seat. The first two rows are pretty much filled up, but the rest are starkly empty. Doesn't seem to be a large turnout. I'm glad I came to support him then. There are maybe fifteen people in the audience. The schedule shows another film playing at the same time in the main theater. I'm guessing everyone's there instead.

There are a few empty rows in the back. But I don't want to appear as though I came alone. In the second to last row, there's an older gentleman with wispy gray hair and a dark leather jacket, sitting in the middle by himself. He's wearing tinted glasses. I find a spot near him, leaving an empty seat between us.

Five minutes go by but no film. The audience is growing restless. A few people get up and leave. I turn to the man and ask, "Excuse me, sir, did they mention when the film is supposed to start?"

"Soon," he says. "But that was a half hour ago."

"I see." I frown and check the schedule again.

"Don't worry. It's normal in the industry. Everything runs late. So you could say we're right on schedule."

"Do you work in film?"

The man smirks. "No, I stay far away from that. I'm only here for the musical aspect."

"Musical?"

"The documentary," he says to clue me in. "You know this film is about the Screaming Trees, don't you? The rock band."

"I know who they are," I say, maybe too defensively.

He smiles. "Thought you might have walked into the wrong screening. From my experience, most people your age have never heard of them."

I can't tell if he's being condescending. "I'll have you know, I came tonight just to see this film," I say.

"Really?" He scratches his cheek, looking genuinely surprised. "You must be a real fan."

"Of course I am."

"Where did you learn about them, if you don't mind me asking?"

"My boyfriend. He introduced me to them. He knows all their music."

"Is that so? And where is he?"

"He—" I go quiet, unsure of what to say. "Couldn't make it."

"Well, that's too bad."

I want to say more about Sam. But there's no time because the lights dim, and everyone rustles around in their seats, facing forward. The tent goes quiet, and I hold my breath as the film begins.

The sound of an engine rumbles over a black screen as the film fades in to an old town street view through the windshield of someone's car. A denim-sleeved hand hits the dial of the car stereo, turning on the music. The second I recognize the guitar playing, a static shock moves across my skin, sending goose bumps up my arms. It's the song "Dollar Bill," a track from

Sam's favorite album, the one we waited in the rain for him to get signed. As the film changes to the next scene, I'm hit with another song that makes Sam swim in my mind again. And then another one. I knew I was here for a documentary on the Screaming Trees, but I wasn't prepared to listen to a curated playlist of the last three years of our lives.

But there's something different about the songs. They seem to have been slowed down, distorted, and rearranged with electric instruments or something. Like brand-new versions I've never heard before. Accompanying the music is a supercut of concert clips, home videos of the band, and television interviews of the members that flash across the screen, all of this overlaid with videos of rippling water and blinking traffic. Almost like two movies are being projected at once. At moments throughout, the lighting changes dramatically, intensifying to create gauzy dreamlike effects that make me squint a little. Twenty minutes in and I still don't know what the film is about. The scenes seem random and out of order, connected only through songs. There's something hypnotic about how everything's been pieced together, and I nearly doze off at one point. When the music fades, and the screen goes black, I wait for more. But then I hear clapping and realize it's over.

"Well that was . . . *interesting*," the man beside me says as the lights come on. He stands, and zips up his jacket. "Glad I made the drive." I wonder if he's being sarcastic.

I look around for Tristan. There are too many people standing and walking around, so I get up. As I scoot into the aisle to find him, I bump into someone else I don't expect.

"Mr. Lee? You're here."

"And so are you—" He holds a glass of wine, and is wearing his usual brown suede jacket, except with a purple flower in the front pocket. Exactly like the ones from the bouquets that decorate the tent.

"I didn't know you were coming," I say.

"I'm always there to support my employees." He nods, and toasts the air. "We're family, after all."

I smile at this. "That's true. We are like a family."

"Tristan will be glad to see you. Have you had a chance to talk to him?"

"I'm trying to find him now."

"Ah, he's been running all over the place, trying to get things in order," Mr. Lee explains, looking around, too. "He might be networking in the next tent."

"Maybe I should check there," I say. "Will I see you at the after party?"

Mr. Lee narrows his eyes. "After party? Tristan never mentioned that."

I press my lips together. *Maybe I wasn't supposed to mention it, either.* "I think it's only for the filmmaker and invited guests," I say.

"Really. And will there be food?"

"I think so."

Mr. Lee sniffs the air. "Seared duck . . ." he says to himself. "I think I shall go to this . . . *after party.*"

"Oh—I think you need a ticket."

Mr. Lee gives me a mischievous look.

I smile and whisper, *"I'll see you there."*

I let Mr. Lee go refill his glass of wine as I keep looking for Tristan. But it isn't for long, because he finds me.

My eyes widen. "Tristan . . . Look at you!"

Tristan straightens up, allowing me to take him in—he's wearing this tailored dark blue suit with satin lapels and a white silk shirt with two buttons intentionally left undone. His hair has been brushed back and styled in a way I've never seen him do before, and he smells pleasant with cologne.

"You look incredible!"

"Oh my gosh, stop," he says, turning as red as the rose he holds in his right hand. "My mom made me wear this."

"She has impeccable taste. Tell her I said so."

Tristan smiles. "So, what did you think of the film?"

"Oh—I'm still taking it in. I thought you said it was a documentary?"

"It is."

"But it was all music and nobody spoke in it."

"Yeah, it's an *experimental* documentary," he explains.

"I see. In that case, I loved it."

"I'm so glad! It's supposed to be one of those things you have to watch more than once to get," Tristan says. "Experimental films are like that." He checks his watch. "Oh—we should go."

"To the after party?"

"No. There's another film I wanted you to see." Tristan takes my hand, and leads me out of the tent. "You're gonna love it."

"*Space Ninjas?*"

"I wish."

"What's the rose for?"

"Oh—it's for you," he says, blushing again. "It was my mom's idea. But you don't have to take it, if you don't want to."

I smile and take the rose.

An usher recognizes Tristan and moves us to the front of the line. We take seats in the "reserved" row of the auditorium. I can't help feeling a little special. Tristan didn't tell me anything about the film, so I'm thrown off guard when the actors speak a foreign language, reminding me how terrible my French is. The story begins with a delivery truck on its way to a bakery, when a bump along the road sends a single baguette out the window without the driver noticing. The rest of the film follows the lost baguette and its journey through the streets of Paris. While the other baguettes are being stacked on wood shelves and taken home by loving families, the lone baguette is run over, picked up, dropped again, mauled by birds, kicked, tangled in a scarf and dragged by a lime-green Vespa across town, before miraculously landing on the front steps of the bakery. But before the baker can come outside to find it, it begins to rain, soaking the baguette, and dissolving it into wet crumbs that wash down the street and into the drain.

When the screen goes black, Tristan hands me his handkerchief to wipe away tears. "I can't believe I'm crying!" As silly as it sounds, I saw myself in that baguette, wanting nothing more than its safe return home. Is that why I'm hanging on to Sam? I want us to go back to the way things used to be. I glance around, and see the entire audience is sobbing as well. I turn to Tristan. "Why did you pick this to show me?"

"I read about this film online and thought of you," he says. "Did you like it?"

"I mean, I did. But it's so heartbreaking."

"Exactly. I knew it would make you sad. Just like you said you want from a film."

"When did I say that?"

"The week we first met," he says, "I asked you what kind of movies you liked and you said the ones that make you cry. You said, you want to cry in a way you've never cried before. Don't you remember?"

I think about it. It does sound like something I'd say.

"I thought about that a lot," Tristan says. "I wondered why someone would want to intentionally experience that. I think I figured it out. You want to *feel* something. Something meaningful, and intense. You want to feel that thing in your heart and stomach. You want to be moved. To care about something, or fall in love, you know? And you want it to feel *real*. And different. And exciting." Tristan glances at the black screen. "And I think this film does that, in its own way. It makes you cry, over bread. You've never felt that before. It's original. It makes you feel . . . *alive*." An usher comes in to clean and arrange the seats for the next screening. Tristan checks his watch again. "Let's get going. There's more I want you to see."

We squeeze two short films in before the after party. One is a romantic comedy, and the other is more action-packed. Around ten o'clock, we follow a crowd toward the main tent where the band's playing. Tristan ties a special wristband on me before we head inside. A champagne fountain bubbles besides silver trays of hors d'oeuvres, as a hundred people or so stand around, socializing. I see Mr. Lee found his way in. I spot him at a table with champagne and roast duck. He smiles at me. I wink at him knowingly.

The crowd is a bit overwhelming, but Tristan never leaves my side. I hold on to his rose as he walks me around the tent, introducing me to other filmmakers, writers, and college students from all over Washington.

"Somebody wants to meet you," he says, pulling me toward the other side of the tent.

I narrow my eyes. "Who on earth wants to meet me?"

There's a man with a paisley tie standing near the corner of the tent, holding a glass of white wine.

"This is Professor Guilford," Tristan introduces us. "He's one of the board members who chose my film. He's also a professor here."

"Great to finally meet you, Julie." He offers me his hand.

"And you as well," I say politely. "But how do you know who I am?"

He laughs. "You're Professor Clarke's daughter, aren't you?" he asks. "She talks a great deal about you. Tells me you're a talented writer."

"She's the best!" Tristan chimes in.

"I'm alright," I say, somewhat embarrassed.

"You know, modesty is the sign of a true writer," says Professor Guilford.

"Oh, she's the most modest person I know," Tristan adds.

I nudge his arm. "*Tristan.*"

"Tristan says you're a senior. Do you know where you're heading to college yet?"

I'm reminded of my rejection letter, and suddenly wish I could disappear from the conversation. "Oh, I haven't decided yet," I manage to say casually. "But Central Washington is still an option for me." I don't tell him it's my only option at the moment.

"Oh really?"

"*Really?*" Tristan repeats.

"It's affordable. And my mom's here." That's really all I can think of.

"Fantastic." Professor Guilford beams. "So I might have you as a student. I understand you like creative writing. Have you thought about writing for film and television?"

"No, I haven't. But that does sound really interesting," I say.

"I offer a screenwriting course every few years. It just so happens the next one will be in the fall."

"Oh?"

"It's typically reserved for upperclassmen," he says with a smirk. "But I've made exceptions before."

"Oh my god—that would be incredible," I say, almost with a gasp. "I never knew classes like that existed. What else do you teach?"

Tristan leaves us to chat for a bit. We have an incredible conversation about some of the projects his students are working on. Apparently, many of them intern in writers' rooms at major television studios over the summers, through his connections with industry members. I always thought opportunities like that were reserved for the sons and daughters of famous producers. It makes me feel hopeful about school. Maybe I could do it, too. Maybe I don't need Reed after all. At the end of the conversation, Professor Guilford invites me to lunch with my mom in the next few weeks to talk about other creative opportunities. After we exchange emails, I go find Tristan to tell him everything.

"Tristan—I'm so glad you introduced us!" I say, still smiling.

"Yeah, isn't he the best?" Tristan says, handing me a glass of sparkling cider. "I'm so happy you might go to school here. We could still hang out. That is, if you're not too cool to hang around, you know, *high schoolers*. Maybe we can work on a project together."

"That's such a great idea. We should!"

"I bet you'd be an amazing writer for films," he says.

"I hope you're right," I say.

The rest of the night is wonderful. I meet Tristan's other friends who worked on the documentary with him, and impress them with my knowledge of Mark Lanegan and the Screaming Trees. We eat chocolate-covered strawberries, and put our names into the raffle. Tristan wins six tickets to the local cinema. One of his friends wins a fancy camera. They all crowd around him enviously, taking turns admiring it. Then one of them whispers something.

"*Did you see him? I can't believe he's here, man.*"

Heads dart back and forth. But I can't tell who they're looking at. Then Tristan whispers, "*He nodded at me after the film. Think he knew I was the director.*"

"What! And you didn't go up and say anything?"

"*I heard he hates being approached,*" says Tristan.

I stick my head into their secret huddle. "Who are you guys talking about?"

Everyone looks at me. Tristan points his chin to my right. "Over there. The one with the glasses."

I turn around, looking. "The tinted ones?" It's the man I sat beside during Tristan's film. "Oh, I talked to him earlier. He was really nice."

Tristan's eyes widen. "What do you mean you *talked* to him?"

"I sat next to him at your screening," I say. "We chatted before it started. It wasn't a big deal or anything. I mostly ignored him."

"Julie . . . tell me you know who that is?"

"Clearly I don't, Tristan."

"That's Marcus Graham," Tristan whispers tensely. "He's one of the former managers of the band. He's old friends with Mark Lanegan and the Connor brothers. He's a big part of their success. He's sort of famous."

"*And he's leaving!*" his friend shouts.

I turn to see his arm disappear through a slit in the back of the tent. How did I not realize who he was? No wonder he was so curious about my interest in the band. As I watch him leave, a sudden thought occurs to me. I need to talk to him again. This is my only chance.

I leave Tristan with his friends and rush out of the tent to find him. It's incredible how much sound the canvas can block from the outside. The cold shift from the night air sends a shiver through me, making my ears pop.

"Wait!" I shout from behind him.

The man stops walking. He turns around, looking for the voice. It's only the two of us out here. He adjusts his glasses. "Something the matter?" he asks.

It takes me a second to think of what to say. "I'm sorry! For not recognizing you earlier."

"No worries," he says with a chuckle. "You won't be the last."

"My boyfriend. He would have loved to have met you. He's a really big fan," I say. "His name is Sam."

"You mentioned him. Too bad he couldn't make it," he says, turning to leave.

I step forward. "He's a musician, too," I go on. "He plays the guitar, and even writes his own music. You guys really inspired him."

"That's nice, kid."

I reach into my bag. "I have one of his CDs," I say. "It would mean a lot if you listened to it." Once I find the CD, I hold it out to him. "Some of the songs aren't finished. But he's really talented."

The man puts his hands up. "Sorry, kid. But I make it a rule not to take unsolicited music. Industry policy."

I step forward, holding the CD out closer. "Please, just listen to it. It would mean so much to him."

He waves a hand in the air. "I said I can't. I'm sorry."

"*Please—*"

"Have a good rest of your night," he says firmly, and walks off.

I stand there with my arm hanging in the air, as a cold night chill sends a shiver through me, and I feel my entire body begin to shake.

I can't let this chance slip away. I have to stop him. I have to do this for Sam. But the man is about to walk off forever.

"He's dead!" I gasp. The words rip through my throat. "He's dead!" When I realize what I'm actually saying, I can't contain myself. "That's why he couldn't make it. That's why he isn't here. Because he died. He died few weeks ago—"

Tears form behind my eyes as my throat swells up. It's been a long time since I heard myself say anything like this. Maybe because I stopped believing it.

The man stops walking. He turns around and looks at me. There's a silence before he says something. "His name was Sam, you said?"

I nod silently as I wipe my cheeks with my hands, trying to stop myself from crying.

"And he played the guitar?"

"Yes," I say through a cracked voice.

He steps toward me, holding out a hand. "Alright then. I'll take a listen."

"Thank you so much."

I hand him the CD. But he can't even take it from me. My grip is too strong.

He looks at me. "Is something wrong?"

"I . . . I just realized this is the only copy I have," I say. "I don't have a lot of his things left."

He lets go of the CD. "Tell you what, why don't you email it to me," he suggests. "That way, I won't lose it and I can respond to you." He takes out his wallet and hands me his card. "Take care now."

I watch him disappear into the parking lot. I don't head back inside. The CD is clenched tightly in my hands. I couldn't even let it go. A stupid CD. Just like the lantern. I wanted to let go of everything but I can't even let go of this. How am I supposed to let go of Sam?

There's something on the ground. I glance down. It's Tristan's rose. I didn't even notice I dropped it.

CHAPTER

SEVENTEEN

The sound of a piano fills the room as I set the table. I smooth out the tablecloth, place down matching ceramic plates, and light a candle. Cardboard boxes are stacked side by side at my feet. I lift one to the counter as I continue unpacking. Silverware tied with twine, coffee mugs, and wooden spoons. At some point, the music changes without me noticing, to "Kiss the Rain" by Yiruma. His song sounds like drops of water falling softly on clay rooftops in the spring. As I touch the drawer handle, I *feel* someone there behind me. Familiar hands move along my waist, and the warmth from them makes me go still. Then a kiss on my neck as I shut my eyes . . .

"How about we take a break . . ." Sam whispers.

We just moved into our new apartment. The floorboards creak and iron pipes snake along the ceiling. Exactly how we imagined it. The place is unfurnished, a bit worn down, and in need of some renovations. But it's full of potential. Just like us.

I touch his hands. "Sam, we've barely started. And there's so much left to do."

Sam kisses me on the neck again. "There's nothing wrong with taking our time . . ."

The music continues to play. Outside the windows is nothing but clouds and clouds, like we're suspended in the sky.

I turn around and take him in—dark eyes a shade lighter than his hair, slender lips that curve gently into a smile. I can't help myself. I bring my hands up to touch his face so I can remember every detail. I take in the contrast of our skin, his golden cheeks against my pale fingers. As I run a hand through his soft wisps of hair, he pulls me in for a longer kiss, and my mind erases everything else in the world except us.

When Sam pulls away, he takes my hands. "So, what do you think of the place?"

I can't stop smiling. "It's perfect."

Sam looks around, his eyes bright with ideas. "I know. Just needs a little work, that's all."

Across the floor are boxes still waiting to be unpacked. In the tiny space that makes up the kitchen, a kettle is simmering quietly on the stove beside a teapot. I note the warm smell of ginger and lemongrass. In an hour or so, I can make something for dinner. We'll pick up groceries because eating out is expensive, and we prefer a home-cooked meal anyway.

The piano music skips suddenly, interrupting my thoughts. Then our record player cuts out.

Sam looks at me, frowning. "I can fix that later . . ."

I let out a laugh as he pulls me to the other side of the apartment that makes up the living room.

"So this is the living room," he says with a sweeping motion of his hand, bringing it to life. "We can put a couch right here, and a little coffee table—and maybe a painting on the wall."

I point at the other side of the room. "Shouldn't the couch go there?"

Sam looks over, his brows furrowed. "Even better," he says. "I knew you had an eye for this."

I watch as he circles the room, taking everything in as he imagines our new home. "We can put a desk here, against the wall, for you to write. I can build you a bookshelf. Since you brought boxes of them. We can put it right there. And we'll need some plants—"

His excitement is contagious. I can't help seeing everything, too. It's a blank canvas for us to paint over. A new beginning to our story. A chance to start the page fresh. Once we fix up the apartment, we'll look for jobs. We'll start saving some money. I'll focus on my writing and reapply to Reed College in the fall.

Sam takes my hands, and our fingers lace together. "So you love it, right?"

"More than you could know," I say, smiling at him. I glance around the room. "I just want everything to be perfect. Like we always planned."

Sam kisses me on the cheek. "You know, Jules, you can't always plan out every detail, though. There will always be things we can't prepare for," he says. "You have to live in the moment sometimes. Let life surprise you."

I don't say anything. I just take this in.

"Listen," Sam says, his eyes glistening. "How about we go out tonight? Somewhere with music. It doesn't have to be anywhere fancy. We'll get something small and share it. You know, find one of those places that gives out free bread."

"But we have so much unpacking to do," I remind him.

"Don't worry. We have all the time in the world for that."

All the time in the world . . . the words echo through me as a breeze comes in through the window, rolling across my skin. I glance at the clock above the doorway. I didn't notice it there before. The hands are missing. Outside, there's still nothing but shimmering clouds. Now that I think about it, how long has the sun been setting out there?

"Is something wrong?" Sam's voice pulls me back to him.

I blink a few times. "No. I mean, I don't think so."

"Then what do you say about going out?"

I purse my lips, considering this. "I guess it is our first night here. Maybe we should celebrate it."

"Perfect."

"As long as we get *some* unpacking done first," I add.

"Deal." Sam kisses me on the cheek again, and then picks a box off the floor. "Where does this go?"

"The bedroom. But it's fragile. So be careful."

"Careful is my middle name."

I give him a look as he slow-walks away, disappearing down the hallway.

Once he's gone, I scan the living room again, deciding what to start next. There's a small box in the corner, illuminated by the light from the window. For some reason, it isn't marked like the others. Sam must have forgotten to label it. I bring it onto the counter and open it first. It's Sam's things, randomly thrown inside. I take out a few of his shirts and fold them on the table. There are other things in here, too. A few records, some photographs, a bunch of birthday cards and letters, and something else that makes me go still. One of the bookends he gave me. I stare at it for a while, along with his things I set on the

table. There's something familiar about having all of them together. Like pieces of a puzzle. As I go through them again, the
pieces come together, and the image hits me like a brick. *This
can't be possible, can it?* There should be something else in this
box. I don't have to look to know what it is. I reach inside slowly
and take it out.

Sam's denim jacket. I stare at it for a long time. This is in the
same box I threw out weeks ago.

As I stand there, running my hand over it, the record player
suddenly comes to life, making me jump. A song comes on that
wasn't playing before, something unfamiliar to me. When it
starts to *screech*, and rise in volume, I hurry over to unplug it.
As soon as I lift the needle from the record, I sense the candles
blow out behind me as the room goes silent. Sunlight fades from
the windows, dimming the apartment. I turn around to see the
table cleared. As I look around the room, the boxes have suddenly
disappeared, too, including the one with Sam's things—the apartment is empty. Where did everything go?

"Sam?"

I call his name a few times but no answer. Is he still here? I
head to the bedroom to look for him. The hallway is somehow
longer than I remember, and seems to extend farther and farther
as I walk. For some reason, there are no doors on either side, only
one at the very end of the hall. It's covered with stickers, just
like the ones Sam has on his bedroom door at home. I touch
the knob, taking a deep breath before I turn it. A couple leaves
roll into the hallway as I open it, followed by a familiar breeze.

Tall grass bends beneath my shoes as I step outside, and find
myself standing in the middle of the fields. I breathe in the air,
taking in the scent of barley. There's something different about
this place. The sky is overcast and I sense a strange vibration

moving under me. A strong wind bends the tops of the grasses, nearly breaking them. There are no sounds of crickets, only a growing rumble coming from somewhere deep inside the earth. As more clouds roll in, I feel the first sprinkling of rain on my skin. In the distance, high above the line of mountains, lightning flashes. A storm is coming, and it appears I'll have to face it alone.

Sam isn't here anymore. Maybe he never was.

I used to live inside my daydreams. I spent hours planning the future in my head, imagining myself ten years from now, finished with college, living in an apartment in the city, getting to write for a living. I imagined the details of the rest of my life—the appliances I would have in the kitchen, the titles of stories I would publish, the places I would travel, who would be there with me. But then you get rejections in the mail, lose that person who meant everything to you, and find yourself back at the beginning with nowhere to go. I try not to daydream anymore. It only tricks me with images of Sam, filling me with the possibility that we can still be together, that there's a future for us, until reality comes in like a storm to blow everything away.

Sam is never coming back. But somehow I keep on waiting for him. I'm not sure how many calls we have left, but the number is winding down. I spent the morning looking through the log of phone calls I've been keeping, remembering our conversations, trying to make sense of things. Since I let him speak to Mika, I noticed each call is shorter than the one before, the static coming sooner. *How many more calls left before I lose you?* It's hard to worry about this when there are other questions we haven't answered yet. *Why were we given this second chance? Just to say good-bye?* It's as if we've been reconnected only to be torn apart again. Sam said that we should appreciate this for what it is, but I can't help thinking there has to be a reason we've been connected again. But there's only so much time left. Maybe I'll never get the answer.

Every time I get off the phone with him, it feels like we're getting closer to the end. Even though I knew this was coming, it still tears me apart inside. *Like I'm losing him all over again. What am I going to do when he's gone?* I wish the world would slow down for us. I wish I could put coins into a machine to buy us more time. I wish I could save these last calls for as long as I can, so we can stay connected. I wish there was something, anything I could do to keep him with me.

"Everything's going to be okay," Sam said in our previous call. "We still have time together. I'm not going anywhere until we say good-bye, alright?"

"But what if I'll never be ready?"

"Don't say that, Julie. You have a whole life ahead of you. There's so much to look forward to. And you're destined to do great things, I know it."

"And what about you?"

"I'll be okay, too. You don't have to worry."

His answers are always vague. I learned not to push him on telling me more. I know he has his reasons.

"Promise me one thing," I said before the call ended.

"What's that?"

"That no matter what, this won't be the end of us. That we'll be connected again someday."

A silence.

"Promise me, Sam," I asked again.

"I'm sorry, Jules. But I can't promise you that. As much as I want to."

It was the answer I expected. But it still fills me with emptiness.

"So you're saying, after our good-bye, it's really going to end? And I'll never be able to speak to you again?"

"Don't think of it like that," Sam said. "It's just a different beginning, especially for you. And you're gonna have a lot them."

"And you? Where will you go after?"

"To be honest . . . I don't really know. I'm sure I'll be fine, though. At the very least, I can promise you that. So don't worry, okay?" And then the static comes, as if on cue. "I think it's time to go soon . . ."

I squeezed the phone. "Where are you now?"

"I still can't say. I'm sorry."

"Can you at least tell me what you see?" I asked.

Sam took a moment to answer.

"Fields. Endless fields."

Rain drizzles down the windshield as we drive up the interstate toward Seattle. As we cross Lacey V. Murrow Memorial Bridge, which floats over Lake Washington, the view of mountains fades behind us, replaced by concrete high-rises that cluster along ocean-blue water. I wasn't planning on coming back here anytime soon. I was hoping to stay in bed all weekend, watching TV shows on my laptop. A trip out to the waterfront was Yuki's idea. She wanted to see it one more time before we graduate and she has to fly back to Japan. When Yuki first asked if I would come with her, I said I couldn't. I've been keeping to myself more lately. Since the film festival two weeks ago, I haven't had much of a yearning for social interaction. But then Rachel caught the flu on Thursday, and I pictured Yuki taking the bus alone and getting lost downtown, and felt a pang of guilt. So I decided to go with her. When I told her yesterday at lunch, Oliver invited himself along, offering to drive. He even convinced Jay to ditch his weekly environmental club meeting and go with us.

I keep my earbuds in as I stare out the car window. Maybe some time away from Ellensburg is what I need after all.

There isn't too much traffic this Saturday morning, so we arrive early to grab breakfast on the pier. Once the rain stops, the four of us take a stroll along the waterfront, pausing at the occasional souvenir stand, looking for our names on key chains. While the others head farther into the arcade stands of Pike Place Market, I take a break from the touristy attractions and find a bench away from the crowds to get some space alone.

A merchant vessel cruises along the harbor, sending little waves against the rocks as I stare out at the water. It's a chilly afternoon on the pier in downtown Seattle. I breathe in the brisk salt air and let it out slowly. It's been a while since I smelled the ocean. It's strange to be back here after a long time away. I forgot how lonely the water can make you feel just by looking at it.

I wish Sam was here with us. The world feels quiet without him in it. It's been more than a week since we last spoke to each other. If only I could call him up for a moment, just to hear his voice. *Know he's still there.* Maybe then I might enjoy this trip, instead of thinking about him every second. I keep my phone in my lap, checking it from time to time. It reminds me we're still connected, even when we can't hear each other. I wonder if our signal works outside of Ellensburg. I wasn't sure if it was a good idea to drive up here and risk it. But since our calls have to be spaced further apart these days, I knew I wouldn't be able to call him this weekend anyway. It's only a few days, after all. I should at least try to have a good time, and spend time with the others. But it's so much harder than I thought it would be.

After a while, someone approaches the bench.

"Can I join you?"

I look up at Yuki. She is holding a compostable tray with two coffees. I move my jacket from the bench, making room for her. She sits beside me, sliding over the tray.

The coffee is warm in my hands. "Thank you. But you didn't have to get me something."

"I think it's the least I can do," Yuki says, staring out at the water. "For making you come all the way out here with us." She looks at me. "You don't seem to be enjoying the trip."

I stare at my phone, feeling guilty. I'm sure she isn't the only one who noticed. "Sorry, I'm not in the best mood," I say. "But I'm glad I came out here with you guys. I just have a lot on my mind."

"What are you thinking about?"

I let out a breath. "The same things . . ." I answer.

We stare out at the water again. A few seagulls cry overhead. After some silence, Yuki asks, "Do you still have those nightmares?"

I think about the crystal I still keep with me. It's tucked safely inside the pocket of my bag. I never leave the house without it. "Actually, I don't anymore. I think what you gave me got rid of them."

"I'm glad it helped."

I take a sip of coffee, letting it warm my throat. I can't tell Yuki what's really bothering me. How I keep imagining a future with Sam still in it. Though I know these calls won't last forever,

I can't seem to let go of our connection, even though it's already breaking. I keep thinking about what Mika said to me the night of the festival. About holding on to Sam.

"This isn't good for you . . . And I don't know if it's good for him, either."

I replay the conversation in my head. What exactly did she mean by that? Am I hurting Sam by holding on for as long as I can? Am I keeping him from something? As much as I love him, I don't want to force him to stay longer. Especially if he needs to move on, wherever that is. This is his choice, too. After all, it was him who picked up my call in the first place. After a while, I turn to Yuki. "Remember what you said about my dreams? The ones about Sam, I mean. How I should seek the opposite to find balance or something . . ."

Yuki nods. "I remember."

"I thought about it," I say, staring down at my phone again, holding it tight. "I think it's obvious what it means now. It means I have to stop thinking about him. That I have to let him go and move on with my life." I let out a deep breath. "I wish it was easier for me."

Yuki looks away, as if taking this in. After a moment, she says, "You know, I don't think you could let Sam go. Even if you really wanted to."

"What do you mean?"

"I guess what I mean is, Sam is still very much a part of your life, isn't he?" she says. "He might be physically gone, but you will always carry a piece of him with you. I know your time with Sam was much shorter than you wanted it to be, but that time together isn't something you can give back. Letting go isn't about forgetting. It's balancing moving forward with life, and looking back from time to time, remembering the people in it."

I stare out at the water again, thinking. If only she understood how different it is for me. I'm the only one who will have to lose him twice.

Yuki touches my hand. "I know this is still hard for you. But I'm glad you decided to come today. I'm glad we're spending time together again."

I smile. "I'm glad, too."

Someone whistles to our left, and we both look up from the bench. Jay and Oliver are standing against the rail of the board-walk, holding churros. The two of them have been inseparable lately. I sense some sparks between them.

Oliver waves at us. "We got churros!"

"Come back up!" Jay shouts over. "There are sea lions."

Yuki and I exchange smirks.

"You know, I really like those two together," Yuki says.

"I really do, too."

As the sky finally clears, we spend the rest of the day on the waterfront. After lunch and some candle shopping, we head to the aquarium to look for otters, because they're Oliver's favorite animal. Jay suggests we buy matching hats to commemorate the trip, and we wear them during our stroll through the sculpture park. Since it's too late to ride the ferry, we head over to Pier 57 and take a ride on the Ferris wheel. When I look out at our view from two hundred feet in the air, I think of Sam, and the memory of us at the fair fills me with warmth.

As the others head back home that night, I decide to stay in Se-attle to spend the rest of the weekend with my dad. He's been asking me for weeks to come visit him. The second he steps out of his car to pick me up, my eyes start watering. I forgot how much I missed him. He's always known how to make things better without needing to ask what's wrong. He even called my mom, asking if I could skip school so we can spend another day together. We do all my favorite things—have pancakes at the diner in Portage Bay where we used to live, drink pour-over coffee in Pioneer Square, and visit my favorite bookstores on 10th Avenue. Being away from Ellensburg was exactly what I needed after all. I still think about Sam from time to time, but the memories are fond, letting me breathe easier. Even though he isn't here, I still see him everywhere. And for the first time, the thought of this brings me comfort.

I arrive at the bus station late Monday afternoon. My mom is still teaching a class at the university, so I have to wait a few hours before she can pick me up. I rest my bag on the floor and check my phone. Now that I'm back in Ellensburg, my calls with Sam should be working again. It's been ten days since we last spoke. It's the longest I haven't heard from him since he first picked up the phone. Ever since our connection broke, Sam and I have been planning our calls several days in advance, one call at a time. Our next one happens to be today. I have the date marked down in my notebook. I was going to wait until I was back in my room, but after being away so long, I can't wait to hear from him again.

There's a new notification on my phone. An email from a name that sounds familiar. I open the email and read it first.

Dear Julie,

Apologies it took so long to get back to you. Spent the morning listening to the songs you sent me. I have to be honest with you. A few of the tracks were fantastic. Sam was a talented musician. He really knew his way around a melody. That's a gift that's hard to come by. And I wouldn't say that if it wasn't true. He was really something special. Again, I'm sorry to hear what happened. A very sad loss.

Anyway, I went ahead and forwarded your email to Gary and a few others from the band (since I know you two are big fans). Hope you don't mind. I'll let you know if they get back to me. They're gonna love knowing you all came from the same hometown.

Hope things stay well. Feel free to reach out anytime.

Take care,
Marcus

I barely contain a gasp as I read the email over again. Marcus Graham, the manager of the Screaming Trees. The man I met at Tristan's screening. I never really expected a response when I wrote to him after the festival. I can't believe he remembers me! More importantly, he loved Sam's music! He said he was talented!

I have to call Sam. I have to tell him right now.

My hands shake with excitement as I make the call. As usual, I hold my breath when the phone begins to ring. It takes a while, but eventually he answers.

"It feels like it's been forever," Sam says. "I missed you."

His voice fills me with warmth. Like sunlight streaming into a room.

"I missed you, too," I say. "You won't believe what just happened. Do you remember Marcus Graham? The manager of the Screaming Trees?"

"Sure, what about him?"

"I met him at the film festival a few weeks ago. I sent him some of your music. He just emailed me back. I have to read this to you . . ."

I read him the email. My voice rises at the parts where Marcus says he loved the songs, how talented he said Sam was, and how he forwarded everything to the others in the band. "Can you believe it, Sam? He said he sent it to Gary! That must mean he sent it to Mark, too. What if they're listening to it right now? Oh my god . . . what if they're talking about you! I wonder what song they like best . . ."

Sam is quiet as he takes this in.

"What do you think? *Say something!*"

"Why didn't you tell me you sent him my music?" Sam asks.

"Because I wasn't sure if I'd get a response," I say. "I didn't know if he would actually listen to it."

"But I thought I told you not to do this."

I go quiet for a moment, surprised by his response. "It's not like I went looking for him. It sort of happened in the moment. Why are you mad at me? Sam—it's the *Screaming Trees.* Marcus Graham said you're—"

"It doesn't matter what he said," Sam interrupts me. "Why are you still doing this, Julie? We talked about this. And yet you're still holding on to my music and my life when I told you there's no point anymore. Why can't you accept the fact that—"

"That what—*you're dead*?"

A silence. I swallow hard, waiting for his response. When I sense there isn't going to be one, I continue, my voice sharper. "I have accepted it. I accepted it a while ago."

"It doesn't seem that way," Sam says. "It seems like you're stuck on this idea that I might be coming back or something. Ever since we started talking again, it's like you can't seem to let me go anymore. And I'm just worried—"

"You don't have anything to worry about," I say back, suddenly furious. "And let me remind you, you're the one who picked up the phone in the first place."

"Well, maybe I shouldn't have."

A shock goes through me. His words silence the both of us. I stand there, completely still, the phone clenched tightly in my hand. *I can't believe he would say that.* I want to say something back, but nothing comes out.

"*I'm sorry.* I don't mean that. Please don't—" Sam starts.

I hang up the phone before he can finish. Because I don't care to hear an apology. I stare down at the pavement, barely processing what just happened between us. Tears form behind my eyes, but I refuse to cry. Not right now. I want to go home. I don't want to wait at the bus station anymore.

I grab my bag from the floor. But before I head off, the phone vibrates in my hand. And then it starts ringing, even though I have it on silent. The last time this happened, it was Sam calling. But we agreed he shouldn't call again. *Because if I don't pick up, it would end the connection.*

I check the screen. The number is unknown, just like last time. So I answer it.

"What do you want?" I ask.

There's a brief silence before Sam answers. As soon as he does, I notice a pain in his voice. "I'm sorry," he says. "But I think I need your help."

"Sam, what's wrong?"

He lets out a breath. "I don't know how to explain it," he says.

"But it has something to do with my family. I have this bad feeling in my chest. I've never felt it before. Have you heard from them lately?"

An ache of guilt in my chest returns. Because I haven't spoken to them since Sam died. I'm ashamed to answer this question. "No, I haven't in a while. I'm sorry."

A silence between us.

"Do you think you can do something for me?" Sam asks.

"Of course. Anything."

"Check up on my family for me, if you can . . . Maybe ask Mika if she knows something."

"Do you think something's wrong?"

"I don't know. I really hope not."

"Let me do it right now—"

Once we hang up the phone, I text Mika right away, asking her if something's happened. She responds almost instantly.

It's James. He never went to school. We think he ran away. Everyone's out looking for him. I'll let you know if we find him.

I call Sam back and tell him this.

"Do they have any clue about where he is?" Sam asks.

"I don't think so," I say. "Mika didn't mention anything."

"Dang it, I wish I was there. I bet no one knows where to look."

"Where do you think he might be? I can help search for him," I say.

"It could be a dozen places . . ."

"We'll check every single one."

"Let me think—" His voice is strained.

"It's gonna be okay, Sam. We're gonna find him."

I write down locations Sam recalls on a piece of paper and

text Mika again. She takes her dad's car to come pick me up, and we go searching for James. Mika and I divide the list of places in half, based on their proximity to each other. Since I'm taking the north side of town, Mika drops me off near the theater and I go running. I check the comic store, the drive-in, the donut shop, and everything in between. When I realize he isn't in town, I run to the lake to see if he's there, but there's no sign of him. So I keep going. It's a long jog to memorial hill, but I have to check. This one isn't on Sam's list of places. I had this feeling James might be there, sitting with him. Once I reach the gates and make my way up the hill, I'm disappointed to find out I'm wrong.

I check the list again. The last few places Sam named are a bit out of the way. They are locations around the old neighborhood where he used to live. One of them is a small park where they used to ride their bikes after school. I don't know what the chances of James being there are. But I leave memorial hill and head for it anyway.

It takes me a while to figure out where the park is located. I've never been to this part of town before. I have to stop and ask people on the sidewalk for directions. When I finally find it, tucked away at the end of a cul-de-sac, I spot a familiar green jacket hanging over a bench. The second I spot James sitting alone on the swing set, staring at the ground, I stop short to catch my breath.

I haven't spoken with him since Sam's death. I don't even know what to say as I approach him at the swings. Although I'm still catching my breath from the run, I keep my voice soft as I lower myself to him. "Hey there, James . . ." I say. "Everyone's been looking for you, you know? You had us all worried."

James doesn't look at me. He keeps his gaze on the ground.

"They're gonna be glad to hear you're not hurt," I continue. "What are you doing all the way out here?"

James says nothing. I'm suddenly reminded of that night at the fair when he wouldn't speak to me. It was the last time the three of us were together, wasn't it? I guess it's been much longer since I've seen James than I remember. I soften my voice again. "How about you and I head on home, alright?"

"No."

"Your parents are really worried—" I start.

"*I don't want to go home!*" he shouts back.

"Is something wrong? You know you can tell me."

I'm sure this has something to do with Sam. But I don't know how to approach the conversation. I can't imagine what it feels like to lose a brother. This is a kind of pain I'll never understand. I try to take James's hand, but he pulls it away.

"*Leave me alone,*" he says, clenching his arms. "I'm not going home. Get away from me!"

It pains me to hear him talk this way. I wish I could make things better. "Can you at least tell me why you ran away?" I ask.

James says nothing.

"Is it because of Sam . . ." I whisper. "Because he's not there?"

"No," James says, shaking his head. "Because he *hates* me!"

"Why would you think that? Of course Sam doesn't hate you."

"Yes, he does! He told me!"

"When did Sam tell you that?"

James drops his face in his hands, trying to hide his tears from me. "When I went into his room and broke his microphone. He said he *hated me.*"

I touch his shoulder and say, "James, listen to me. Sometimes people say that when they're mad, but they don't mean it. Sam doesn't hate you—"

"But he stopped talking to me!" he cries. "He was ignoring me! Right before he died."

My heart breaks from hearing this. I wipe my eyes and take James by the hands. "Sam loves you, okay? Brothers fight all the time and say things they don't mean. If Sam was here, he would tell you this himself."

James wipes his tears with his sleeve. "You don't know that. Why do you even care? You don't even like me!"

"Of course I do—how could you say that?"

"You don't care about us! You only liked Sam! You only came to see him."

"That isn't true," I say. "You and I are friends, too. I care about your whole family."

"*That's a lie!* Cuz when Sam died, you never came over, and you never talked to us again! It's like you died, *too.*"

A sharp pain stabs through my chest as the weight of this hits me. I can barely fight back the tears. I open my mouth, and find myself unable to speak. I should have come by and checked up on his family after Sam died. I never thought about what James must be going through. "I—I'm sorry, James. I shouldn't have left you like that. I should have tried . . ." My voice gives out. Because I don't know what else to say to make James forgive me. Maybe the reason I avoided their family was because I couldn't bear to see them without Sam. Because I didn't want to be reminded he was gone. But this doesn't matter. I should have been there for James. Instead, I made things harder for him. I abandoned him, too.

"*I'm not going home,*" James cries.

I wish I could get through to him. But he won't even look

at me. I can't blame him, though. If only there was something I could do to make it better. It pains me to see him like this. I need to do something, but I'm not sure what. I think of Sam. He would know what to say if he was here. He's the only person James will listen to right now. A thought occurs to me. Our connection is weakening, but I need to do something. I can't let James spend the rest of his life thinking Sam hated him.

As I step away from the swing set for a moment, I pull out my phone and call Sam again. He picks up after the first ring.

"Did you find him? Is he okay?"

"I'm with him now. Don't worry."

Sam's voice floods with relief. "Where was he?"

"At the park. Just like you said."

"I'm so glad he's safe. Why did he run away?"

"It's a bit complicated," I say. "But he thinks you hate him."

"Me? Why would he think that?"

"James told me you said it to him before you died," I tell him. "I tried to explain how you didn't mean it, but he won't listen to me. I'm not sure what else I can say. But I'll make sure he gets home safe and everything."

"Thank you," Sam says. "For finding him."

"Of course," I say. Then I look back at the swings. "But, I need a favor from you now."

"What is it?"

"I want you to talk to James," I say.

"Julie . . ." Sam starts.

"I want you to do this for me, okay? Please, before this call ends. He needs you."

A brief silence as he considers this. "But our calls are weak as it is . . . this could really harm our connection," Sam warns me. "Are you sure?"

I take a deep breath. "I'm sure."

James is staring at the ground as I approach him again. I kneel down to him, holding out my phone.

"Listen, James. There's someone I want you to talk to, okay?"

He looks at me. "My parents?"

I shake my head. "Why don't you see for yourself? Here . . ."

James puts the phone to his ear, listening. I know the moment he hears Sam's voice, because his eyes widen, as if he's making sense of it. After a minute on the phone, when James starts weeping into his shirt, I know he realizes it's truly Sam. And the two of them are suddenly reconnected. I stand back quietly, giving them this brief unexplainable moment together. I catch a few things from their conversation. They talk about being strong for their mom, about taking care of the family while Sam's gone, about how much Sam loves him.

But since our connection is breaking, the call doesn't last too long. When James hands the phone back to me, Sam and I only have a few seconds to speak.

"Thank you for this," he says. "But I have to go now."

"I understand," I say.

And then the call ends. Just like that.

James and I hold hands as we leave the park together. I text Sam's mom for the first time in a while, letting her know I found James and that we're on our way back. When Sam's house rises into view, his mom is there standing at the driveway, waiting for us. Her face breaks into a smile when she spots us, as if we haven't seen each other in years. When she puts her arms around me, we hug each other tight, and I don't know which one of us starts crying first. Sam's mom takes James by his other hand as we walk inside the house to greet his dad. After I help set the table, the four of us sit down together for dinner for the first time in what feels like too long.

CHAPTER
EIGHTEEN

I have a lot of time to myself these days. Time to think and process and catch up with the rest of the world. Ever since my last call with Sam, I don't find myself waiting by the phone anymore. Instead I'm spending more time with my friends and focusing on school again. I finished up my final essay for Mr. Gill's class, and am set to graduate. I also found time to work on my writing sample, even though I won't be submitting it anywhere soon. Who cares if no one else reads it right now. I found peace in writing something for myself for once. Peace in remembering those moments makes me feel connected to Sam, especially when our calls are broken. Those memories of us are something I'll always have. Even after he's gone. I only wish he had a chance to read it. But I try not to think like this, though. I'm thankful for this temporary hole in the universe that we found ourselves floating through these last few months together.

It's hard to believe graduation is a few days away. I still don't know what my plans are after. Since I'm lacking options, it's as though I no longer have a say in the matter. Like things are being decided for me. I'm not used to this feeling. I like the idea of making plans, looking ahead, and seeing what's in front of me. But every time I do, life seems to get derailed. Sam always told me to be more spontaneous and let things be a surprise. He never warned me that surprises are not always good things. That's something I had to learn on my own.

Sam and I have one phone call left. This will be our final call. The last time I ever get to talk to him. I'll have to say good-bye this time. Sam said this is the only way to end our connection and let us both move on. The call will take place the night of graduation, and will only last a few minutes. And according to Sam, the call should be made before midnight, otherwise we might lose our chance. A part of me wishes I could save this call for as long as I can, but I have to be strong for both of us.

It's been a few weeks since we last spoke on the phone. It still pains me to be away from him for so long, like he's moving further away from me with each day. But at least there's been one silver lining from our distance. My mother and I have connected again. We've spent these last few weeks together, having dinner every night, watching TV in the living room, shopping, and taking weekend trips to the beach—things we used to do. She said she missed spending time with me. I didn't realize how much I missed it, too.

Cars honk impatiently as my mother and I sit in traffic. We are on our way to the outlet mall in search of a graduation dress. Evergreen trees rise from the side of the road. We've been stuck on the highway for almost an hour. My mother has her meditation podcast on low volume as I stare out the window, watching clouds.

My mother glances over at me. She's in her yoga clothes even though she didn't have her class this morning. She says it helps her focus while driving. "So, have you looked at the course catalog for Central yet?" she asks. "They get filled pretty quickly."

"I skimmed through it."

"Looks like they have a writing course in the spring. You must be excited."

"Over the moon."

"No clichés in the car. Your own rules."

I let out a breath. "I'm sorry. But it's hard to be positive when you didn't get in anywhere else."

"You know, you only have to stay there for two years," my mother says, lowering the volume. "And then you can transfer somewhere else. Lots of students do that, Julie."

"I guess you're right," I say. "It just wasn't part of the plan. None of this was . . ." *Getting rejected from Reed. Having to stay in Ellensburg. Losing Sam.*

"Plans don't always work out how we expect them to."

"I'm learning that . . ." I say, resting my head against the window. "Don't put too much effort into things. You'll only end up being disappointed."

"That's a bit pessimistic," my mother says. "Sure, life ends up more complicated than we want. But you figure it out."

I sigh. "You'd think at least one thing would work out, though," I say. "Sometimes I wish I could skip a few years into the future to see where I end up. So I don't waste all this time planning things out, only to have none of it go right."

"That's not a way to live life," my mother says, her hands gripping the wheel. "Always worrying about what comes next, instead of living in the moment. I see this in a lot of my students.

And I'm seeing it in you . . ." She looks at me. "You're living ahead of yourself, Julie. Making decisions, and wanting things done, only to set up the future."

"What's so wrong with that?"

"Life will pass right by you," she says, her eyes focused on the road. "And you end up missing the little things, the moments you don't think matter—but they do. Moments that make you forget about everything else. Just like with your writing," she adds out of nowhere. "You don't write to get to the end. You write because you enjoy doing it. You write and don't want it to end. Does that make some sense?"

"I guess so . . ." I think about this. *But what if I don't like the moment I'm living in?*

When we finally pull into the parking lot, my mother shuts off the car and leans back in her seat. Her fingers tap against the wheel. "Is there anything else on your mind?" she asks after some silence. "You know you can always talk to me."

I stare out the window again. It's been a while since I opened up to her. About what's really going on in my life. Maybe it's time I change that. "It's Sam . . ." I tell her. "I'm still thinking about him. About how he won't get to finish school or graduate with us, you know? I mean, how am I supposed to think about college and the rest of my life, when his was cut so short? I know it's not good for me. But I keep wishing he was still here."

My mother turns to me, and runs a hand through my hair. "I do, too," she says softly. "And I wish I knew what to say to make things better, or at least tell you how to go through this, Julie. But the truth is, no one experiences grief the same way, and we all come out of it differently. It's okay to wish for those things, and even imagine him here with you. Because those moments inside our heads are just as *real* as anything else." She taps her forehead. "Don't let anyone tell you otherwise . . ."

I look at her, my head slightly titled, wondering what she means. For a second, I almost ask if she knows about the calls, but I don't. "I know I have to say good-bye soon," I say. "But I don't think I can let him go."

My mother nods silently. Before we leave the car, she wipes a tear from my eye, and whispers, "Then you shouldn't. You should keep him with you. Help him live on somehow."

My mother's words stay with me for the rest of the week. I try not to stress too much about things that haven't happened yet, and try to enjoy my final days as a senior. Oliver brings me and Jay to a party near the lake on Saturday, and the three of us go hiking the next morning. Mika got accepted after being waitlisted at Emory University, and will be moving to Atlanta at the end of the summer. Even though I'm so thrilled for her, I hate that we'll be so far away from one another. But she says she'll come back for Thanksgiving and Christmas break, and I promise to visit her once I save up some money. At least Oliver will be studying at Central with me. We went through the course catalog the other day, looking for classes to take together. Maybe it won't be so bad there. Especially if I get into the screenwriting class. I email Professor Guilford, and he tells me to show up the first day, so I'm keeping my fingers crossed. And my mother's right. I can still transfer after two years if my grades are good enough. I could even apply to Reed College again. I have to stay cautiously optimistic.

It is the night of graduation. Blue and white balloons float along the chain-link fence of our football field as families file into the bleachers of the stadium. My mom and dad are sitting together somewhere in the middle of the crowd with Tristan and Mr. Lee. The band is in full uniform, playing a mess of unrecognizable songs so loud it's hard to hear anything else. After they finish with what I believe is the national anthem, the ceremony begins with a performance from our choir, featuring a beautiful solo from Yuki. I stand up on my chair and cheer her name at the end. A few speeches are made, the music changes, and it's time to for us to walk. Oliver was supposed to walk with Sam, so the school lets him stand in between me and Mika as we march, arms linked, toward the stage. Beneath each of our gowns is something that belongs to Sam, in memory of him. Oliver is wearing the plaid shirt, Mika one of his sweaters, and me his Radiohead T-shirt. Maybe it's all in my head, but it feels like the crowd cheers the loudest for us.

I only have a few minutes to change into my new dress before a million pictures are taken in front of the stage. Tristan gifts me a bouquet of yellow roses. My mother makes me take group photos with everyone around us, including David from history class, who I've never said more than five words to. Yuki introduces me to her parents, and they invite me, Rachel, and Jay to their home in Japan next summer. "A reunion!" Rachel cries, her face beaming. When the music dies, and the sun starts to set, I check the time. *I need to go soon.* Once the crowds dissipate a little, I go find the others to say good-bye.

The last call I have with Sam is tonight. I need to hurry home, get to my room, and be ready to say good-bye. I know he'll ask me all about today. I only wish he was here to celebrate it with us instead . . .

"What about the graduation party?" Oliver asks me. "You can't miss that—it's gonna be lit."

"I have something I need to do," I say.

"Are you sure?" Mika asks. I give her this look and she nods knowingly. "Maybe you can meet us after. Just text me, okay?"

"I will," I say, and hug them both.

With my phone clutched in my hand, I turn to go but—someone tall from the football team *bumps* into me. The impact is so hard, my phone is knocked out of my hands and hits the concrete, shattering the screen. I don't even hear their mumbled apology. The world becomes a tunnel . . .

A chill runs through my body. I'm too terrified to move a muscle. My heart pounds as I reach down for my phone. But it won't turn on. No matter what I try, *it won't turn on.* The screen is black and shattered, and I don't know what to do. I just stand there completely frozen, trying to process the full weight of what I've done.

Mika must have noticed something was wrong because she appears at my side.

"What is it?" she asks.

"My phone—*I broke it*—Mika, I broke it!" I keep repeating as she's trying to calm me down, telling me it's okay, when it isn't. The buttons aren't working. The screen remains black.

I turn to her. "I need your phone—" I grab it and call Sam's number but it doesn't go through. I try a few more times but the call keeps failing.

Oliver arrives. "What's the matter?" he asks.

"Julie broke her phone," Mika says gravely.

"Dang, I'm sorry. I'm sure we can go get it fixed tomorrow—"

"*No.* I need it tonight—let me see your phone—"

I take it from his hands before he can say anything. The call fails again. And again.

"Who's she calling?" Oliver asks as I pace around, desperately trying the number again, holding his phone up to maybe get a different signal that Sam can find. I must appear out of my mind, because a crowd has formed around me, watching. *Why isn't this working?*

I remember something Sam said. His voice echoes in my head.

Only our phones are connected.

I shove Oliver's phone back at him as my mother arrives at the scene. She asks me what's wrong, but I don't have time to answer. I grab her phone and call Sam again, even though I know it won't work. *Nothing will.* But I don't know what else to do. The calls only work through my phone, and it's *cracked* and *broken* because I was so stupid, I didn't watch where I was going. I need to figure something out. *I need to fix this.*

Sam expects me to call him tonight. I can't leave him waiting forever. *What if he thinks I forgot about him? What if he thinks something is wrong?* My heart is pounding harder than ever as a rush of adrenaline pumps through me, making it hard to breathe. I have to go find him. I have to find Sam. I'm not losing the last call I have left. I'm not losing him all over again. Not like this.

I turn to my mom. "I need your keys—" I take them from her hands without answering any questions. "Have Dad drive you home!"

I get into the car and start driving without knowing where I'm going. I drive through town, circling the streets, looking in store windows and coffee shops where we used to go, to see if Sam's there—*but he isn't*. I park the car and run into Sun and

Moon, ignoring the looks from strangers, and check the table where we used to sit.

"Sam? Sam!" I call his name.

But he isn't here. Of course he isn't.

Then I remember it was him who went looking for me. I get back into the car, and the next thing I know I'm driving up route 10, where he crashed that night, again. I pull down my window and look out to see if he's walking along the side of the road, searching for me. But Sam isn't out here, either. Another chill goes through me. I glance at the clock and see it's ten past eleven. *I'm running out of time.* If Sam isn't here walking along the roads, where would he be? Where is he going?

I remember something else. During one of our phone calls. I asked him what he saw.

Fields. Endless fields.

Of course! I turn the car around at once and take the next exit, toward the fields where he brought me. I take the shorter road Jay found and reach the path in no time. As soon as I get out of the car, I am swallowed in darkness. My heart is pounding, and I can barely see a thing as I race up the path toward the fields. Tree branches reach over my head like thin hands. For a moment, I think about turning back to the car, but I push forward. Sam is waiting for me somewhere out there. I can't let him down.

Where are you, Sam? Why can't I reach you?

Something pulses in my pocket. When I feel a warmth, I reach inside to check. *The selenite.* The crystal Yuki gave me that I carry everywhere. It's glowing! I hold it out in front of me and let its light illuminate my path, banishing the darkness. I can *feel* its energy radiating through me and into the air. I raise the crystal to the sky and see the moon lower itself toward me, granting me more light. I see everything now. The fields have never looked clearer than they do in this moment. And then it starts snowing. *In the middle of May?* I look around, wondering what's going on. As the snow falls on my hair and shoulders, I realize it isn't snow at all. *It's petals. It's raining cherry blossom petals?*

This must mean he's close.

I know you're here, Sam. I can feel you. Because you're everywhere. You were back in the coffee shop, there at the lake, somewhere waiting in these fields. All this time I've been wondering why we've been given this second chance. But maybe we're always connected, even after you're gone. Because I can never completely lose you. You're a part of me now. You're everywhere I look, falling from the sky like petals.

I reach the fields, and wade through the barley, calling out his name, searching for him. I think I spot the top of his head and rush toward it, but nothing's there. I think I catch his scent—of pine, of cologne, but I can't grab ahold of it. I keep running, up and down and through the fields, until my legs are trembling. I run until I'm so exhausted, the next thing I know I've collapsed in the grass, trying to catch my breath.

I don't think Sam's here anymore. I'm beginning to doubt he ever was. What's wrong with me? Why did I come here? I check the time again. 12:35 a.m. Already past midnight. My heart stops. It's too late now. I lost him again. The petals have vanished.

After everything Sam's done for me, I broke our promise. He asked me to call him one last time to say good-bye, and I let him down. What if he waits for me forever? What if he needed me to say good-bye to move on? I take out my broken phone and try to turn it on. Nothing. I'm so devastated, and disappointed with myself, and terrified of what I've done, I hold my phone up and talk to him anyway. If we're always connected, maybe there's still a chance . . .

"*Sam—*" I start. "I can't hear you . . . but maybe you can still hear me. *I'm sorry!* I couldn't get to you in time. I know you wanted us to say good-bye. I'm sorry I ruined everything again. Please don't wait for me, okay? *You can go.* You don't have to wait. You can move on now!" My voice cracks. "I'm going to miss you so much. But I want to tell you one last thing . . ." I take a deep breath, fighting back tears. "You're wrong about something. You did leave your mark on the world, Sam. You left a mark on *me.* You changed my life. And I'll never forget you, okay? We're a part of each other. Do you hear me? *Sam—*" My voice gives out.

Why can't I call you with another phone? Why is it only through mine?

I hear his voice again. It echoes in my head.

Only our phones are connected.

I think about this. About our connection. About it being between the two of us. *Only our phones.* I repeat the words over and over in my head until it hits me like a bolt of lightning. My heart jolts. Of course. Why didn't I think of this before?

As soon as it hits me, I get up and leave the fields, hurrying back to my car. The drive back is a blur in my mind. The next thing I know I'm parked in front of Sam's driveway, racing toward his house. The key under the mailbox is still there. I unlock the door and hurry inside. Thank god no one else is home. His family is spending the week with his grandparents, so I don't have to be quiet as I rush into his room and go through his things. I rummage through a dozen boxes, tearing through plastic bags, until I find it. The box of Sam's things they found at the crash site that night.

Inside the box are his wallet, ID, key chain, and cell phone. Exactly what I was looking for. I take his phone, switch out our SIM cards, and turn it on. The light from the screen blinds me for a few seconds. It's 1:43 a.m. There is just enough battery life left to make a call. So I dial his number.

Only our phones are connected. Maybe that means his, too. I take a deep breath and hold it in.

The ringing sends shivers through my body. I sit down on his bed and try not to freak out. It keeps ringing, until a voice comes on the line.

"Julie—"

"Sam!" I gasp. I hold back a cry as my entire body bursts with relief. "I didn't think you'd pick up!"

"I don't have a lot of time," he says.

"It's okay," I almost shout, trying hard not to cry. "I just needed you to know that I didn't forget you."

"What took you so long to call?" he asks.

"I broke my phone. I'm sorry—"

"I'm so glad you're okay. I was starting to worry."

"I'm here now," I tell him. "I'm so happy to hear your voice. I thought I lost you forever."

"I'm happy to hear you, too. I'm glad you made the call. Even if it's late. But it's time to say good-bye now, okay? I have to go soon—"

There's an ache in my chest. But I can't let Sam go knowing this. I have to be strong for him. I swallow down the pain. "Okay, Sam."

"I love you, Julie. I want you to know that."

"I love you, too."

Some static comes through the line. I have to say what I need to say faster.

"Thank you, Sam. For everything you've done. For picking up the phone because I needed you. For always being there for me."

A silence.

"Are you there?"

"I'm here. Don't worry," he assures me. "But I need you to say good-bye now. Okay? I need to hear you say the word."

I swallow hard. The words come out cracked and broken. "Good-bye, Sam."

"Good-bye, Julie."

Right after, he says, "I need you to do one last thing for me, okay?"

"What is it?" I ask.

"After we hang up . . . I'm going to call you again. And I need you to not pick up this time. Can you promise me that?"

He needs me to break our connection for good. He needs me to move on.

"I can . . ." I whisper, even though it kills me inside.

"Thank you. I'm going to hang up now. Okay?"

"Okay."

"I'm glad we were able to speak one last time," Sam says. "Even if it was just for a few seconds."

"Me, too," I tell him—but the call has already ended.

My body goes numb as I sit on his bed in silence, waiting for the call. And then the phone rings. The number is unknown but I know it's him. I squeeze the phone tight, wanting to pick it up so badly, desperate to hear his voice again. But I can't do that to him. I made a promise. So I let it ring. I let it keep ringing until it stops, the screen turns black, and I'm alone in the room again. My heart shatters, and sinks into the pit of my stomach. I set the phone down, and curl up on Sam's bed, letting myself cry.

Our connection is over. Just like that. I'll never get to speak to Sam again. I should get up and go home, but I can't seem to move. So I lie there in the dark for a while. In his bed, alone in the emptiness of the house, wishing things were different. And then something happens.

A chime goes off from somewhere in the room, followed by a blinking light. I lift myself up from the bed to see what it is. *Sam's phone.* I grab it and turn it on.

A hundred notifications fill the screen. I go through them and see text messages and missed calls from Mika, my mother, and everyone else who couldn't reach me these past few months. Here they are, flooding back to me, right after I ended my last call with Sam. Like the phone's been reconnected to the world. Like everything is moving again.

There's a new voice mail. One dated from tonight. But the number is unknown.

I listen to it immediately.

Sam's voice comes through the phone. "Hey—so, I'm not sure if I should do this . . . Or if it will even work. I probably should have said this to you over the phone, but we ran out of time. Or maybe, the truth is, I was scared you would think of me differently . . . That is, if you knew why I picked up the phone that first time—" He pauses. "Before we hung up, you said something that made me feel a bit guilty. You said I picked up your call that night because you needed me. I guess part of that is true. But that isn't the reason I answered." A long pause. "The truth is . . . I picked up because—because *I* needed you. I needed to hear your voice again, Julie. Because I wanted to make sure you didn't forget me. You see, I took you to all those places—like the fields, to see the stars that night—so that you'd always remember. So that whenever you looked up at the sky at night, you'd think of me. Because I didn't want to let you go yet. I never wanted to say good-bye, Jules.

And I never wanted you to, either. That's why I stayed as long as I could. So don't blame yourself for anything. It was me that was keeping you from your life. Maybe it was a bit selfish of me. But I was just so scared you'd forget. I realize now I made it a lot harder for you to move on. And I hope you forgive me for that."

Sam pauses again. "Remember back in the fields, when I asked what you wanted . . . if you could have anything? Well—*I* want those things, too, Jules. I want to be there with you. I want to graduate with you guys. I want to move out of Ellensburg, and live with you, and grow old together. But I *can't*." Another pause. "But *you* still can. You can still have all those things, Julie. Because you deserve them. And you deserve to fall in love a dozen times, because you are kind and beautiful, and who wouldn't fall in love with you? You're one of the best things to ever happen to me. And when I think about my life, I think of you in it. You are my entire world, Julie. And one day, maybe I'll only be a small piece of yours. I hope you keep that piece."

Static comes through the line.

"I love you more than you can ever know, Julie. I'll never forget the time we had together. So please don't forget me, okay? Try to think of me from time to time. Even if it's only for a moment. It would mean so much. You have no idea." A long pause, followed by static. "I should go now. Thank you . . . for not picking up the phone this time. Good-bye, Julie."

The voice mail ends.

I listen to the message again. I listen to it on the way home, and several more times before I fall asleep. I listen to it the next morning when Mika comes over and I replay it for her. I listen to it again that night and the day after that. I listen to it on the days I miss Sam most and want to hear his voice again. I listen to his voice mail until I have it memorized, and I don't need to play it anymore.

EPILOGUE

But I still think about him. I think about him throughout my first week in college when I'm walking under the cherry blossoms. I think about him whenever I'm in town, grabbing coffee at Sun and Moon. I think about him when I'm on the phone with Mika, and we talk for hours. I think about him after an awkward blind date Oliver sets me up with. I think about him after a better first date with someone from my English class. I think about him after I finish writing our story and submitting it to a writing contest. I think of him when I win an honorable mention, and it gets published online. I think about him when I visit his house for Sunday dinners with James and his family. I think about him on my last day in Ellensburg, as I get ready to move to the city where we always planned to live together. And I think about him whenever I close my eyes, and see us together again, lying out there in the fields.

ACKNOWLEDGMENTS

You forget how much time has passed until you have to sit down to write your acknowledgments. In publishing, you learn pretty quickly that everything happens all at once or nothing happens at all. And for most of my life, nothing was happening. Anyway, there are a lot of people I want to acknowledge who got me to this point in my life. The person I want to thank first is my sister, Vivian. What a long journey, right? You were there when this book was nothing but an idea in my head. You became my first critique partner. You gave me some of the best and harshest feedback I've ever received to this day. There are so many of your thoughts and ideas in this book, I can hardly distinguish them from my own anymore. Most important of all, thank you for always being the biggest fan of my stories.

Thank you to my agent, Thao Le. You don't know how excited I was when I got your email saying you were halfway through and loved it so far! After our phone call, I knew you were the right person for this book. Thank you for helping me get this book into the right shape. And thank you for all your support and championing of me. You are truly the best in the business, and it is wonderful to work with you. Thank you to everyone at the Sandra Dijkstra Literary Agency for all that you do. A special shout-out to Andrea Cavallaro for taking this book overseas. And thank you to my wonderful film agent, Olivia Fanaro at UTA.

Thank you to my editor, Eileen Rothschild. You truly helped take this book to levels I didn't expect. I think that's because you understood it in ways no one else did. You helped bring Sam to life and I am incredibly grateful that we got a chance to work together. Thank you to the Wednesday Books family. Mary Moates and Alexis Neuville, you guys make things so much better and more fun! Thank you for all you do behind the scenes. Thank you to Kerri Resnick for your genius and kindness. Thanks for finding Zipcy, who illustrated the best cover I could ever have asked for. Thank you to Tiffany Shelton. And thank you to Lisa Bonvissuto. It is such a joy to get the chance to work with you on this book!

To my friends and family. Thank you to Jolie Christine, my friend and CP. You really helped me through my revisions. Thank you to Julian Winters and Roshani Chokshi for your friendly support throughout the process. Thank you to Judith Frank at Amherst. You gave me space to work on this book when you didn't have to. Thank you to my friend Ariella Goldberg, who helped me with the prologue when I felt stuck. Thank you to my brother, Alvin, for always being there, and for supporting my stories. And thank you to my mom and dad. From the very beginning, you guys always believed in me.